SNAKE IN THE
GRASS

FAIRY TALES OF A TRAILER PARK QUEEN
BOOK THREE

SNAKE IN THE GRASS

FAIRY TALES OF A TRAILER PARK QUEEN, BOOK 3

KIMBRA SWAIN

CRIMSON SUN
PRESS

Kimbra Swain
Snake in the Grass: Fairy Tales of a Trailer Park Queen, Book 3
©2018, Kimbra Swain / Crimson Sun Press, LLC
kimbraswain@gmail.com

Cover art by Audrey Logsdon
Formatting by Serendipity Formats: https://serendipityformats.wixsite.com/formats
Editing by Carol Tietsworth: https://www.facebook.com/Editing-by-Carol-Tietsworth-328303247526664/

CRIMSON SUN
PRESS

CHAPTER ONE

Tears rolled down my cheeks. "It's the most beautiful thing I've ever seen in my entire life. It's big, sparkly and makes my heart thump," I whimpered.

Levi looked at me incredulously. "Grace, it's a trailer."

"It's a triple wide with a garden tub, so now you can keep your bare chesticled self out of my bathroom!" I replied.

"I'm all for that," Dylan interjected. He stood behind me with his arm around my waist as the workers from the mobile home delivery service anchored my shiny, new triple wide in the spot where my last trailer had burned down on Christmas Eve. Damn Trolls.

"It's huge!" I exclaimed.

"That's what she said," Dylan quipped.

"Oh, you think you are funny?" I asked.

"Nope. Just seemed appropriate," he grinned. Juvenile penis jokes. Men.

Winnie was in Levi's arms covering her ears as the big truck backed up with a squawking alarm. "I don't know why you are worried about a trailer when you have Dylan's house," Levi said.

"Because, it's Dylan's house. Not my house!" I protested. I felt

Dylan's chest bump my back a couple of times as he suppressed a laugh. I'd lived with Dylan for the month since my trailer burned down and even though we really had no issues other than trying to figure out how to please a six-year-old little girl, I couldn't wait for the new trailer to be delivered. There were times I actually missed fighting with him, even when it was fake, it was fun. However, not fighting had been heavenly.

"What are you going to do when you get married? Dylan, you moving into the trailer?" Levi scoffed.

"I go where she goes," he said.

"Bullshit!" Levi declared.

We both laughed at him. Frankly, we hadn't discussed it in depth. As far as we were concerned, here or there, as long as we were together it didn't matter. But I had to have a trailer; that wasn't up for discussion. The siding was a nice tan color with candy apple red shutters. Of course, they were fake, but it gave it that extra little something. High-class mobile home. I was a queen after all.

"Ooo Wee! She's a beaut," Tater said behind me.

"I've never seen anything so wonderful in all my life," Cletus said.

"See," I poked Levi.

"Yes, let's go on the opinion of Beavis and Butthead," Levi said.

Tater and Cletus began to mimic the cartoon idiot's laugh perfectly. Dylan put his head on my shoulder as he laughed. "What put a stick in your craw, Levi?"

"Kady," he said.

"I told you pegging wouldn't be fun," I said.

"Grace! I swear to God, you are the most vulgar woman on the face of this earth," Levi exclaimed covering Winnie's ears which were already covered by her own tiny hands. She gazed up at him and smiled not knowing what we were talking about. "There was no pegging."

"Alright, ma'am. It's down. You can go in," the foreman said.

I clapped and giggled like a girl getting her first dolly. Dylan released me as I ran to the trailer. The workers barely got the temporary wooden steps laid before I bounded up them to the door.

"Can't you control her?" Levi asked Dylan.

"Why would I want to?" Dylan returned.

"I heard that Levi Rearden," I said as I stepped into the trailer. The guys walked in behind me with Winnie.

"It's got that new trailer smell!" I gushed. "Come here, Winnie. I'll show you your room."

"My room is at Mr. Dylan's house," she said.

"Well, you have a room there and a room here," I said.

"Two rooms?" she asked.

"Yes, ma'am," I replied.

She clapped, giggling just like me, and we ran off to the front of the trailer together where I showed her the room.

"Can we decorate it?" she asked.

"Yes, how do you want to decorate it?" I replied, as Dylan stood in the doorway.

"Well, what do you want, Winnie?" he asked.

"It should be different from my other room," she said. "So, I think we should make it a secret garden."

"Oh, how fun. How about butterflies too?" I asked.

"No, I want my garden to have foxes and deer like the ones that hear Uncle Levi play his guitar," she said.

"Oh, like woodland animals," I said. "That would be cute."

"I love it," Dylan said.

"Love what?" Levi asked joining us.

"Winnie wants to decorate her room in the animals that come to hear you play your guitar," I said. Levi had been working hard on his musical magic. He had most of the forest around Dylan's house enthralled. He and Winnie would sit on the back porch as he played. All manner of creatures would come to listen. I inherited Levi Rearden by accident. His uncle, a Sanhedrin operative, sent him to Jeremiah, my contact in the zealots group. Jeremiah dropped him off at my doorstep and had remained out of sight pretty much since. It didn't matter. Levi was family now. No matter how much I ribbed him. I loved him to death.

"Can I have toys here, too?" she asked.

"Of course! What would a room be like without toys!" Levi said. I cleared my throat. "Shut up, Grace."

"Shut up is not a nice thing to say, Uncle Levi," Winnie scolded him. I giggled.

"You are right. I'm sorry," Levi said, then rolled his eyes at me.

"Come see my bathtub!" I said, grabbing Dylan's hand. Pulling him to the other end of the trailer, I opened the door to an extra-large bedroom. Well, it wasn't as big as our room back at his house, but it was huge for a trailer.

"We will have to christen this," Dylan's said nibbling at my neck.

"Not just this. The whole damn thing!" I said.

"Mmm, yes!" he agreed as his lips found mine.

I pulled back a little. "I didn't mean now. Winnie's here," I smiled.

He sighed, releasing his hold on me. "Tease," he said.

"Yep," I replied opening the door to the bathroom. I jumped into the dry garden tub with my clothes on and pretended to bathe.

"I'm going to have to go in the other room," he said.

"See if there is room for you too," I said.

"No, Grace, not while Winnie is here," he countered.

"Ugh! Fine! But you will test it out later with me, right?" I pouted.

"Maybe," he said, walking into the other room.

I climbed out of the tub taking one last look to admire it. At one time, I wanted a tub surrounded by candles, but after Taylor had burned my house down with candles, I decided the next candle I saw would be too soon. Twirling the engagement ring around my finger, I remembered the night the candles were all around Dylan's room. He went from dead to happy, sexy time in less than an hour. Such was life in Shady Grove, Alabama, where I was the Queen of the Exiled fairies.

Absurdity knew no bounds in this town full of misfits. The thirteen Yule Lads decided to move into town. The mayor and a business associate of Remington Blake's got together and were building a huge apartment complex for the influx of new residents. I complained that it was an eyesore. We already had a trailer park with lots. Seemed to me an apartment complex didn't keep with the character of the town. I was overruled. Which was fine, because before long, we would have a fairy council where I would be the deciding vote on all things fairy. The power was already getting to me.

"Grace, come on. You don't want to be late for your first day at work," Dylan called from the kitchen.

"I'm coming," I groaned as I blew a kiss to my garden tub. "Be back soon, my love."

CHAPTER TWO

Wrapping the white apron around my waist, I realized it was too big. "No, like this," said Nestor Gwinn, the owner of the Hot Tin Roof Bar and my grandfather. He wrapped the ties around my waist twice doubling up the apron, tying it in the front. It was time to learn the family business. Sometime while sitting around Dylan's mansion bored, I decided I wanted to work. Dylan had earned his money over the years, because as a phoenix-thunderbird mix, he didn't threaten people like an unseelie fairy queen. He was able to work various jobs, and even though I didn't know exactly how much money Dylan had amassed, I knew he was wealthy.

Now that I could, I decided to make myself useful, even if it was only bartending. Dylan assured me that tits would be enough to do the job. Nestor said it was more than just a pretty face. I just wanted to learn a skill other than seduction, plus this would keep me in touch with most of the townsfolk.

The Queen of the Exiles gig didn't pay well. In fact, it didn't pay at all. Perhaps when we held elections for fairy council, I could suggest a pay raise. Fat chance.

"Today, you watch, and dry glasses," Nestor said as he threw a towel at me.

"You dry these glasses over and over," I said.

"Well, at least you pay attention," he smirked.

I still hadn't been able to call him anything other than Nestor. He was my mother's father. My mother was a siren and concubine to my father, Oberon, King of the Wild Fairies. Her name was Ellessa. I'd patterned my glamour after her. I spent most of my days as a young brunette with dark brown eyes, but when I dropped my disguise my true fairy form burst through. I was Gloriana, a winter queen, with platinum hair and turquoise eyes. The looks I received from my father. I stored power in an intricate tattoo on my right forearm which depicted a glittering ruby encased in a fancy filigree. When I transformed into Gloriana, the red stone turned to a deep sapphire, I wielded the power of the darkest cold night. That part of me walked the edge of evil, so I avoided it at all costs.

I started drying glasses as Nestor described how to make drinks. I sipped on a cup of coffee too. Nestor's coffee was a magical soothing elixir that he only shared with family. It was only a few months ago I was alone in this world with no known family, besides my dachshund, Rufus who had abandoned me for Winnie as his favorite person.

But from the moment Jeremiah Freyman dropped Levi into my lap, I'd gained a misfit sort of family. Dylan Riggs, my fiancé, was once the sheriff of this town. He had just applied to the state to be a private investigator. Nestor was my grandfather who served me drinks for years, but never told me of his relation to me until recently. His girlfriend, Mable Sanders, was the local gossip fly and spy for my father in Shady Grove. Finally, little Miss Wynonna Jones was my daughter. Not by blood, but by heart. Her mother passed away on Christmas, and Winnie became mine. She missed her mother and wore a special key around her neck given to her by a Yule Lad that connected her heart to her mother in heaven. I didn't think the key had any special magical properties, but a child's belief in a mother in heaven was more powerful than any blizzard I could conjure. Winnie was human, but we loved her as our own.

"Where's Levi?" Nestor asked.

"Well, I'm not sure. Yesterday at the trailer he acted like he and

Kady were on the outs again, but he disappeared early this morning from the house. I know he was anxious to get back into the trailer and away from us. He probably went to buy some furniture for his room," I said.

"Those two are never going to work out," Nestor said.

"I tried telling him that, but there must be something about her. It's not like there aren't any other choices," I replied. "The contractor working on the apartment building has a really cute daughter. Levi just turned his nose up at her. Whatever. I try to stay out of it."

"Grace, you know I love you, right?" Nestor said.

"Um, yes?" I replied not sure where he was going with this.

"Don't be mad at me, but Levi compares every woman to you. Until he finds his own, fairy queen, he won't be happy," Nestor said.

"Bullshit," I said.

"It's true."

"Levi is not in love with me," I said.

"No, no. Not in love with you. Just the model which he bases all his relationships on," Nestor said.

"There are better models," I said.

"I agree," Nestor replied. I tapped him on the arm as he grinned.

The bar door swung open, and our first patron of the day showed up.

"Mighty fine new 'tender you got there, Nestor," Remington Blake said. He was with the apartment contractor. Remington and I had a fling a few years back before I moved to Shady Grove. He was my lawyer now. He'd stayed away since I moved in with Dylan, but he always took the chance to flirt. It wasn't really flirting because it was the flowery language he used with all women. Not just me.

"She's okay," Nestor said. "A little rough around the edges."

"I like it a little rough," Remy said winking at me. I was thankful Dylan wasn't here. He'd punch him out just for flirting. Remy couldn't help it. He was Star-folk, a child of the great Native American legends. Only Remy grew up in New Orleans, so he had a debonair personality that derived from the exotic tone of that city. I didn't know a woman that could say no to him, except me. "Let's have a little whiskey for me and my friend here." I watched Nestor pick up two glasses, putting ice in each. He poured dark liquor in each one. I hadn't drunk much since Dylan came into my life permanently, but the sweet smell of whiskey permeated my nose. It smelled so good.

"Afternoon, Mr. Babineau," I said greeting the contractor.

"Afternoon, Grace. How are you this fine day?" he asked in his jovial manner. He and Remy both crawled up toward Alabama from New Orleans. When the town wanted to build the apartment complex, Remington suggested Mr. Niles Babineau. I wasn't sure who was funding the monstrosity, but I couldn't hold it against him for building it.

"I'm well, except for learning this new job," I said.

"You will make a fine bartender. I'm sure of it," he smiled sipping his drink.

"She makes everything fine," Remy flirted.

"Remington Blake, you are so full of shit that your eyes are brown!" I laughed.

"That may be, my dear, but when I'm right, I'm right," he said finishing off his drink. "When is this council meeting?"

"Tomorrow night at the community center," Nestor answered.

We were finally getting together to discuss a fairy council for the town. We had so many new inhabitants that we desperately needed to get everyone on the same page. There needed to be rules and limitations. Otherwise, we would have the thirteen days of Christmas all over again. I never imagined I'd be interested in having rules. After my experiences running from the Sanhedrin, I hated the restrictions they put on me. Now the Sanhedrin could back off the fairies in this town because we intended to police ourselves. The council and I would handle issues as they arose. Just hopefully quicker than we dealt with the Yule Lads.

"Alright. I'll be there to give legal advice, of course," he grinned.

"That would be great," I said.

The bar door opened again as a young woman entered. Her Asian features were muted, but her large almond shaped eyes gave away her heritage. Around her, I saw the faint glow of a fairy. She was slender with long copper locks that shined like a new penny. She nodded to us as she found a seat on a stool.

"What can I get you, Miss?" Nestor asked. Remy and Niles eyed her closely. She was strikingly beautiful. Her unique features would have every fairy man in this town going nuts, which made me think of Levi.

"Something fruity. Can you make an apple martini?" she asked with her soft uber-feminine voice.

"Sure thing. You got some I.D. on you? Sorry, I have to ask everyone," he said.

"That's no problem," she opened her tiny clutch pulling out her driver's license. Nestor showed me where to look on the I.D. to determine the persons age. The I.D. was issued in Ohio. She was twenty-three years old according to it. I imagined she was much older, but you never could tell with fairies.

"Thank you, Ma'am," Nestor said handing it back to her. He showed me how to fix the drink even though I'd made lemon drops at home before I got hooked on the darker liquors.

I took it over to her, sitting it down on the bar. "Here you are. It's a good drink. I used to drink them all the time," I said.

She smiled. Around her neck hung a silver bead about the size of a marble, but it sparkled like a diamond. She took a sip, "Ah, yes, it is very good." Her tiny hands grasped the drink as if it were her lifeline.

"What brings you to Shady Grove?" I asked.

"I hear this town is different," she said.

"It's unique. That's for sure. I'm Grace," I said, offering my hand.

"Hi, Grace. I'm Misaki. You are the one they speak of, right?" she said, shaking my hand. Her grip, if you could call it that, was clammy and delicate.

"Depends on what they say," I teased.

She smiled, but her eyes didn't show it. "You are a protector. Yes?"

"Of those who need it. I am. Well, at least I try. It's kind of a new gig," I said.

"And you are bartender?" she asked.

I chuckled. "Actually, it's my first day. My grandfather owns the place, and I needed something to do."

"Ah. I see," she said as her finger twirled around the edge of the glass of bright green liquid. "I am in need of protection."

"You are welcome here in Shady Grove. Where are you staying?" I asked.

"In motel," she responded showing the first sign of broken English.

The Cahaba Motel was just down the street. It was the only one in town so I assumed that's what she meant. "There are a few houses for rent around town. I'll write down a few of them for you, if you plan on staying," I said. "Do you work?"

"No, I have daddy's money," she replied.

"I know how that is," I said.

"Your father is King?"

"Yes, but not here," I replied.

"Daughter of King is a hard job," she said.

"I take it you know that," I replied.

"Yes, I know too well," she said as she finished off the drink. "I have particular problem."

"We all do, honey. What's yours?" I asked.

"I cannot speak of it here. Perhaps we meet somewhere else later," she said.

"Of course. Will you be okay until then?" I asked.

"Maybe. Maybe not," she said.

Lordy mercy. Mo' fairies, mo' problems.

"Maybe you should stick around here. The peanuts are free. Or you could go over to the diner. Betty and Luther are familiars. Damn good food, too," I replied.

I looked up to see that someone else had entered the bar. My bard, Levi, and his raging hormones locked eyes with the beautiful girl. His jaw dropped. He wore a long sleeve t-shirt, a Kevlar motorcycle jacket and a pair of jeans that hung low on his hips. Even though Levi was only half fairy, his looks definitely came from his father's side of the family. Dark blue brooding eyes and scruff on his chin made all the girls swoon. I bought him a Harley for Christmas, upping his hot factor. The damn thing scared me to death, but I knew he wanted one.

"Levi, you are drooling," I said.

He put his hand to his chin, then realized I was joking. "Shut-up, Grace." He stalked over to where Remy and Niles were chatting with Nestor, but kept looking at us. Could that boy be any more obvious? God bless it.

"He should be punished for his disrespect," she muttered.

"Ah! That's just Levi. He's my bard. I make him pay on the regular," I said.

"Oh, he is your sex slave," she said.

"Oh, no! Not like that. I just give him hell," I said. I couldn't wait to rib Levi about that one. My sex slave. I suppose I could include that in his list of duties. Dylan would likely object.

"He deserves lashes," she replied.

"We don't do lashes around here. Besides, he might like that kind of thing," I said.

Finally, she blushed catching my meaning. I looked back at Levi when she did, and a pretzel fell out of his mouth.

"He is staring," she said.

"Well, Misaki, you are a beautiful girl. Levi likes beautiful girls. He's harmless though, unless you don't want him to be," I said. "In fact, if you need someone to keep an eye on you until we can talk, he would fit the bill."

"Fit what bill?" she asked.

I reckoned she'd not heard southern speech before and probably only caught on about half of what I was saying along the way.

"I meant that if you needed protection, someone to look out for you, that Levi would be happy to do it," I said. "Maybe he could show you around town."

"Um, I do not know him," she said. I realized she definitely wasn't going to go for the bodyguard route. "I will stay here if that is okay."

"Sure honey. You are safe here. You want another drink?" I asked.

"Yes, please," she replied.

I walked back over with the empty glass. "She wants another," I told Nestor.

He pulled a fresh glass as I bent over the small sink to wash the glass. "My god, she's an angel," Levi purred.

"Levi, if you don't stop fucking her with your eyes, she's going to run. She says she needs help. Now quick gawking," I scolded him.

"I'm not fucking her with my eyes," he protested.

"Yeah, you are," Remy said.

"Fuck off, Remy," Levi spouted.

Remy and Niles laughed, and I couldn't help but smile.

"How's Kady?"

"Fuck you too, Grace," Levi said, stomping out of the bar. Even Nestor chuckled at poor Levi. He brooded on the regular. Hell, if he wasn't brooding, I'd think he was sick.

"Let me go catch him," I said. Nestor nodded.

I ran out of the bar as he put his helmet on. He'd climbed on to the denim blue Harley.

"Hey, what's going on?" I asked.

He hung his head. "I'm really done this time," he said.

"With her?" I asked.

"Yes, I can't do anything right," he replied.

"Honey, she does nothing but torture you. Frankly, I think I am the only one allowed to do that. What happened this time?" I asked.

"I forgot our monthiversary," he said.

"Montha-what?"

"Apparently, we'd gone a whole month without breaking up, and I forgot. She got me a pair of biker gloves. I didn't know there was such a thing, Grace," he whined twirling the fingerless gloves in the air.

"There isn't. She made it up to make you feel bad. So, go buy her something," I suggested.

"No, she said it was too late now."

I grabbed his hand sending tingling wave of fairy touch through both of us. He shivered. "Levi, be done with it. Once and for all. There are other girls."

"Yeah, like that one in there. Damn, Grace. She's beautiful. What's her story?"

"Fairy. Needs protection. Same song, different verse," I said.

"I'll protect her," he said.

"I suggested that, but she seems a little skittish. Why don't you just hold your horses on that one? I'll let you know," I said.

"Okay. I'm going to meet the furniture folks at the trailer. They should be there with my stuff," he said.

"Alright. Be safe on that hog," I said.

"I will," he said firing up the guttural engine. As he pulled away, a red Camaro approached the bar. My heart flip-flopped.

Dylan stopped the car and climbed out. Long legs and sandy hair. Hot damn. Without a word, he wrapped me up in his arms, kissing me. "Yum. What did I do to deserve that one?"

"Uptown shopping for downtown business," he said.

"Oh really?"

"Later," he grinned. "What are you doing out here with Levi? It's freezing."

"The cold doesn't bother me," I said. He smirked.

"It does me," he said pulling me back into the bar. His eyes locked on Misaki. Stopping in his tracks, his body tensed.

"What's wrong?"

"Thunderbird warning went off in my head," he said. I'd learned more about his Thunderbird heritage over the last month. The Phoenix in him allowed him to use fire magic and rise from the dead. The other part of him was a protector much like the role I now found myself in. Keeping the law and protecting his people. He made me want to be a better person. I thought about the last few years as I worked with him. He was an excellent lawman. I knew he missed it. Later this week, he would go to Montgomery to complete his private investigator license. I was happy to see that he would be getting back to something he loved, even though it would put him in danger. I'd realized though that with Shady Grove growing, we were in constant danger.

15

"She says she's in trouble. Needs protection," I said.

"Hmm," he replied.

"Hmm, what?"

"Just think she may be the trouble," he said.

"Most women are," I replied.

"Don't I know it!" he laughed kissing me on the cheek. "Now get around there and fix me a beer!"

I slapped him on the arm. "You are a butthole," I said. When I turned away from him, he popped me on the ass. Spinning around on him, I paused because of the devious look on his face. He winked at me. The flush of embarrassment spread up my neck to my cheeks.

He leaned over to my ear. "You are so damn beautiful."

"Okay. I forgive you," I said.

"Howdy, Dylan," Nestor said already cracking open a bottle of piss water.

"You keep that beer mouth away from me," I told him.

"You sure about that?" he said, taking a swig.

"I'll get back to you," I said, returning to Misaki.

"He is your mate," she said. She'd watched the whole exchange closely.

"Well, sometimes. When I claim him," I joked.

She smiled. "I will claim him if you don't."

"Whoa there, honey, hands off my man," I replied light-heartedly.

"You said sometimes," she said watching Dylan.

I laid my hand on the bar, twisting my ring back and forth. "He gave it to me. I'm his. He's mine. You will get used to me. I joke around a lot."

"Still. He can protect me," she said.

"Yes, he's a protector, too," I replied. "We have many in this town who are capable."

"I want him," she said. Perhaps she didn't understand the concept that Dylan was my fiancé. A language barrier or cultural barrier. I wasn't sure.

"Want him how?" I said.

"He must make me a baby," she said.

"The fuck he will," I said loudly. Nestor approached.

"Everything okay?"

"No, she wants Dylan to make her a baby," I said.

"What?" he said.

"Look, Misaki, Dylan isn't making babies with anyone but me," I said.

"I am?" Dylan said.

"At least practicing," I returned.

"He must take me before they arrive," she said.

Fucking fairies. I hated this shit-town.

CHAPTER THREE

"Misaki, I'm Dylan Riggs. Perhaps you tell me what kind of trouble you are in, and we will see if we can help," he said.

We'd moved her over to a small table where Dylan and I sat to talk to her. She seemed shy around him, but she was clearly attracted to him. I couldn't blame her. Not just handsome, Dylan carried himself as the strong, silent fighter. If provoked, that façade faded into a burning fury.

"There is a man following me. He is my betrothed, but I want to choose my own mate. If I can procreate before he arrives, he will break off our engagement," she said.

"You cannot guarantee that you will get pregnant," I said.

"I will. My kind is always ready," she said. "I would like Mr. Riggs to do it."

Dylan put his hand over my arm to calm me. The last woman that even mentioned Dylan that way ate my fist. "Misaki, I am sorry, but that's not possible."

"She has not given you baby," she said.

"There is a cultural difference that you do not understand," he tried to explain. I seethed. Dylan did need an heir, and it wasn't like we were trying to prevent that from happening. It just hadn't yet.

19

"I will not settle for a half-breed," she said.

"There are many fair-folk here, if this is truly what you want to do. We will introduce you to them," Dylan said.

Her face crinkled. "I only have one day, then he will be here," she said.

"What are you?" I dared to ask.

"I am Kitsune from Yokai traditions," she said.

"Fox," Dylan said.

"Yes," she replied.

"Kitsune are usually old and wise. Forgive me but you seem young," I said knowing a little about the Japanese fairy.

"I am unblemished," she replied shyly.

I tilted my head sideways. A kitsune was a unique fairy especially for these parts, but a virgin, human or otherwise, was damn near an urban legend. "I wouldn't broadcast that honey. You'll have every man in the county ready to jump you."

"Then perhaps I should tell them all," she replied.

"Better not. There are a lot of fairies here and some lycans, but not all are as reserved as we are. I wouldn't want anyone to take advantage of you," Dylan said.

"Who is coming? Another Kitsune?" I asked.

"No, he is a demon," she replied.

"Oh, joy!" I said. "How did you become betrothed to a demon?"

"Demons are not always bad. Oni can be very good sometimes," she said. "But I do not want to marry him."

"Outside of impregnating you, is there another way?" Dylan asked.

"You could kill him," she offered.

"I was thinking more like banishment like Levi's demon," I said.

"I will do some digging to get information about this type of demon. In the meantime, I can take you back to your hotel room," Dylan offered.

"Wait, what?" I asked.

"Yes," she purred, as if she had suddenly lost all innocence. She stood and walked to the door. Glancing back at Dylan, she fluttered her eyelashes. A fox skin purse would be nice.

I looked at Dylan pleading with him not to go. "Either you trust me or you don't, Grace," he muttered.

"I trust you. I don't trust *that*," I said pointing to the fox.

"I already have one sex crazed fairy. What would I do with two?" he smiled.

"Wear yourself out," I attempted to joke.

His kissed me. "I'll be right back."

CHAPTER FOUR

"CALL HIM," LEVI SAID, LOOKING AT HIS WATCH.

"No, he will think I don't trust him," I replied.

Dylan left around lunch to take Misaki back to the hotel. Looking at the clock, my anxiety reached a new level. It was almost 6 p.m. The fairy council preliminary meeting was in an hour, and he hadn't returned. No call. Nothing.

"I'm driving down there," Levi said, grabbing his helmet. He'd come by the bar for a cup of Nestor's magical coffee. I'd already drank 3 cups.

"Levi, don't," I pleaded.

Ignoring me, he went out the door. I looked at my grandfather. "Call him, Grace. Better if he's mad at you than something be wrong."

Pulling out my cell phone, I dialed. It rang several times then went to voicemail. I dialed again.

"Grace," he answered. "I'll call you back." He hung up.

"What the hell?" I said. "He hung up on me."

"What did he say?" Nestor asked.

"Said he would call me back. Something is wrong," I said.

Nestor sighed. "Wait for Levi to get back, then you two go over to the meeting."

"I can't go without him!" I said.

"Grace, you took in this role before you and he were together. You can do it without him for one night until we can find out what's going on," he said.

I took a glass, pouring Crown into it. Nestor shook his head as I threw it back. It burned, and my eyes watered. I coughed. It had been a while. Feeling it burn through my throat into my chest, I prepared myself for what I was sure would be a fairy circus. Contrary to his belief, my heart belonged to Dylan when I accepted this shit job. Even if I hadn't admitted it yet.

"His car wasn't there," Levi said.

"We gotta go. He answered the phone, so it's not like he's hurt or something. I'll deal with it later," I said.

"You are freaking out," Levi said as we walked into the community center. He left his bike at the bar, riding with me in Dylan's truck.

"Doesn't matter," I replied. We walked into a boisterous gathering of people. More than I imagined. "Goodness gracious."

"I didn't know there were that many fairies in Shady Grove," Levi said.

Looking around the room, I saw many people that I knew were fairies. Some I didn't know. There were a few lycans, like Sheriff Troy Maynard and his girlfriend Amanda Capps. Trying to gain confidence, I walked through the middle of the room to the front. Off to my left, Remington Blake stood next to Niles Babineau and his daughter.

"Settle down," I said projecting my voice with a touch of power. The room silenced. "We are here this evening to discuss election for fairy council. There are a few things I want to say before we get started."

Dylan and I had talked over the last few weeks about the possibilities of mayhem that could erupt in a meeting like this. So, we planned on setting some ground rules from the start. He was supposed to be here to help me keep the peace. The thought pressed on me that I would have to do it alone, and my confidence sank.

"Go ahead, Grace," Levi said encouraging me quietly. Levi spoke up at just the right time. I wasn't alone. My bard had my back.

"This will be a civil discussion. The moment it isn't, we will adjourn and trouble makers will be dealt with accordingly. Secondly, if you have something to say, you may approach the podium to speak, however, if you speak out of turn, you will be removed," I said. I looked at Levi who nodded. I supposed he would be the enforcer. "Today's topics will be how many council seats, election rules, and election date. Now, one by one, please speak your opinion."

First to the microphone was peg leg Lamar, the eldest of the Yule Lads. "My Queen, I know my brothers and I want to thank you for your tolerance, considering we caused a lot of trouble here. My suggestion is that we have a census to make sure all fairy factions are represented equally," he said as the crowd began to murmur.

"I'm not sure that is feasible, Lamar. Many of our kind came here to hide. Not to have their identities recorded," I rebuffed. I knew I didn't want my name recorded anywhere. "I think it is safe to say that we only have four groups of supernatural. Those are Seelie, Unseelie, Lycan and what I'd call miscellaneous."

The murmur of the crowd rose as people discussed my distinctions. Lamar sat down as Betty from the diner stood up. "Technically many of us fall under the unseelie category. We could have more representation than the other groups, plus just because we are Unseelie doesn't mean we are wild like some," she said defiantly.

"No one said anything about being wild," I replied. "However, I don't see us having more than four seats. No group should be held higher than another, but all groups should be represented." I felt the tension growing in the room. It was up to me to control it.

Before I could speak again, Deacon Giles joined Betty at the microphone. "This is just another way to alienate those of us who were banished versus those who chose to leave the Otherworld," he said.

"Some of us don't go smashing witches with our hooves," the feisty older lady replied referring to an incident on the Winter Solstice where Deacon Giles transformed into Krampus, his monstrous fairy side. He subsequently smashed a human witch that I had frozen solid with his hoof.

"One at a time please. Betty are you finished with your remarks?" I asked calmly. She crossed her arms, sneering at me. It hurt, because I loved Betty and Luther. He looked at her from his seat trying to get her to sit down.

"This ain't over," she said plopping down next to Luther. Her frustration surprised me. She and I had always been friends. Even before I realized that she was a fairy. My fairy detection skills had developed with the acceptance of my role here in Shady Grove, but I still had issues determining the exact variations. There wasn't a handbook; I asked.

Betty's frustration was only the tip of the mountain. As they got up and spoke, the crowd became unruly. At one point, Troy Maynard stood up and shushed the crowd, to which an unseen voice yelled, "Sit down, dog!"

At that moment, the back door of the room opened, and Dylan appeared. I hoped the look I gave him made him melt inside. However, relief spread over me that he was here and safe. As the room descended into chaos, he mouthed, "I'm so sorry."

I stood to my feet pushing power out of my tattoo. As it turned from red and black to silver and blue, my glamour dropped releasing my true self on the room. The temperature dropped as I yelled, "Cease!" The command rocked the room. Several people clasped their hands over their ears, but everyone shut up. My power over the room felt stronger than any other time in this form because they had given me authority over them as their Queen. I hadn't realized how intoxicating it could be.

Levi stood next to me, watching the crowd. I knew that he could stop me if I lost control. However, his concern was turned toward the crowd. My eyes cut to Dylan who folded his arms and leaned on the back wall. A devilish grin crossed his face. The bastard looked so damn hot doing it, I almost lost focus on the room full of angry fairies.

A short stubby man with ginger hair stood in the back. His brown eyes fixed on me. He waddled into the aisle. Dylan tensed, unfolding his arms. I'd never seen him before today. Nothing about him stood out. Even his reddish hair was a muted tone.

"I propose we limit the power of the Queen. We accepted her in desperation of an obscene need for freedom. Her will could crush us all as we stand here. Surely you felt the wave of power roll over us as she unleashed the command. With respect, you, *my Queen*, have not earned your station. There are many here with royal blood who would be far better for the position than you," he spoke wagging his finger at me. His manner drew the attention of everyone in the room.

"Forgive me, Sir. I do not know your name," I tried diplomacy which I was terrible at in the first place. Thought I'd give it a shot.

"That's another thing. You don't know me. I dare say you don't know half the people in this room. How in the world do you get to be judge and jury when you can't even tell what kind of fairy I am?" he questioned. The mob responded in agreement. Fuck diplomacy.

"I don't see anyone else volunteering for the job," I replied.

An evil wind passed through me and I shuddered at the coldness of it. Colder than me. Almost colder than my father. The stout man grinned while motioning to the back door. "I present an alternative. A long-standing member of this community who has always had our best interests at heart."

The back doors slowly opened with no help, and as the raven-haired beauty stepped into the room, my heart sank. "Fuck," I muttered as Stephanie Davis, Dylan's ex-girlfriend slithered into the room. She stopped to greet people as she made her way to the podium. She stood several inches shorter than me with a thin frame. She was so thin, I wanted to make her a biscuit. With butter. Or better yet, gravy.

Stephanie was a high-born Seelie elf, her skin glistened with an unnatural illumination when she wanted it to which was right now, apparently. Her violet eyes twinkled like stars as she stared at me. Dylan moved to the edge of the room working his way to the front. He didn't step on the platform, but he was within a few steps of it. I didn't know if he was there to prevent me from doing something or if he wanted to confront her.

A seductive smile crossed her face when she saw him. His jaw tightened. I felt Levi move closer to me, and her glare moved to him. She winked at him. Bitch.

She leaned forward showing her cleavage to the room and said, "I declare my candidacy for Queen of the Exiles and Head of the Shady Grove Fairy Council."

The room erupted. Some protested. Others cheered. She clapped delightfully. I wanted to slap the whore who disrespected Dylan for years by fucking around behind his back. She made delighted faces at all the cheers and the jeers alike. I've never wanted to throw down more in my entire life.

"Silence!" I ordered as the power swept over the room. They made me Queen. Until they voted differently, I still held the power.

The room waited to see how I would respond. I looked her in the eye, returned her wink and said, "Good luck." The crowd erupted again.

Her face looked like she had swigged dill pickle moonshine. Instead of calming the crowd with my voice, I mouthed to her, "Watch this."

I let the screams and taunts fill the room. Power built up like a spinning top. Arguments started between long-time friends. People shouted across the aisle. Just as I felt it grow to the point where punches might be thrown, I sucked in power from the room.

Dylan's voice floated through the cacophony, "Grace!"

I shot my hands into the air palms out bending my arms at the elbows with a clear signal to stop. The whole room froze. The floor iced over, snowflakes fell inside, and the windows crackled with the sudden temperature change. Once again, all eyes were on me.

"There will be four council seats. One representing each group I mentioned. Election rules will be posted tomorrow, here at the community center. All fairies are allowed to vote for every seat, not just their representative. Nominations are due tomorrow. You must have a petition of twenty signatures to nominate yourself for office. The election will be held in two weeks. Any objections?" I paused watching the room stare at me.

The dumpy man spoke, "And what about Stephanie's challenge?"

Pulling darkness from deep within I stared at her coldly. She realized that I was serious about my commitment to these people. Perhaps she remembered me as the flippant woman in the trailer park. It didn't matter. I wasn't that woman anymore. I didn't smile. No sarcastic remark or quip. I simply said, "Challenge accepted."

CHAPTER FIVE

TURNING ON MY HEEL, MY EYES MET DYLAN'S. HIS BLUE EYES twinkled with amusement, but darkened when he saw my face. I'd pulled deeper into Gloriana's power than I ever had. I'm sure it showed outwardly. I needed Stephanie to know that I wasn't a pushover, and that even though I'd made a comfortable life here, I knew how to fight. I would fight her for what was mine. The silence ended, but the roar of voices was muted.

As I reached the edge of the platform, Dylan offered his hand to me. I hesitated. Even though he made me worry, I knew that he was mine. Taking his hand, I squeezed, fighting the urge to rip it off and beat him with it. The time had come to tuck the evil fairy queen away.

He leaned into my ear, "I know you are pissed, but you are so hot when you are mad." I elbowed him, and he laughed.

"Don't test me right now. Surely you feel the power I just dipped into. Do you want to try your luck? Be my guest, sweetheart," I sneered, with a smile on my face like only a southern woman can do properly.

"As long as there is angry sex involved, yes," he snickered. The comment stopped me in my tracks. I grimaced, because no matter how mad I was at him, angry sex sounded good. He took the grimace to mean that I'd met my limit of his humor instead of how incredibly turned on it made me. "Okay. Okay. Let's go."

We walked out hand in hand like a happy little couple. I'd seen many elections over the years where the dutiful spouse stood by their mate. I didn't want Dylan standing by me to be a show. I wanted our partnership to be real. He just better have a damn good explanation for worrying me to death. Especially with this meeting. I knew it would be important, but I could have never predicted a challenge to my claim.

We greeted friends on the way out of the center. Nestor hugged me. "It will be okay. Come have some coffee."

"Thanks, Nestor, but Dylan and I need to talk," I replied. He looked alarmed, but nodded.

"Leave Winnie with us tonight. We will take her to school in the morning," he offered.

"Thank you, Nestor," I said.

We walked into the cool night, and the sounds of the room were muted. "Do you want to ride home with me?" Dylan asked carefully.

"I need to take Levi to his bike. Will you follow?" I asked trying not to sound pissed.

"Yeah, sure," he said, then hugged me. The warmth if his arms melted all the anger inside me. He kissed me on the forehead.

Pulling away, I realized that Levi had claimed the driver's seat of the truck. I shook my head at him. "Someone doesn't mind provoking you," Dylan smirked.

"Yeah, he knows I can't hurt him. Not really," I replied as Levi started the truck. He hadn't looked at us, but I could see the edges of a smile form on his face. It hit me what he was doing. "Levi Rearden!"

He shifted the truck into gear, leaving me behind. Dylan tried not to laugh, but he couldn't help it.

"I guess I owe him one now," he said.

"You already kissed him once," I smirked.

Dylan's face turned red remembering the accidental kiss while under an enthrallment spell. It was my favorite piece of ammo against Mr. Sandy Hair. I deployed it at the least expected moments, and he always blushed.

"I'd probably get further with him tonight than you," he tried to joke back.

"Take me home, Dylan," I said, ignoring his jest.

"Yes, my Queen," he groaned.

To be honest, I wasn't in the mood for Dylan's nonsense tonight. The ride back to the house was quiet. We should have picked up Winnie on the way home, but Nestor insisted that she stay with him and Mable. If she was with us, I could count on her to dominate the conversation. Otherwise, the ride was silent and uncomfortable. I knew if I said anything it would be taken wrong. Therefore, I waited on him to explain when he was ready. Fuck that.

"I needed you there with me," I said.

"I know," he said simply.

"That's all you have? I know?"

"When we get home, I will explain," he muttered.

Once we were home, he stopped in the kitchen. Taking out two cans of orange soda, he waved one at me. I definitely needed one. Actually, I needed more than orange soda, but it would have to do. I took several burning sips when he started to talk.

"Grace, I took Misaki to the motel, then remembered a contact I have that lives up on Parson's Ridge. I drove up there to talk to him about the kitsune. I lost track of time," he said. "It's not a good excuse. However, you didn't need me. You owned that room. You dipped into power that I didn't know you could control." Parson's Ridge was at least a forty-five-minute drive. He'd spent an hour and half on the road, leaving plenty of time that he needed to give an account.

"One thing at a time, so I don't lose my shit here," I said. "What contact?"

"Mr. Takahashi is from Japan. Like old Japan. When I got to his house, he invited me in, but I had to go through the traditional rituals to respect him and his home. I took off my shoes, waiting while he made tea. We drank tea, and then, and only then was I allowed to ask questions," he explained. "He said a kitsune can be very dangerous or harmless. However, he also said there are demons out there that will pose as a kitsune to draw attention. To be honest, I'm not sure that Misaki is a kitsune."

"What about the demon chasing her and needing to mate?" I asked, because the information was interesting. Also, the conversation was allowing my anger to settle.

"He said that it's possible, but it could very easily be a lie. But when it comes to an Oni, they are always evil. Misaki said they weren't," he said.

"So, you actually learned nothing," I replied. "We are still in the same spot as before you left me alone to the wolves."

"Grace, I never intended to stay gone that long. Once I was in his house, it would have been rude to leave. Besides, you had that handled," he said.

"Until your fucking ex-girlfriend crawled in," I spouted. Nope, the anger simmered instead of settled.

"I was as shocked as you were," he said. "Everyone in this town knows that she's a whore. There is no way she would ever beat you for the job. Besides, she only wants it because you claimed it and me."

"Mostly you," I said.

"Probably," he replied.

"I can unclaim you," I spouted.

"Grace, you can unclaim me all you want, but my heart is and will always be yours," he said.

"Don't fucking say sweet shit like that when I'm mad," I steamed.

"Why? Cause you can't handle it?" he teased.

"Dylan Riggs! I'm warning you," I said feeling a smile working its way to my face. I couldn't give in now. I had an argument to make. I was right, damn it!

34

"What are you going to do? Go sleep in the trailer with no bed?" he said.

"There is a bed there now. Levi's furniture arrived today. I'm sure he'd be happy to share," I said.

He sobered. Walking to me, I had no defense from him. I wanted to melt into his arms. I wanted to forget being the Queen of the Exiles. At this point, I never wanted to step foot in town again. "Don't threaten me with Levi. I know you don't mean it. You are upset about everything that happened tonight. I was wrong not to be there," he said, wrapping his arms around me.

I tensed. "You said that you would be right back," I started to sob.

"Yes, I know."

"You could have called or something," I said, as he traced a finger down my cheek.

"Yes, I should have," he admitted.

"Damn it," I said, pulling his mouth to mine. I kissed him furiously. "Don't do it ever again." I tried sounding tough, but it was a whimper at best.

"Yes, my Queen," he said.

"And quit fucking calling me that," I said.

"Forgive me, Grace. Please. I want to make love to you. This mad fairy shit is driving me wild," he purred.

"No," I said defiantly, but it was a losing battle with his lips sucking on my neck. "Stop that. All I need is trying to run for office with a hickie on my neck."

"You claimed me, so I get to claim you," he countered.

"There are better places to suck," I supplied.

"Oh, that's it," he said picking me up like carrying a bride over a threshold to his bedroom. Our bedroom.

I woke up feeling his warm body next to mine. His heavy breathing indicated that he was still sleeping. Angry sex was fantastic, but I was exhausted after fighting him for control in the bed. We needed to do it more often. It wasn't long before he stirred. It was like he didn't miss a beat.

"How are you controlling that dark power now?" he asked.

I sighed. "I dunno. I think it's just a willpower kind of thing. You know, I just go on instinct. Instead of it taking over me, I demanded it to work in my favor. However, I may have frightened quite a few people."

"It was strong. They all obeyed you with just a hand gesture," he said.

"That wasn't my power. That's the power they gave me when we stood in the Grove on that Sunday last year, and Matthew Rayburn proclaimed me as the Queen of the Exiles. I've always felt it there, but never used it."

"You were afraid to use it," he said.

"Why do you have to know so much?" I complained. Granted, I'd asked him plenty of questions since we reconciled our differences. He was always open to explain, but my natural instinct was distrust. Not that I distrusted him specifically, but I'd spent my whole life on the run for the most part. Skepticism was natural for me.

"I've watched you for years, Grace. I know you," he smiled.

I rolled my eyes. He liked to remind me that all the years we spent working together he was attracted to me all along. Like I was oblivious to it. I wasn't, but he had a girl. The viper that walked into my meeting last night, in fact. The snake that used to live in this house with him. The serpent that slept around on him while he remained faithful to her. Shady Grove didn't need her kind roaming about spreading venom through the masses. There was only one good snake in my book. A dead one.

"They are going to drag me through the mud," I said.

"You will rise above all of that. I'll be there with you. There is nothing she can say that will harm you," he said. "Fairies moved here from all over the world to be under your protection. They won't let her sway them."

"I'm not that naïve. We need to prepare for the worst," I said, climbing out of bed.

"What is the worst?"

"That I stole you from her. That I'm some whore that fucked every man in this town and every other town I've lived in. She will bring up my arrest. She will bring up kissing Levi. Being engaged to

Levi. I'm willing to bet she will bring Winnie into it, and so help me, if she does I won't hold back," I rattled off all the crazy things she could use for an attack. Dylan slid out of the bed catching me in the middle of the rant.

"Stop," he said softly. "I've got plenty of dirt on her."

I raised my eyebrows at him. "Huh?"

"I lived here for five years. I was a cop. I know everything there is to know about Stephanie Davis, and she knows that I know," he grinned.

"I don't want to stoop to her level," I said.

"Since when did you become all high and mighty?" he laughed.

"Since my fiancé is the most honorable person I know, and I have a lot to live up to," I replied.

"I love you, Grace, but all I've ever wanted was for you to be you," he said.

"There you go being sweet again," I said.

"Does that mean I can get angry sex again?"

"We will see," I teased. He groaned as we pulled apart to go about getting ready for the day. It was still early. "I want to talk to Betty. She surprised me a little last night, but you came in after her outburst."

"Really? She went against you?" he sounded surprised as I started the shower in the bathroom. "What did she say?"

"It was the old Unseelie versus Wild fairy distinction. Some Unseelie fairies are rather tame, like Betty and Luther. Others are pretty wild like Deacon Giles," I replied. "She just acted like they should be separate. I disagree. However, she is my friend. I want to talk to her because I don't want this election to come between us."

"I'm going to make coffee," he said, leaving me in the shower to think.

Every part of me cringed at the idea of having to compete with Stephanie Davis. She was a respected lawyer. Her fiancé was a partner in the law firm where she worked. Her mother had lived and died in Shady Grove. She stayed with Dylan for five years until he left her for me. However, it would look like I took him from her no matter what we tried to explain about the situation. Our personal lives would be exposed to the whole of Shady Grove. The election could prove to be very dangerous for the fairies in Shady Grove. The world at large knew little of fairy beings, other than tales and legends which were embellished for the most part to appeal to the human population.

I was unemployed trailer trash. The fact was, despite my reputation, I'd only slept with two men in this town. Dylan and Remy. She'd slept with many, many more than that. I'd see her flirting at the bar, but because of my working relationship with Dylan, I never broached the subject with him. I didn't know the nature of their relationship. Their relationship made no sense to me, even now.

Finally, I had everything I'd never dreamed of, a sweet daughter, a dedicated fiancé, and a purpose in life. But when she walked into that room last night, I wanted to punch a 'ho. Going forward, I knew I had to be true to myself, but I was a brash, vulgar-mouthed, and impulsive trailer queen, which would get me into more trouble than gaining votes. My very being was in conflict with what I needed to be to win.

Stepping out of Dylan's shower in this enormous house, I suddenly felt completely out of place. Rufus stood at my feet lapping up the shower water on the floor. What was I supposed to do? Go head to head with a woman who could outtalk and outclass me? Shrink away and give up? Neither of those things sounded promising to me.

"Grace," Dylan's voice broke through my thoughts.

"Huh?" I said as he handed me a cup of coffee.

"Get over yourself. You aren't going to back down. My girl is a fighter," he grinned.

"Can you read minds?" I asked.

He laughed, "Just yours." For a moment, I thought he was serious. "No, Grace, I just know you. Stop stressing it. She was here in the limelight for much longer than you. Never once did she give a shit about anyone, but herself. That will be the difference. People will remember. We will remind them."

"You my campaign manager?" I asked.

"I'm your everything," he said winking at me.

"Cocky bastard," I laughed.

"It's true."

"Still cocky," I replied.

"Get dressed, and I'll take you to town," he said. I started putting on jeans and a sweater which was pretty much my staple outfit when it was cold outside. Dylan had bought me a really cute black leather jacket because he knew how much I loved his. However, I loved his, because it smelled like him. The one he gave me wasn't the same, but it came from his heart. If I stayed in this fight, it would be for him. He believed in me. I couldn't let him down.

CHAPTER SIX

ABOUT 2 MILES OUT OF TOWN, IT STARTED. FIRST WAS A ROYAL BLUE sign on metal stakes under a mailbox with elegant lettering. It said, "Vote for Stephanie." Next was a small billboard with her fair face in a sensible dress proclaiming, "No one knows Shady Grove better than Stephanie Davis. Vote for Stephanie."

"Fuck a duck," I muttered.

"I'd rather…" Dylan started.

"Shut up!" I quickly shot back.

"Just ignore it. A couple of signs. No big deal," he said.

As we pulled on to Main Street, it got worse. More signs and royal blue ribbons lined the streets. Several shops along the row had blue "Vote for Stephanie" signs. I even saw, "Stephanie is the best!" on a marquee.

We pulled into the diner and proudly displayed in the line of bushes in front was a royal blue sign. My heart sank. If Betty and Luther weren't voting for me, there was no way the half of Shady Grove that I didn't know was going to.

"I don't want to go in there," I muttered.

"I'm hungry. You can sit here if you want," Dylan said, hopping out of the truck. He stood in front of it with his hands on his hips watching me.

Opening the door, I slid out of the truck. The town almost smelled different. As we approached the door, I could hear the patrons inside talking. The jukebox was playing an old Johnny Cash song, "Ballad of a Teenage Queen."

Stepping inside the small diner, the five patrons turned from their discussion to look at us. "Golden hair and eyes of blue, how those eyes could flash at you," Johnny sang.

"Morning Betty," Dylan called to the white-haired waitress behind the bar.

"Morning Mr. Riggs," she smiled. She nodded at me.

"Hi Betty," I muttered.

"What can I get for y'all?" she asked taking her pencil out from over her ear.

"I'll have the big breakfast plate. You know how I like it. What do you want, Grace?"

"Coffee," I replied.

"Eat something," Dylan urged.

"And a bowl of grits," I added.

"Sure thing. Luther, hungry folks out here. Speed it up," Betty called to him. She jeered him constantly, but never meant a word of it.

"Calm down! It takes time and love to make good food. Morning Dylan! Grace!" Luther was exuberant as ever.

I waved at him. "Morning!" Dylan called back.

Looking at the other diners, I recognized them all. Juanita and Diego Santiago were Mexican immigrants. Both were bear shifters. Many people considered the Mexican Grizzly Bear to be extinct, but in actuality, they continued to walk the earth, but moved from their homeland because they were hunted vigorously. There were supernatural hunters in the United States, but Shady Grove wasn't on most maps, so we managed to stay out of the limelight.

Malcolm Taggart sat next to his partner in crime Caleb Joiner. Malcolm, a Seelie fairy, was kicked out of the Otherworld for being too much like an Unseelie fairy. Caleb, a changeling, had a Gwyllion mother and a human father. His father died not long after he was born, and his mother, being the hideous creature that she was, left him to die. He was rescued by a kind-hearted Sanhedrin by the name of Jeremiah Freyman.

I'd learned over the past few months that I wasn't the only fairy that Jeremiah took pity on. In fact, I knew of at least a dozen fairies that lived in Shady Grove that were brought here by the old coot. He'd called me a couple of days after the mayhem at Christmas asking about Winnie. I berated him for not being here to help with the chaos leading up to Christmas, but he just apologized saying he was very busy. I imagined he'd show up shortly with another forlorn fairy in need of protection. Only now, it might not be me protecting them. It might be Stephanie Davis. I wondered what Jeremiah would think of that. Hell, what did the Sanhedrin think about Stephanie? Caiaphas, the head of the zealots, had pretty much endorsed my ascension. Did they have an opinion on Stephanie? The Sanhedrin were Seelie fairies who posed as religious zealots that hunted wayward fairies. They hunted me for hundreds of years until Jeremiah had pity on me. I lived under their contracted rules until a few months ago when I accepted the Queen of the Exiles role. If I didn't win, would it mean that I'd get a new contract? The thought caused goosebumps to rise on my arms. Dylan instinctively rubbed my arm with his warm hand.

The final patron in the diner sat at the far end alone with a newspaper blocking his face. I knew who it was. Chubby fingers clasped the edges of the paper. Freckled hands with a touch of ginger hair indicted to me that it was the man who introduced Stephanie last night.

Turning to Dylan, I said, "Who is he? Do you know him?"

Dylan groaned, "Yes, he's been to the house a couple of times with Stephanie. He's one of her fairy servants, but he works as a legal secretary at the law firm. For a secretary, he's pretty high and mighty."

"For a servant, you mean," I said.

Dylan smiled. "Yes, for both. He's smarmy."

"What does that mean?"

"You've never heard of smarmy?"

"Well, yes, but tell me what you mean by it," I asked. I knew there had to be a story there.

"He's smug, but will butter up anyone if he thinks he can gain from it," he said.

"Yuck. A brown-noser," I said.

"Yes, and slicker than chicken shit on linoleum," Dylan replied.

"Fairy? What kind?"

"We are going to have to get you a book," Dylan teased. I smacked him on the arm.

"Don't beat that pretty man, Grace," Betty chided. I thought she was just joking, so I started to smile, but the look on her face could have skinned a cat.

"Yes, ma'am," I said looking to Dylan to see if he caught it.

"Maybe after the election you can mend fences with her," he suggested.

"Maybe," I replied sadly.

"He's a brownie. Low level Seelie fairy. He will do whatever she tells him to do," Dylan explained going back to the secretary.

"Name?" I asked.

"My name is Kyffin Merrick. If you wanted to know my name, *Queen*, all you had to do was ask, but since you have no time for such things, I suppose getting your wencher to explain things is just as well. However, don't insult me by thinking I can't hear your foul mouth," he droned.

"Thank you, Mr. Merrick for the information. Go fuck yourself," I said. Malcolm and Caleb found it to be funny and began making a ruckus by laughing.

"Grace Ann Bryant, you will not talk like that in this establishment! We have good paying customers who don't have to come in here and listen to your vulgarities," Betty spouted. The men stopped laughing, returning to their breakfast.

I immediately stood up and left. Dylan caught me at the car. "Grace, where are you going?"

"I can't even speak like I always have anymore. I'm going to get coffee with Nestor. Go back in and eat. I'll be fine," I said.

"Hang on a minute," Dylan said. He walked back in and talked to Betty who sweetly patted his hand. He gave her a wad of cash, then hurried back outside to me. "I'll go with you. Let's walk." He offered his arm to me. I latched on, leaning into him.

"I can't do this," I said.

"You can, but you are going to have to think before you speak," he said.

I pulled away from him. "You said you have never wanted me to be anyone but me."

"That's true. However, it seems obvious if you want to continue as Queen, you are going to have to decide how you want to approach it. You can continue to be the brash woman that I adore. Or clean up your act, if only for the election," he said trying to coax me back to his arms.

"Brash, huh?"

"That I adore," he repeated.

I took his arm back, and we continued to the corner where Hot Tin Roof sat. "I don't know that I can be anything else, but me."

"Really, because it wasn't so long ago that you were a trailer bound, unemployed, contracted, Unseelie fairy. Now you are free, employed, and a church goer!" he teased.

"It's not that kind of church," I replied. Our Baptist church was actually a portal to a magical grove where a Druid service was held every Sunday. It's how I got to know most of the fairies that lived in Shady Grove. Or at least, I thought it was most of them. Apparently, quite a few of them didn't attend services.

"Still you are different. You have a devastatingly handsome fiancé, too," he added.

"Yes," I replied.

"Yes? I'm devastatingly handsome?" he prodded.

"Yes, I'm different. You are moderately handsome," I replied.

"I'll take that," he smiled as he opened the door up to the bar. He was right though. I fell to pieces inside every time I looked at him.

"Nestor?" I called out.

"He must have taken Winnie to school this morning," Dylan said.

I walked behind the bar, starting the coffee pot. Nestor always kept the pot ready to brew just in case I showed up before he came down from his apartment over the bar. "Maybe I'm in over my head," I groaned.

"There is no doubt about that," Dylan said. I scowled at him. "But you can swim."

"Do I look like a mermaid to you?" I asked.

"Dunno. Turn around and shake your tail," he laughed. I threw a bar towel at him.

The door swung open, and Levi entered.

"Morning, Bard," I said.

"Morning, Grace. Dylan." He looked pretty rough. "Coffee not ready?"

"Not yet. We just got here," I said. Dylan stood up from the bar stool. "I'm going to get the food. I told Betty to pack it up."

"She probably spit in mine," I replied. "Let Levi eat it."

"Why would she spit in your food?" Levi asked.

I told him about my little outburst with Kyffin Merrick, and how Betty jumped down my throat about vulgar language.

"This is from a woman who smacks her boyfriend on the ass, regularly," Levi said.

"That's true," Dylan agreed. "I'll be right back."

"Dylan!" I said.

"I mean it!" he laughed as he went out the door.

"So, help me God, if he doesn't come back this time," I said pouring Levi a cup of coffee.

"What? You are going to leave him?" Levi asked. He knew I wasn't.

I sighed. "No."

"That's what I thought," Levi replied while sipping the coffee.

"Am I too vulgar?" I asked.

Levi laughed. "Yes, but that's just who you are. Don't change that because of all of this. I'm sure that Merrick fella deserved whatever you dished out at him."

"It was a command to go masturbate," I replied.

Levi spit coffee across the bar. I wiped it up with a bar towel, laughing at him. "Damn, Grace," he said wiping coffee off his chin.

"You missed a spot," I said, rubbing his jaw with the towel.

"Thanks," he replied.

"Why do you look dog tired? Don't like the new bed?"

"No, it's fine. Kady called in the middle of the night apologizing," he muttered.

I grimaced. His on and off girlfriend was trying my nerves. I'd already punched her once for asking about Dylan's dick. She best lay off my bard before I jerked a knot in her. "Please tell me you didn't forgive her?" I asked.

"No. I didn't," he said staring into the coffee cup. I walked around the bar and hugged him. That familiar tingle as our skin brushed vibrated through my body. "What's that for?"

"'Cause you needed it," I said.

"Thanks, Grace. If the people here can't see that you are a good person, let them get what they deserve," he said.

Dylan walked back in with two bags. He stopped when he saw me standing so close to Levi, but he kept on after the slight hesitation.

"Apparently, they are out of grits. I got you a biscuit," he said.

"He needed a hug," I explained.

"I need one, too," he replied. So, I hugged Mr. Jealousy, and he grabbed my ass.

When I jerked away from him, because it startled me, he winked at Levi who rolled his eyes and snickered.

"There you go flirting with him again," I said. Levi turned red, but Dylan shoved a biscuit in his mouth. "I could go a lot of places with that big ol' biscuit in your mouth, but I'm trying to tone down my vulgarities."

Dylan shared his breakfast with Levi. I didn't eat. My mind was on Shady Grove. I'd claimed it as my town. How dare she show back up out of the big city and act like she cared what happened here? Why did she care? Those thoughts were probably the key to figuring all of this out, but what was I supposed to do? Walk up to the bitch and ask her why she cared all of a sudden? I doubted I'd get a straight answer.

It wasn't long before Nestor returned from taking Winnie to school. We discussed strategies, and the awful blue signs covering every patch of green along the roads.

I thought purple signs would be the best, but Dylan said I should go more traditional like red. Make it a signature color. Wear red to match my tattoo. I'd planned to keep my tattoo covered. However, I needed to accept that there were things about me I would never change. The tattoo, even if I could, was one of those things. It was a part of me. Besides, I didn't need to revamp myself. I just needed to be a more polished version.

"I need to go shopping," I said.

"Call Mable. She will go with you," Nestor said.

"No offense, Nestor, but Mable and I don't really share the same tastes. I know who to call," I said. Picking up my phone, I dialed.

"Dr. Tabitha Mistborne," she answered.

"Hey, I need to get new clothes for this election thing. Want to go shopping?" I asked.

"Heck, yea! We can find you some really cute stuff. When do you want to go?" she asked. Tabitha and I had become friends after my sickness around Christmas at the hands of the Cane Creek Coven. We got together frequently having lunch, watching movies, and goofing off. I'd never had a female friend, but she was awesome.

"Whenever you can. Are you working today?" I asked. She was a doctor at the med center in town.

"Nope. I've got three days off!" she replied. "We can get you some signs made too. I hate these damn blue signs everywhere. I'm thinking red."

"Great minds," I replied.

"Oh, you want red too?" she asked.

"It was Dylan's idea," I admitted.

"Great minds, indeed. Where are you?" she asked.

"At the bar. Having coffee."

"I'll pick you up in an hour. I've been lazy all morning. I'll get up and get a shower. See ya soon," she said excitedly.

"Bye," I replied, hanging up.

"All set?" Dylan asked.

I nodded. "You busy today?"

"Not really. Want me to go buy some more furniture for the trailer?" he offered. "Unless you want to pick it out yourself."

"No, that's fine. You can do it. Just don't turn it into a man cave. My only request is a big, comfy recliner," I said. Furniture shopping didn't appeal to me. I was glad he offered.

"For two," he smiled.

"I said big," I reminded him.

"I thought you were talking about something else," he smirked.

"Ew," said Levi.

We teased Levi until Tabitha arrived. I got a nice, long kiss from Dylan who told me to have fun. Levi still looked forlorn, but it was a perpetual state for him. I needed to find him another woman. Tabitha and I headed off to Birmingham to search for clothes.

CHAPTER SEVEN

TABITHA AND I TALKED ABOUT THE ELECTION ALL THE WAY TO THE mall. Thankfully, she was on my side. She never once said I needed to change who I was. She assured me that plenty of people in the town knew me and appreciated what I'd done for them.

We spent the whole day shopping. By the time we were finished, I was sick of red. However, I had the feeling that I'd be seeing a lot of it for the next couple of weeks. We also visited an office supply store and designed campaign signs. They were red, too. All sorts of variations of vote for Grace. Grace Ann Bryant for Council Lead. We had to avoid fairy terminology. There were still normals living in Shady Grove. I needed to get home and finish up the rules for the election.

I called Levi to meet us at the bar with his laptop, so I could type them up. Tabitha said her goodbyes, taking a bunch of signs with her to put up around her house and the med center. Levi brought the laptop. As I sat at the bar finishing up the rules, Misaki came in.

"Hello, Queen Grace," she said with a slight bow. I wasn't sure if I was supposed to return the bow or not. I just dipped my head to her hoping that was enough.

"Hello, Misaki. How are you feeling today? Any demons show up to claim you?" I asked.

"No. My betrothed has received word that I am pregnant," she said.

I spewed coffee all over the laptop. Wiping it down before it got sticky, I asked, "How do you know if you are pregnant?"

"Oh, it only takes once," she said.

"Well, that's great for you," I said, hoping I'd cleaned the coffee off the laptop sufficiently. I wondered who obliged her need to procreate. She provided me with the answer promptly.

"I want to thank you for understanding the position I was in," she said sitting down on the stool. "I would like to stay here in Shady Grove to keep the child near his father."

"It's a boy?" I asked.

"Most definitely. I also want to thank you for allowing Dylan to help me," she said.

I didn't spit the coffee out. Instead, I dropped the entire cup. The plain white cup hit the tile floor of the bar, shattering into a million pieces. A woozy feeling rushed over me, and my cheeks grew hot. "How did Dylan help you?"

"In the only way, he truly could. Like I said. I am very thankful for your understanding," she said.

Standing up off my stool and backing away from her, I said, "You are a liar. I didn't allow him to do anything. He didn't make that thing with you."

"Oh, my! I thought you knew," she said. "It took persuasion, but he agreed it was the best way to protect me. He is wonderful man. You are lucky woman."

Nestor came in from the stock room. "Grace, what's wrong?"

I slapped the laptop closed, dialing Dylan as fast as I could. The phone rang, but he never answered. Telling myself to stay calm, I looked at the kitsune. There was no way. She was lying. I dialed again. No answer. "What is the purpose of having a phone if you don't fucking answer it?" I yelled.

"Grace! What is wrong?" Nestor tried getting my attention. My chest heaved with hard breaths. I had to stay in control. If I released the evil inside me, I'd kill this woman and Dylan's child. But no, it wasn't his, because she was a liar.

"I think I upset her," Misaki said.

"What did you say?" he asked.

I backed against the wall near the jukebox, dialing Dylan over and over. "Please answer," I muttered.

"I thanked her for allowing Dylan to save me from the demon," she said staring at me. Along the corners of her eyes, I saw amusement. Running to the door, I heard Nestor yell at me, but I kept running. The trailer wasn't far from here, and the bus would bring Winnie home soon. Hoping I'd beat her home, I ran all the way to the trailer park to the trailer, then into an empty living room. No furniture. Dylan must be still out buying furniture.

"Grace?"

"Fuck!" I yelled. "You scared the shit out of me, Levi."

"What's wrong?" he immediately knew something was bothering me.

Shaking my head, I tried to gather my thoughts. "Call Dylan. He's not answering for me," I said.

"You need to sit down. Come in here," he grabbed my hand shooting the tingle through my arm. He'd pulled power to coax me to calm down. "Now sit here on my bed. Take deep breaths." I obeyed, because I didn't have a choice. He picked up his phone and dialed Dylan.

"Hey, man, where are you?" he asked. "You need to come home. Right now. We are at the trailer." He paused to listen to Dylan. He handed me the phone.

Barely holding it in my hands as they shook, I answered, "Hello?"

"What's going on?"

"Misaki is pregnant," I muttered.

He paused for a moment. "Grace, why does that matter?"

"She said, you are the father," I sobbed.

"You believed her?!" he shouted.

"No, but the way she looked at me. It felt wrong. I ran. I ran all the way home. I've called you twenty times, and you didn't answer. Levi called once," I barely got the words out.

"I have no missed calls, Grace. Stay there. I'm on the way," he growled. The line went dead. Sliding off the edge of the bed, I landed on the floor with a thud. Levi crouched before me. He put his hands on my cheeks. Less power this time. Just a soothing tingle.

"Tell me what happened, that way I can tell him when he gets here. You guys can't fight right now. This election is too important," he said.

"When did you grow up on me?" I asked.

He grinned. "You are just seeing it like that for the first time?"

Leaning forward I rested my head on his chest letting the prickles surround me. He wrapped his arms around me. I always forgot how strong he was until he was wrestling me when I was fighting mad, or when occasionally I'd get a good hug. Starting at the moment she walked in the bar, I told him everything. "And so, I ran here," I said.

"You know he didn't do it, right?" Levi asked.

"I know. It just upset me," I replied.

"When he gets here, I'll meet him outside and try to calm him down. Tell him what happened. I admit that this is a selfish thing for me," he said.

"How so?" I said leaning back and wiping the tears off my cheeks.

"I know that Lisette is back in the bayou. The demon was dispatched. But I have nowhere else to go. You and Dylan are my family. My crazy best friend and her fiancé. He's like a brother. I'd do anything for you," he said. "Plus, if you get mad at him, you will be here, and I really like the garden tub!"

"What! Levi Rearden, you didn't!" I pushed him away from me.

"Popped that bathtub cherry," he smirked.

"Did you really?"

"No, but I wanted to prove that Dylan having a kid with someone else was secondary to me using your new bathtub," he laughed. I swatted him on the arm. "Git up." He stood pulling me to my feet as we heard Dylan's car pull up outside. He kissed me on the forehead with one last tingle. I shivered as he ducked out to meet Dylan. Sitting on the end of the bed, I waited.

It didn't take long. Dylan peeked around the corner into the bedroom. Closing my eyes, I felt ashamed for letting it get to me. I felt him approach, and just like Levi, he put his hands on my cheeks. No vibration, just warmth. "Open your eyes, and look at me," he said softly. I did as he asked. "Would I ever do that to you?"

"No. I know you didn't. It was just frustrating," I said.

Levi stood in the small hallway outside of his room. Dylan swatted the door closed, then pressed me down on the bed. His lips met mine in hot kisses as if he was trying to prove his faithfulness to me.

"Awe, come on, you guys. Don't do that on my bed," Levi whined.

"Shut up, Levi," we yelled back to him. A huge smile crossed Dylan's face.

"This damn town," he muttered. "Let's just go."

"You sound like me now," I said.

"If you don't win the election, we are leaving," he said.

I nodded. Before he could finish what he'd started, the squealing brakes of the school bus echoed through the trailer. He sighed. "We can finish it later," I said.

"I love you," he said.

"I love you, too."

"Aunt Grace!" Winnie yelled, running to me as she tried holding on to her backpack. I wrapped her up in a big hug.

"How was school?" I asked. She was in first grade at Shady Grove Elementary. I'd spoken to her teacher after the holidays. Miss Castle was sad to hear of Bethany's death, but she was happy to know that Winnie would have a more stable life. I started to explain to her that my life was far from stable, but I knew Dylan and I offered her more stability than her drug addict mother had. Definitely more love.

"It was good. Everybody wants to be my friend, but not the boys. They have cooties," she explained.

"Do I have cooties?" Dylan asked.

"No, men don't have them. They outgrow them," she replied.

"That's debatable," I interjected.

She hugged Dylan and Uncle Levi, then ran off into the house to start her homework. Levi went with her. He was the designated homework helper. Dylan and I could only do so much considering neither of us had any traditional schooling. We both had records saying we went to school, but they were fakes. Levi was in school not too long ago, so he got stuck with the job. He loved it.

"What subject today?" Levi asked.

"Math," Winnie said making a gagging noise.

"I like math," Levi said.

"You do?" she asked.

"Yes, especially when you are counting money," he replied.

"Oh, I like money," she said.

"See math isn't so bad. Let's see what we have to do," he said as she took out a sheet with addition and subtraction problems. Levi helped her complete it, but she was smart as a whip, knowing how to do most of it herself.

"I did buy some furniture," Dylan said. "It will be here tomorrow. Including a nice big recliner."

"This election is going to drive me crazy," I said.

"Short drive," he replied. I punched his shoulder. It hurt me more than him.

"Tab and I had some signs made today. We need to put them up, but I left them at the bar," I said, remembering I'd ran home in a frenzy.

"Let's go get them. Levi, you got Winnie for a bit?" Dylan asked.

"Yeah, sure. We can do homework, then color or watch TV in my room," he said.

"Yay!" she responded.

"Okay. We will be back soon, then go home for dinner," Dylan replied.

I kissed Winnie on the forehead, and she giggled. Dylan drove us back to the bar where we found a relieved Nestor. He said that Misaki left earlier.

"I could have sworn she was already showing," Nestor explained.

"If I got that woman pregnant, it was the least memorable sex ever," Dylan joked, but then quickly looked at me. Shaking my head at his terrible joke, I laughed anyway. However, it wouldn't be the first time a fairy seduced someone and made them forget it. "These signs are great. I'm glad you decided to go with the red."

"We bought a ton of red clothes, too. Although it seems a little silly. Red is like blood. That's got to be a bad omen," I said.

"Red is the counter to blue," Nestor said.

"Winnie would have said Pink," I offered.

"Pink is too girly. We need you to seem tough, yet feminine," he said.

"I just need to be less vulgar," I said.

"I need you to be more vulgar," he said lifting his eyebrows. The red blush traveled up my next to cheeks. Nestor laughed, uncomfortable with the comment.

"Let's go put up some signs," Dylan said.

"We have to stop by the community center and put up these election rules," I added.

"I've got some coffee to go," Nestor said, pouring the magical java into to-go cups.

"Thanks, Nestor. You are the best," I said.

We loaded up again. Stopping on the busiest corners, Dylan got out strategically placing a red sign among the plethora of blue signs. As we approached the community center, there was a group of people waiting for me to post the rules. The rules were simple and concise.

Everything from no public brawling to not removing campaign signs was listed. Dylan looked up local election rules, and together we adapted them to what we thought would be needed for a fairy election.

Dylan took the rules and posted them on the community center board while everyone gathered to look. The nominations were to be turned in at the Hot Tin Roof Bar in a box Nestor placed on the counter. We'd given Mable the key to the box, so she was the only one with access. We put all of this in the notice with the rules. Stephanie and Kyffin were suspiciously absent. Troy approached the car.

"Good afternoon, Sheriff," I greeted him.

"How are things going?" he asked.

"I guess they are okay. How's the law business?" I asked.

He sighed, "It's been quiet, but I got the feeling this election is going to keep us busy. For what it's worth, Grace, you have my support. I'll endorse you publicly if need be. Most of the department is behind you, too. The guys all know how Stephanie treated Dylan. Heck, several of them have slept with her. None of them would vote for her though. She's not part of this community anymore. She moved to Tuscaloosa. I doubt she even is a resident here. Can she even be eligible?"

"I'm sure she owns her mother's old place. When her mom passed in October, I'm sure Stephanie inherited everything," I replied.

"That's right. I'd forgotten about that. Just looking for angles to help you," he said.

"I appreciate it," I said.

"Hey Troy," Dylan said returning to the car. He shook hands with Troy.

"Hey, man, just telling Grace that she has my support," he said.

"Thanks. I'm sure we are going to need as much support as possible," Dylan said.

"Have you both considered getting married before this election?" Troy said. "I think it would be a good comparison. You are the married woman with a child. She is the unmarried woman who slept with half the town."

"No. We aren't getting married for an election," Dylan said which surprised me. He'd been pushing for a date, but I hadn't decided. It wasn't because I didn't want to marry him. I just couldn't decide on the best time of year to do it.

"We could if needed. She's engaged to Sergio Krykos, the head partner at her law firm," I reminded them. "She's as stable, if not more so than I am."

"What am I? Chopped liver?" Dylan teased.

"Ew, I don't eat liver," I said. Realizing the implication, I quickly added. "Don't you even say a word!" I saw the light in his eyes. Who knows what he would have said if I hadn't stopped him. And I was the vulgar one!

The low rumble of a large vehicle approached. Around the corner came the largest monstrosity I'd ever seen. A huge private motorhome drove up with Stephanie Davis' face plastered on the side of it. The huge thing came to a stop with hisses and grunts. When the door opened, Stephanie and Sergio dismounted the steps like gymnastic gazelles. I'd never seen anything more graceful. I climbed out of Dylan's car leaning next to him. We took in their cheerful greetings to all those who had gathered there.

"Can I put my face on the side of your Camaro?" I asked Dylan.

"No, but we can buy you an RV," he offered.

"I thought you loved me more than your car," I pouted.

"The car wouldn't do your face justice," he said.

"Nice backpedal," Troy said offering Dylan a fist. They bumped.

Her icy stare met us. She raised her hand and waggled her fingers at me as if we were old friends. I waggled mine back, but left the middle one up for a measure. She rolled her eyes.

"At what point can I kick her ass?" I asked.

Dylan sighed, knowing I didn't mean at the ballot box. "You can't. If you want to win."

I sighed, too. "If I get to the point where winning isn't as important as kicking her ass, then I can do it."

She walked over to the posted rules while Sergio took pictures of it. They conversed in low tones while Kyffin Merrick fended off the adoring public. I hadn't even seen him get off the bus. Looking with my fairy sight, I saw the bright purple glow of royalty around Stephanie. Merrick was outlined with a lighter shade of purple showing that he was a royal servant. Sergio Krykos glowed a bright blue.

"Hmm," I uttered.

"What?" Dylan asked.

"He's blue," I replied.

"Krykos?"

"Yep. I'm blue, too" I replied. I knew Krykos was Greek, but there were very few beings in the Greek myths that would be considered fairies. Most were gods and children of gods. Creatures like my friend, Chris Purcell, did fall within that category. Chris glowed with a pale tan color which was almost white. I'd never seen Krykos before the memorial service when I thought Dylan died. Surprised that he was blue, I looked again just to be sure. He was most definitely Unseelie royalty. However, that group included hundreds of fairies. Most of which I'd never met.

"Maybe you could ask your father for some insight on the colors." Dylan offered.

"I probably should before this gets out of hand. I wonder if Mable would help me. I hadn't approached the subject with Mable Sanders, my grandfather's girlfriend, about her spying for my father. To be honest, I didn't care what she told Daddy about me. However, if she had information that would help me with the election, I should talk to her. "We need to go pick up Winnie. It's getting late, and I want us to have dinner together."

"Alright," Dylan said, opening the door for me.

"Oh, Miss Bryant, do wait a moment," Stephanie purred.

"Shit," I muttered. "Please make it quick, Miss Davis. I need to get home to my child."

"Your child? Oh, that's right. You know I heard that Bethany Jones died. Very sad for poor Winnie to be forced to live with a woman like you."

"Yes, poor Winnie," I agreed, just to make her shut up.

"My lawyer is going over these rules that you made up. I think that we might have a few disputes on the way these are worded. You really should have hired a lawyer to look them over before posting them," she said.

"I did the research on the rules, Stephanie. They are in accordance with state and local regulations, but adapted for our people," Dylan supplied.

"Just the same, you will hear from my lawyer on this matter," she said. "My intention is to win this race. If you haven't noticed, we've put a lot of money into this campaign. I do hope you are prepared to lose. If you do, you will be the first fairy banished from my kingdom."

My body tightened. I felt the cool burst of anger travel down my spine as my glamour dropped, and the icy fairy queen emerged. "Stephanie Davis, let's get one thing straight. You might think you could banish me from my home, but you would be wrong. I dare you to try. I'm not leaving Shady Grove. This is my home and these are my people. Perhaps you think I'm just a piece of trailer trash. Please keep thinking that because when I wipe the floor with you, I'm going to let you live here. Just so you can see me ruling here every day. Something tells me that if you lose, you'll suddenly forget your residence here. Have your lawyer send me your complaints. I'll forward them to Mr. Remington Blake."

"Remy is a joke, but I admit he's a good lay," she laughed.

I didn't surprise me that Remy had slept with her. By Nestor and Dylan's admission, Stephanie had slept with half the town. She'd probably slept with half of Tuscaloosa too.

"He was good in bed, but he's an even better lawyer," I said.

"If he was so good, then why be with Dylan," she laughed.

"Because, I love Dylan," I replied flatly. Dylan smiled as he guided me into the passenger seat of his red Camaro.

Climbing in the driver's side, he said, "Thank you for that."

"I don't know what you are talking about," I smiled. "At least we don't have to paint your car. It's already red." We laughed, as he drove off leaving Stephanie in a cloud of exhaust.

CHAPTER EIGHT

We picked up Winnie and went home for a nice meal. I made spaghetti.

"I love 'sketti, Aunt Grace," Winnie said.

"Well, that's why I made it," I replied.

"Makes my belly fat," she said pulling up her shirt to show me her belly.

Since Winnie came to live with us, she had gained a lot of weight. No more hungry bedtimes. She told me one night as we read our bedtime story that she had "grumbly" stomach at night. It was so loud she couldn't sleep. My heart broke. All those years with her little self across the street from me in the trailer, going to bed hungry. I did as much as I could for her, but I don't think I realized the depth of the poverty that she'd faced. Never again.

"Time for bed, little girl," Dylan told her.

"Aw, do I have to?" she begged.

"Yes, ma'am. You have school tomorrow," he said.

"Will you read to me?" she asked, fluttering her eyelids. She was already charming the men. She wrapped Dylan and Levi around her little fingers whenever she saw fit.

"Of course," he replied. She ran up the stairs to the bedroom that he'd made for her even before her mother died. A perfect little girl haven with rainbows and unicorns.

Dylan occasionally had this creepy intuitive part of him. It's almost like he knew one day that both Winnie and I would be living here. Of course, I had my trailer now, but most of my nights would be with him. It didn't matter which home. I stood outside the bedroom door while he read her a book. Something about green eggs. Sounded awful, but it was a cute book.

When he finished reading, she said, "Mr. Dylan, I never had a daddy."

"I know, Winnie, but you have Uncle Levi and me to take care of you," Dylan said.

"Will you be my daddy?" she asked. My eyes welled up in tears.

Dylan's voice cracked, "Are you sure, Winnie?"

"Yes," she whispered.

"I would be honored to be your Daddy," he said, kissing her on the forehead.

"My Daddy has an awesome red car!" she excitedly said. She'd always loved that red Camaro. It made me giggle. Dylan looked back at me with the biggest grin on his face.

"Night, Winnie. I love you," he told her.

"I love you too, Daddy," she said. "Night, Aunt Grace."

Once again, I was pushed down the line in Winnie's love, but it didn't matter. She was too darn sweet.

I blew her a kiss. "Night, Winnie."

Dylan shut the door, then wrapped his arms around me. He picked me up.

"Oh, my god! That was amazing," he said. "Let's have ten more."

"Wait! What?"

"At least one," he said.

"At least one," I agreed.

"But if we had more, I'm fine with that," he said.

"I think I'd need one of those fancy quadruple-wides," I replied.

"Ugh, you and the damn trailer," he laughed. "Let's get started."

"On having kids?" I asked.

"Yes!" he said scooping me up to carry me to the bedroom. I laughed, having no desire to stop him. He plopped me down on the bed, climbing up over me. "Get these damn clothes off!"

Suddenly, he was in a baby- making frenzy thanks to Winnie's profession of love. I kept giggling as he yanked and pulled at my clothes. He paused for a moment, looking into my eyes.

"Why did you stop?" I asked still giggling.

"You do want to have a child with me, right?" he asked.

"You are asking me now? It's a little late isn't it considering how many times we've done this," I said.

"Well, I didn't want to assume," he said.

"You were already an ass, so go ahead and assume," I laughed.

"Answer me," he said.

"I have apprehensions, but I think all women do. However, seeing your face light up in there when she asked you that, I'd give you as many babies as you would like," I admitted.

"Okay, the rest of the clothes, please," he demanded.

"Yes, Daddy," I purred. He growled and was on me like white on rice.

Winnie was eating cereal when Dylan came downstairs looking pretty worn out. "Morning, Darlin'."

"Ugh," he grunted.

"Caveman need coffee?" I teased while Winnie giggled.

"Ugh," he grunted again.

"Daddy is a caveman!" Winnie proclaimed. Dylan's smile returned.

"Here you go, Daddy Caveman," I said handing him a cup.

"Thank you, my Queen," he grinned.

"Ugh," I replied. Winnie thought all of this was hilarious.

"Why does Daddy call you Queen?" she asked.

"She is the Queen of Shady Grove!" Dylan said.

"I am not," I replied. "Just the fairy part." I winked at Winnie.

She winked back, only it was both eyes instead of one. Thankfully, at Christmas, she still had a sense of wonder about her when she saw me transform into Gloriana. She thought it was fun dress up time. I wasn't sure how we would handle it going forward, but Dylan assured me that we would figure it out. I imagined at some point she would have to be told the truth. Kind of like the lie of Santa Claus only lasts for so long.

She slipped her key necklace around her neck. "Okay, it's time to go."

"I'll get my keys," Dylan said.

"I can take her in the truck," I replied.

"You sure?"

"Yeah, I'll do it. Then I'm supposed to work at the bar today," I said.

"Okay, I'll bring you lunch," he said.

I kissed him. Winnie made smooching noises. He hoisted her up in the air letting her fly over his head. She squealed and giggled. He hugged her tight, then let her down. She took off running to the truck.

"See you soon," I said.

"I'm gonna shower, and I'll be there as soon as possible. If I'm not, you call me fifty times until I answer," he joked.

"I will," I said.

"Love you, Grace," he said. He never let me go anywhere without saying it. He told me he never wanted me wonder if something ever happened to him. I cursed him for mentioning such a thing.

Dropping off Winnie at school, I noticed considerably more blue signs around town, but more red signs in the yards of homes. I pulled up at Hot Tin Roof, and Nestor had put up a huge red sign that said, "Vote for Queen Grace." I loved it. It was big and gaudy like me.

"I declare Nestor that sign is the most beautiful thing I've ever seen. Well, maybe not as beautiful as my new trailer, but it's nice," I said, taking off my jacket. "It's like a big red apple ready to be cooked for a pie!"

"You like it?"

"Love it! I'm thinking all of my signs need glitter to make it just right," I laughed.

"Too gaudy," he said.

"No such thing!" I replied, pouring a cup of coffee.

"I saw the RV," he said.

"Now that is too gaudy," I laughed.

He dried glasses as he talked, "It's a monstrosity."

"I couldn't agree more," I said.

"You should be out campaigning instead of working," he suggested.

"I am campaigning. The good folks that come into this bar have votes just like the rest of them. This is my core," I boasted.

"Oh, really? The drunks?"

"Hey, like I said, even drunks vote," I replied.

We talked about the election. I told him about her threatening the rules last night. He suggested I call Remy sooner rather than later to give him a heads up. "If she means to cause trouble, she will. She's never been anything, but trouble. I was happy the day Dylan came in here all tore up about her. Of course, I know now that he ran her off, so he could come after you."

"I'm not sure that's what happened, exactly," I denied. It was exactly what happened.

"What about the kitsune?" he asked.

"What about her? Dylan says he wasn't with her. I believe him," I said.

"Of course, he didn't, but if she's pregnant, someone did it," he said.

"I'm not sure that affects me," I said.

"What if it was your bard?" he offered.

I laughed. "She didn't want a half-breed as she called him."

"Maybe she got desperate," he said.

"Even if he did, I'm fine with it. Better than Kady," I said, pulling out my phone to call Remington Blake.

"Morning beautiful," he answered.

"Morning Remy, I might have a legal issue with Stephanie. She doesn't like the election rules. We based them on state and local election rules. I'm not sure what she has, but I'm sure I'll hear about it today. Mind taking a look at the rules for me?" I asked.

"Anything for you, my dear," he replied. "She's hell on wheels. Sweetheart, you have nothing to worry about with this election. When it's all said and done, her true colors will show."

"I certainly hope so. I don't have the same confidence," I said.

"Just be yourself. We all love ya," he said. "Email me the rules and call me when she stirs the pot."

"Thanks, Remy," I said.

"That man would do anything you asked him to do," Nestor said.

I groaned. It was true, and I tried not to abuse it. However, I paid him to do my legal work. So, I didn't feel too bad. As long as he didn't expect anything else out of the deal.

Levi came in the door with a blue plaid flannel shirt and jeans. He scratched his head because he'd let his hair grow out. It was getting a bit too long.

"Bikers don't wear flannel," I told him.

"Heh," he responded while pointing to the coffee pot.

"I ain't yo' mamma. Get it yourself," I told him. "Levi, did you sleep with that kitsune?"

He spit coffee across the bar. "What the hell, Grace? No. I didn't."

"I just wondered," I said. "You gotta stop spitting coffee everywhere."

"I wouldn't if you didn't say such things," he accused.

"You love it," I replied.

"I do," he admitted with a twinkle in his eye. "She was hot. The fox. I did some digging on them on the internet. They can be pretty seductive. Shapeshift. She could be pretty deadly if she wanted to be. So, why would she be afraid of a demon?"

"Any new fairy in town is a potential threat," Nestor offered. "The kitsune. The demon that chases her."

"Stephanie," I added. Levi gave me a high five.

"Yes, even Stephanie. Grace, you need to be careful. She is ruthless. If she wants something, she will get it. I've heard that when she started working for the law firm, she told everyone she wanted to be engaged to Sergio. She made that happen. He was with someone else, but she's disappeared. I'm not implying that she offed her or anything, but maybe. If she wants your job, she will do whatever it takes."

"Why should I be afraid of her?" I asked. "It's not like she can hurt me. She's only an elf."

"She is a royal elf with many servants," he said. "You have Dylan and Levi."

"No, I have Dylan, Levi, You, Remy, Troy, Amanda, Mable, should I keep going?"

"I'm sure you could add thirteen Yule Lads and a Krampus to that list," Levi said.

"Exactly. I'm not afraid of Stephanie Davis," I said confidently.

೭

"That fucking bitch," I yelled looking at the paperwork her lawyer delivered. "She's gone after every single rule. This stupid election was not supposed to be about me!"

"Sit down and eat," Dylan coaxed. He'd brought me a cheeseburger and fries from the diner which was my favorite meal from there. However, Miss Davis' antics left me with a bad taste in my mouth that no cheeseburger will fix. "Send the paperwork to Remington."

"She's even mad with the hours to vote. It's the same as the state elections! Except we added a few hours at night for the fairies that don't do daylight," I groaned.

"Don't let her get to you," Dylan said, sitting on a bar stool watching television. I slapped the paperwork down on the bar, taking one of Dylan's fries. He tried to steal it back. "You have your own. Quit eating mine."

"Eating yours is more fun," I said. He visibly flinched.

Closing his eyes to fight off whatever it was that hit him, he looked at me, "Could you not?"

"That's fine. I won't eat yours anymore," I teased.

"Yuck!" Levi exclaimed.

"Jealous," I said to him.

"Right now, yeah, I'm jealous of anyone getting some," he grumbled.

"Oh, good grief. It's only been a couple of days," I said.

"Four whole days," he moaned.

"Poor baby," I teased.

"Grace, eat!" Dylan ordered.

"*Grace, eat me!*" I mocked his tone. He cleared his throat, trying to forget what I had really said. "Who the hell told her we were having an election, anyway? She doesn't even live here."

"Can I have your cheeseburger?" Levi asked.

"No, go get your own," I complained.

"You are pitching a hissy fit, and it's getting cold," he said.

"He's right," Dylan added.

"Nestor, you said these two were on my side, but ever since they kissed I'm pretty sure they team up against me. Bromance style," I whined. Even though I was wound up tighter than a ten- day clock, I could still joke with these two. However, Stephanie not only challenged the rules. She challenged them all. We might have to actually find a judge to rule on her complaints. This was getting out of hand quickly.

Kadence Rayburn entered the bar. Levi turned to see who entered, then promptly turned his attention back to the television. I watched him, then her. She scowled at him.

"Grace, my dad wants to speak to you, but he won't come in the bar," she said.

Her father, Matthew Rayburn was known as the local Baptist minister to the common folk, but to us, he was the head Druid who held services every Sunday in a grove only accessible through the doors of the Shady Grove Baptist Church. To keep up appearances, he never entered the Hot Tin Roof Bar.

Unfolding my apron, I told Nestor I'd be right back.

"You good?" Dylan asked.

"Yep. I'll holler if I need you," I winked at him, heading out the door with Kady. I had no desire to talk to her. No matter whose fault it was, I was going to be on Levi's side when it came to their on-again, off-again relationship.

"How's Levi?" she asked boldly. I'd already punched her out once for blatantly asking about the size of Dylan's dick after confessing her crush on him.

I stopped, putting my hands on my hips. "He's great, Kady. Why ask me? He's sitting right in there," I said, pointing back in the bar. "I think he's waiting on his date to get here." I hated the lie after I said it, but the look on her face was worth it. A mixture of hatred and hurt. She deserved it for constantly torturing Levi. I supposed she had a pussy like skittles because he kept going back to taste the rainbow. There wasn't a pot of gold at the end of it either. Just more grief and heartache.

"Oh, I see," she muttered.

"Grace, it's good to see you," Matthew met me with a hardy handshake.

"Morning, Reverend. What can I do for you?"

"Well, I'd like to talk to you about this election. I don't want it interfering with our services," he said.

"I'd never campaign at church," I said.

"I know, but Miss Davis contacted me to let me know she would be attending services while she was in town for the election," he said. "I just wanted to give you a heads up that she will be there. For what it's worth, you have my vote. I can't endorse you or anything like that, but I do believe you are here for a reason. You are the one that stepped up when we needed you."

I smiled. Matthew was a kind man. His wife died when Kadence was younger, and he raised her the best he could. She was most definitely a daddy's girl. "No worries, Rev. I promise. No politics at church."

"Thank you, Grace," he said.

"Anytime. I appreciate your confidence in me. It's the reassurance of people like you, that keep me focused on this election. As much as I loathe the entire business, I should have known it wouldn't be easy," I said.

"Never is," he replied.

"Nope. Have a good one," I said as he climbed into his Yukon with a pouting Kady. "See ya later, Kady." She didn't even look at me, but Matthew shot me a look.

"Trouble in paradise?" he asked.

"Isn't there always when women are involved?" I replied. He laughed.

"See you Sunday," he waved as he pulled out.

Walking back into the bar, Levi didn't bother to look. "It's just me, Dublin." He visibly slouched.

"I hate her," he growled.

"Hate is a strong word, honey. You might want to rethink that one," I replied.

"Do you hate Stephanie?" he asked. Levi liked to do this to me. No matter what kind of instruction or help I tried to give him. He liked to turn it back on me.

"Yes, I do," I replied as Dylan chuckled.

"*Hate is a strong word*," Levi mimicked my tone.

"In this case, it's not strong enough," I said.

CHAPTER NINE

A COUPLE OF DAYS WENT BY WITHOUT ANY DISTURBANCE. REMY AND the lawyer from Stephanie's firm came to an agreement about her protests to the election rules. Most of them were resolved in my favor. Small victories were important in a local election. I wasn't sure I could take any of it much longer, and it had just started.

Saturday morning, I showed up at the Hot Tin Roof around 10am to get things stocked up for Nestor's biggest day of business. I hoped to talk to people from town as they came in for drinks. Maybe get them talking about the election and win some votes.

Like a good little candidate, I wore a red shirt. It was a plaid button down, and I tied it below my breasts like I had always done, but at the last minute I'd untied it. Too hussy. I didn't need to give Stephanie ammo. The shirt was tight enough to have some sex appeal. I wore tight jeans and cowgirl boots. Proper work attire.

"Morning, Grace," Nestor said stumbling down the steps. I'd known him since my first day in Shady Grove. I walked in the door seeking alcohol to calm my nerves after signing the contract with the Sanhedrin. Back then it didn't occur to me that he was a fairy. It's a shame that at first, I found him a tiny bit attractive. Too old for my taste, but he looked just like Sam Elliot. Sexy Sam Elliot from Roadhouse with Patrick Swayze. There were a few older men in this world who carried that kind of sex appeal. Nestor, however, didn't have the suave approach or the voice like Sexy Sam. He was just plain ol' Nestor. My grandfather. Thank God I never tried to make a move on that. "What the hell are you thinking about?"

"Oh, crap. Sorry," I said. "You don't want to know."

"I never do, but you always tell me," he laughed.

"First time I saw you I thought you looked like Sam Elliot," I replied.

He chuckled, "I've heard that before, but it usually doesn't do me any favors with the women."

"You got Mable," I replied.

"Not because I look like Sam Elliot," he replied. "Even if I did pattern my glamour after him."

"Wait, what?" I asked. It never occurred to me that it was a glamour.

"Grace, honey, you are so damn naïve sometimes," he laughed. "When is the last time you saw an old fairy?"

He was right. I was stupid. Fairies don't age after they reach adulthood. I didn't even think about it. Most fairies wore glamours in this world. "Why did you pick Sam Elliot?"

"Cause the women like him," he laughed. "But I needed to be older to pull off the barkeep gig, and people don't notice that you age well if you are already aged."

"Oh, crap," I said. "I'll have to age my glamour."

"Yes, if you stick around, you sure will," he said. The realization that I might have to look old sunk in. I pouted with my bottom lip stuck out. "Get over yourself."

"That's not very nice," I said.

"I know," he laughed. "I'm having fun picking at you. Usually Dylan and Levi get to have all the fun when you aren't torturing them."

"I love torturing them," I said.

"I noticed," he laughed. "You might lay off Levi though. He's struggling. He was here last night."

"Here? Drinking?" I asked.

"Yep. He didn't get drunk. I guess he was just scoping out the women. He's still getting used to this whole fairy thing," he said "Could you go out to the storage shed and bring in a new box of rocks glasses. I dropped three last night. It's time to get a new box."

"Why are you dropping glasses?" I asked. "Are you okay?"

"Yes, one a patron dropped. The other two just slipped out of my hand," he said.

"I've never seen you drop a glass. What's wrong?"

"My attention was diverted," he admitted. "Go get the box."

I flinched at how his tone turned gruff. Something happened last night, and he was going to tell me what it was. I decided to go get the box first though. It was actually warm today. That's what you get in Alabama. In the middle of winter, it can be 80 degrees outside. Next thing you know we'd be having tornados. Or snow.

Stepping into the small storage shed attached to the bar, I flicked on the light to find the right box. Nestor kept all the liquor inside the main building, but all the other bar items were kept out here like glasses, napkins, bowls and miscellaneous stuff for the pool tables. The door was attached by a spring, so it slammed shut behind me as I moved deeper into the shed. I looked over the names on the boxes, searching for the rocks glasses. Opening the lid, I checked to make sure I had the right thing. When I realized it was the correct box, I closed the lid. Light cascaded into the shed as someone stepped inside with me.

"Malcolm Taggart, you scared the shit of me," I said.

"Sorry, Grace. I saw you come in here, and thought you might need some help," he said.

"Naw. I'm fine. Just grabbing this box for Nestor," I said, grabbing the box. I didn't know why he was here so early. Alarm bells went off in my head. He rushed up beside me, brushing his hands over mine to pick up the box. I jerked my hands back as the familiar tingle of touching another fairy ran up my arms.

Malcolm's blue eyes flashed at me with fairy magic. I could have sworn his eyes were green. His tousled light brown hair shimmered with flecks of gold in the early morning sun that flowed through the window of the storage shed. When he smiled, his lips always dipped a little to the right. A sexy, crooked grin.

"You okay?" he asked, sharing that grin with me.

"Yeah, just forgot you were a fairy. The tingle, you know," I said.

"Well, it's not a feeling you should forget, Grace. You are one of us. I know you are with Dylan. He's not exactly fairy. Some people might look at it like we weren't good enough for you," he said, standing to full height. Not exactly fairy was right. Dylan felt completely different from any fairy I'd ever touched, and I'd touched a lot of them over the years.

"I, I thought your eyes were green?" I stammered.

"They are whatever color I want them to be. Or whatever color you want them to be," he said. Quickly they flicked back to green, then back to blue. "Dylan's eyes are blue. I just thought you liked blue better."

"Malcolm, why are you here?" I asked.

"You don't have to be afraid of me, Grace," he said.

"Well, you are in this shed, very early in the morning," I said.

"So, you are accusing me of something other than just being neighborly, and helping you out?" he asked. The grin faded as he looked genuinely hurt. He turned, hiding his face from me.

"No, that's not it at all," I said, backtracking my words.

"Perhaps what they say is right," he said.

"Who says what?" I asked.

He turned back to face me, stepping close. He brushed his fingers up my arm. "That you've forgotten what it's like to be one of us. You've spent so much time trying to hide who you are that you need to be reminded."

I did not like the sound of that, mostly. "Oh, really? And who is supposed to do the reminding?" I smirked nervously.

"Doesn't matter. It just needs to be done," he said. "I bet your bard would happily do it for you. Hell, I'll volunteer. You are in love with Dylan Riggs, but he could never make you feel like a fairy could. You remember what it was like to be with Remington Blake." I totally remembered my short fling with Remington. When I touched him for the first time, it was like coming home.

"I don't like this conversation. Get the hell away from me," I said, pushing him in the chest. He caught my hand in his, crushing my fingers in his tight grip. His green eyes flashed feline. His dark black hair curled down around the temples of his face. Slowly he brought my fingers to his mouth, sucking the tips. I tried to jerk them away.

"No, Grace. Let me remind you," he turned up the fairy charm. My breath hitched at the wave of seduction that rolled over me. "See, you forgot what it feels like."

"Get away," I gritted through my teeth. My chest heaved. I felt needy. I'd never felt like I was missing anything. Malcolm's touch made me crave him, instead of my fiancé.

Dylan. Dylan. Dylan.

I kept saying his name over and over in my head.

"How can you lead us if you shun your own people?" he asked, tracing my hand with his tongue.

"I love Dylan, but I don't shun any of you. I would never," I said.

"How long do you think he will stay with you now that Stephanie is back? You know they were together for a very, very long time," he said pressing his body to mine. The tingles ramped up to full blown throbbing. He was right. I did forget this. The closest I'd come to remembering it was the night I came on to Levi to prove a point, but I was in control of that situation until Levi diffused it. Malcolm was in full control here. "She gets what she wants."

"He wouldn't," I replied.

"I saw him with the kitsune," he said. "He followed her right into that motel room."

"He and I have already been over this. He did not sleep with Misaki," I replied.

"Damn, he's got you good," he said as he leaned down over my lips. He hovered there waiting for me to move. In a panic, I reached out to the only person I knew that could help me. The response was immediate. In fact, he was already on the way.

"Please, Malcolm, don't do this," I said. My resolve to resist him wavered. One taste to remind me. I thought about when I kissed Levi, and how good it felt. Levi was only half fairy. Malcom's lips parted sucking in air. His tongue trailed across his bottom lip sending my fairy hormones into overdrive. If he kissed me, I would be done. Dylan and I would be done. The power of seduction pressed into me as if I'd already let him inside me. It was like swapping gravy with Levi times a million. The temptation, a sweet, but bitter fruit, begged me to yield to him. It spoke to the deepest, darkest parts of me. I quivered at its power to convince me to give in. My body craved it, my heart rejected it, and my mind teetered in the middle.

Speaking of Levi, the door to the shed flew open. "Get away from her," he growled, as the green jewels from his tattoo pulsed with power under his sleeve. His connection to me. The power we shared.

"I should have known. He's your servant. Nice move, Grace, because you and I both know you crave it. You wouldn't have been able to stop me," Malcolm laughed. He released my hand, patting Levi on the should as he walked out.

"What the hell?" Levi asked.

"He tried to seduce me," I said. "It doesn't take much without defenses. I hadn't worried about such a thing, but he's strong. He must be an incubus. I knew he was Seelie, but that would explain a lot." My hands trembled.

The fire in Levi's eyes cooled as he approached me. "Are you okay?"

"Levi, what do I do if someone corners me like this again? I had nothing to resist him," I said. "Dylan would never forgive me. He wouldn't understand."

Levi wrapped his arms around my shoulders and pulled me to his chest. The tingle hit me again, but it was subtle compared to the power of Malcolm. "Then you call me. Just like you did. I'll come, but you need to tell Dylan that this happened."

"Stop being all grown up on me," I said, but I squeezed him back. "Thank you, Levi."

He planted a chaste kiss on my forehead. "Now what are you doing out here?" he asked.

"Getting that box for Nestor," I said pointing at the box of glasses. He turned around to lift it up, motioning me to get the door. We walked into the back door of the bar together. Nestor looked confused. "Look what I found in the shed."

"You found a bard?" he asked.

"Well, I was thinking more like a slave to carry boxes, but yes, a bard," I replied. I couldn't see Levi's face, but I was pretty sure he rolled his eyes. Nestor laughed, but still looked confused.

Levi sat the box down. He started pulling the glasses out, sitting them on the bar. "Wash 'em up, Grace," Nestor said. "And you can tell me why he was out there."

"Malcolm was out there," I replied.

"No, shit?" Nestor cussed. A rare occurrence for him.

"Did you just cuss?" I asked.

"Nope," he replied. "What did Malcolm want?"

"He had his paws on her," Levi growled.

Nestor stepped back with shocked eyes. "Grace, he's an..."

"Incubus. Yes, thanks I know that now," I replied. "Thanks to Levi, I'm not his thrall."

"Why would he come after you? He knows you are with Dylan," Nestor asked, knowing that even some of the worst seducers in the world wouldn't cross the line into another fairy's relationship which made Stephanie Davis even worse. She had no qualms about doing it.

I paused not wanting to repeat what Malcolm said to me. Some of it made sense. It never occurred to me that the fairies in town might take a slight that their queen had chosen a non-fairy mate. Yes, Dylan had his own set of powers, but he wasn't from our realm. Much like Chris Purcell, my friend the flying werehog, they were mythical creatures that walked the earth.

"Grace?" Levi prompted. "I'd like to know too."

"I need to talk to Dylan," I replied.

"Talk to me about what?" Dylan said as he walked through the door.

Did he arrive exactly when I spoke his name? What were the chances of that? It caught me off guard. Thoughts swirled in my head. I couldn't lock on to a single one of them to make a coherent sentence. Flashes of Malcolm's lips almost touching mine. The pressure on my fingers as he sucked the tips.

Dylan. Dylan. Dylan.

"Shit. He got to her," Nestor muttered.

Dylan saw my distress, rushing to my side. I felt his warm arms envelope me. His breath on my hair. "Grace Ann Bryant, talk to me," he whispered in my ear. The confusion faded.

"Incubus," I muttered.

"Who?" he growled. Apparently, he knew about the power of one.

"Doesn't matter. It's what he said that I can't seem to grasp," I replied.

Nestor and Levi watched us intently. "Come on," he said dragging me back out the back door of the bar. Once the door closed behind us, he put his hands on his hips and waited. "Tell me."

"He was in there," I said, pointing to the shed. "He said that there were fairies in Shady Grove that would never trust me, because I didn't choose a fairy mate. He said that I forgot what it was like to be with a fairy." I saw the fury in his eyes burning blue, but his shoulders sagged indicating that he realized the importance of what Malcolm said to me.

"Who was it, Grace?" he said, his tone calm and steady.

"Malcolm," I replied.

He stepped closer to me, putting his hand on my cheek. I leaned into it craving his touch in this deeply insecure moment. "How did you resist him? Because what I know of them, it's impossible."

"Levi interrupted him. He backed down," I said. "I told him multiple times that I loved you."

"Yes, your brain still says the right things, but your body does something completely different," he said.

"You act like you've come across one before," I replied.

"I have. There was one here before Malcolm. We made him

leave Shady Grove. He was seducing every woman and fairy he could get his hands on. They were helpless to resist him," he replied.

"When you were Sheriff?" I asked, leaving his hand to put my arms around his waist. He understood. He knew how awful it could have been for us. He embraced me. Fairy or not, no one on this earth could make me feel like Dylan. The tingle was nothing compared to the heat between us.

"Yes. You were living here, but I only saw you when you helped me with a few cases. It was very early on. I didn't call you in on that one. I didn't want to give him a reason to stay in Shady Grove," he said. "Someone needs to be with you at all times to prevent him from taking advantage of you. I hate to think it's true, but I know my ex-girlfriend. She probably sent Malcolm after you. She probably fucked him."

"Seriously?" I asked.

"Look at it this way. What he did in there made you question the loyalty of the fairies in this town, right?"

"Yes," I replied.

"Secondly, any further action on your part or his would have driven a wedge between us. I know that she hates the fact that we are together. It doesn't matter if she is engaged or not. She wants every man she can get her hands on. That's what they do," he said.

"That's what who does?" I asked.

"We have got to get you a fairy handbook," he smiled.

"What is she?" I asked.

"Leanan sidhe," he replied.

"Whore fairy," I scowled. He laughed. "What's so funny?"

"Never heard them called that," he said.

"Yeah, well, all of us are whores to some extent, but it's bad when even the whores call you a whore," I replied.

"I love you, Grace," he continued to laugh.

"You wouldn't, if Malcolm would have had his way in there," I said.

"I'll admit that I'm not sure how I would have handled it, but it wouldn't stop me from loving you," he said.

He knew how to disarm me by being sweet. I had nothing to say in return. "I love you, too," I muttered.

"Now let's go wash some glasses, but seriously you can't be alone. She won't stop," he said, still convinced that Stephanie sent Malcolm after me.

"I will be able to handle it next time. I've just got to be more aware of that kind of thing," I said.

"Let me ask you something. I want you to be completely honest," he said.

"Okay?"

"You used to be paranoid of everyone before you realized half the town was like you. Why do you suddenly trust everyone?" he asked.

I thought back over the times I hid myself away from the humans of this world. I cowered at the idea of another fairy finding me. He was right. I didn't suspect anyone anymore. It was like my paranoia lessened when the rest of our little corner of the world became familiar. I shouldn't have. If anything, I should have ramped it up. Not all fairies were nice. We were damn lucky to have some good people here. "I guess realizing that I wasn't alone. But we aren't all the same, are we? Exiles, yes. However, some of us are very bad and easily persuaded."

"Grace, I know you want to see the good in the people here, but I'm begging you to just keep your wits about you. I don't know what I'd do without you," he said.

I kissed him on the cheek, then on the mouth. "Too bad you are stuck with me."

"Right where I want to be," he replied. "Let's go back inside."

He followed me back into the bar to find Nestor and Levi staring at the door. "What?" I asked.

"Well?" Levi replied.

"Well, what? It was a private conversation," I said.

"You guys are fine?" he asked looking at Dylan.

"We are like peas and carrots, Levi Rearden," Dylan replied.

"God help us all in this box of chocolates," I added.

"Huh?" Levi missed the reference. Dylan and Nestor laughed.

"It's from Forrest Gump, Dublin," I said snatching the wash rag from him.

"Oh, speaking of movies. Nestor, anyone ever tell you that you look like that guy from Roadhouse?" Levi asked.

We all cracked up. God bless Levi Rearden.

CHAPTER TEN

THE RUSH HAD DIED DOWN. I LEANED ON THE BAR TALKING TO Dylan and Levi. Nestor picked up glasses from around the abandoned pool table. The last game died down about thirty minutes ago. The sound of shattered glass made us all pause.

"Fuck," Nestor growled.

I walked over to him, stooping to help pick up the pieces. "What the hell is wrong with you? You better tell me," I said.

"I can't," he replied.

"Are you sick?" I asked.

"No," he said. "Don't worry about it, Grace." He walked over to the sink to begin to wash the remaining glasses.

"He dropped two last night," Levi said.

"Thank you, tattletale," Nestor said.

"Seriously, Nestor, what's wrong?" I asked.

"Leave. It. Alone."

I'd never heard Nestor use that tone, ever. Dylan's eyes looked alarmed, but he made a motion with his hand trying to get me to back-off. I sucked in a deep breath, knowing that backing down was not one of my finer traits.

Walking back over to Dylan, I wanted to talk to him more about what Malcolm had said. It didn't bother me that Levi was sitting there. The connection I had to him grew every day. I hadn't had a servant in a very long time. I never intended to make Levi mine. Not in that way. I knew that I could separate the part of me that wanted to own him from the part of me that found such a thing disgusting.

"What Malcolm said," I started.

"About?" Dylan asked looking up from his coffee.

"Do I need to leave?" Levi asked.

"Shut-up, Dublin," I said back to him. Dylan laughed. "I'll start this by saying there is no way in this world I'm breaking up with you for some damn election, but what is the best way to make everyone feel more at ease? I don't want people thinking I chose you because you weren't a fairy. It's such nonsense."

Dylan's brow furrowed. He looked down at the coffee rotating the cup around watching the magic swirl around in it. "I'm not sure, because I don't know if anyone thinks that or not. It's possible that they do. It's possible that Stephanie is playing an angle."

"Either way, it takes votes away from me. I don't want to give Shady Grove up," I said.

"We could tell everyone that Levi is more than just your Bard," Dylan said.

"What?" Levi and I both said.

"Everyone has already seen you kiss him," he said.

"I'm not the only one that kissed him," I replied.

"If either of you think I'm getting into some polyromance bull-shit, you've lost your minds," Levi teased.

"What do you even know about that?" I asked.

"Internet," he said.

"You realize the internet is controlled by a demon, right?" I asked.

"It is not," he replied. "Is it?"

Dylan began to giggle. Levi whacked him on the shoulder making Dylan laugh harder.

"We, Dylan, are non-negotiable. We have to figure out how to prove to everyone that it's not a shun on anyone." I turned the conversation back to the original issue.

"I just don't think it's a problem. I think it's something she made up. Many people in this town have congratulated me on, well, I don't know how to put it without sounding arrogant," he said.

I groaned. "Just say it."

"Nah, you know what I mean," he said.

"But you want to say it," I replied.

"They congratulate me on getting you," he said with a devilish smile. "Now if I can just get you to set a date."

"You haven't set a date?" Levi asked. "Why not?"

"Been a little busy, Levi," I said.

"Just name a day," Levi said.

I scowled at Dylan. He started this shit just to get me fired up. "Dylan Riggs, if you think for one second that I'm going to get mad enough to fuck you angry, you've lost your damn mind."

Levi fell off his barstool. "I gotta go," he muttered climbing up off the floor.

"Levi, wait!" I yelled at him. "Look what you did!"

"He didn't leave because of anything I said," he laughed. "Let's go home, Gracie."

"Don't you Gracie me," I said, leaning back from the bar. He pushed up on the bar stool, grabbing me by the back of the head. He pulled my lips to his as I resisted, but the moment they touched mine. I gave into the heavenly warmth of my fiancé. "Damn, that's good."

"Let's go home," he repeated.

"I'll go upstairs and get Winnie," I said.

She was asleep on Nestor's couch. Mable sat in the recliner watching television. She smiled as I picked her up. She was heavier than she used to be, which was fine with me. Finally, she was healthy. When I reached the bottom of the stairs, Dylan took her from me.

"Sorry, I didn't think about her being asleep," he said.

"Let's go home," I repeated with a smile.

After tucking her into bed, Dylan sat with me in our room. "I know we joked about it, but maybe if you stayed in the trailer during the election, it would help you win."

"Dylan, if winning Queen means I have to give you up for one single moment, I don't want the job," I said. "And, I don't want to hear anything else about it."

"Yes, ma'am," he said. "That was kinda sweet, Grace. Are you feeling okay?"

"If you don't shut up," I warned him.

"What?" he asked. I knew then he was trying to rile me up again. "What are you going to do?"

"Ignore you," I said, plopping down in the bed. I pulled the covers over my head. He was on top of me instantly trying to wrestle them off of me. Holding on tight, the only point of entry he found was along my side where he stuck his hands in to tickle me mercilessly.

Finally, I relented, but instead of pulling the covers off, he crawled under them with me.

In the middle of the night, Dylan's phone rang. "Hello," he muttered.

I heard Troy's voice on the other side. Dylan handed me the phone as he climbed out of the bed. He started to get dressed as I answered, "Hello?"

"Hey, Grace, sorry to bother you so late, but we have a fairy problem. I think I need your help," he said.

"Um, okay. I've got to find someone to look after Winnie," I said.

"I'll stay here. You go," Dylan said. "Call Levi to meet you there."

"Why doesn't Levi just come here?" I asked. "Or we could take her to him?"

"I don't want to wake her," he said. "Send Levi here, but I'm not going to leave until he gets here."

"Where are you?" I asked Troy.

"I'm out at Caleb Joiner's place on Woodland Road past the water tower," he said.

"I know the place. I'm on the way," I said hanging up. "Are you upset?"

"Yes, I was enjoying a good sleep next to your fine body," he grumbled.

I grabbed jeans sliding them over my hips. He tossed me a sweater that I pulled down over my head. Dylan's warm hands wrapped around my waist before I got it on all the way. "Be careful until I get there. Stay away from Malcolm if he is there."

"Why would he be there?"

"He and Colby get into trouble together. Plus, it may be Stephanie again," he said.

"You've got to stop thinking everything is her!" I said, kissing the little pout on his lips.

He held me tight and groaned. Swaying us side to side, he leaned down breathing heavily in my ear. Shit, he had me turned on again. "She's trying to ruin my life," he muttered.

"Not going to happen. I'll quit before that happens. Do you want me to stay?" I asked, knowing the answer.

"Hurry down there. I'll call Levi. Take your phone," he said, releasing me. "I love you."

"Love you, too. I'll have it taken care of by the time you get there," I winked at him.

It was a short drive to Woodland Road. I wished Troy would have given me an idea of what the problem was considering I hated surprises.

Pulling up in the drive, I knew I was in the right place. There were three deputy cars sitting in the yard. I was pretty sure the department only had three cars, maybe four. Climbing out of the car, I was met by Sgt. Kwaski. I hadn't seen him since my in-trailer confinement while I was accused of murdering two human children.

"Hello, Miss Bryant. Sheriff Maynard asked me to take you inside," he said.

"Okay," I nodded, following him into the ranch-style home. When I walked into the living room, I groaned. Troy held Caleb Joiner against one wall. Amanda Capps and another officer held Malcolm Taggert against the other wall. Blood ran from Malcom's nose. The skin on his knuckles was split. Caleb didn't look much better.

"Fuck," I muttered as I walked in the door.

"See, I told you she wanted it," Malcolm spouted at Caleb.

"You are an idiot," Caleb screamed back at him.

"Hey, honey, I'm glad you are here," Malcolm said to me. The sweet smell of spring time and sunshine rolled over me. Fucking Seelie Fairies. My eyes locked on his. I took my hand and rolled my engagement ring around my finger once. He flinched.

"That's right. I'm ready for you this time, you bastard," I spouted at him.

"He did come after you?" Troy asked.

"Yes," I replied. "He failed."

"Only because I walked away," he said. "If I wanted you Grace, you'd be begging for my cock right now." With that Amanda hauled back on his right arm that she had twisted behind him. He yowled in pain.

"Another vulgar word from your mouth, Taggert, and I break this arm off. Hope you are left handed," she said.

"His cock hopes he's left handed," I added.

Caleb laughed at him. "You thought you could get her. You are so damn stupid. I told you that woman was no good."

"What woman?" I asked.

"Stephanie Davis," Caleb said. Dylan was right.

"We are going to have a civilized conversation. Troy let Caleb sit down in that chair," I said. Troy let Caleb go. He sat down in the chair, crossing his ankle over his other knee. Looking to Malcolm, I unleashed power from my tattoo. The room turned colder. "Mal, sit down on the couch." With unbridled power, the command struck Malcolm who instantly bent his knees to sit. Amanda and the other officer dragged him to the couch. I narrowed my gaze at him. He gulped.

"Amanda, you and Officer Tully go meet Riggs when he gets here," Troy said. "I think we are fine here now." They nodded, leaving Troy and I with the best friends.

"Now, Caleb, tell me what happened?" I asked.

"Why does he get to go first?" Malcolm whined. I threw my hand up at him without looking. He tried to speak, but he couldn't open his mouth. He started mumbling something, then let out a long whine.

"Don't fuck with me," I growled at him. "You pushed your luck this morning. It won't happen again. Sit there and be a good little incubus." I could have done the same with him this morning had I expected his advances. He was powerful once he lured you in, but now he had nothing on the Queen of the Exiles.

"He told me what he did to you this morning. I told him when Stephanie came to talk to both of us about the election that she was trouble. I don't know how she made him do it, but I guess he did it. He's an idiot. Please don't banish him. I hate him, but he's my best friend," Caleb said.

"I'm not banishing anyone. Tell me more about this visit from the fairy whore," I said.

"Oh, you know what she is?" Caleb said.

"Yes," I replied.

"She told us that you didn't know what any of us were," he said.

"I'll admit that I don't know what most of you are, but I've only been at this a few months. It's been on-the-job training," I replied as I heard the low rumble of a V-8 engine arrive outside. "I know what you are too, Caleb. I think my fiancé is here." Malcolm whined behind his magical duct tape.

Waiting on Dylan, I paused to think. He came bounding in the door. The muscles in his face tensed. An action that rippled down his body as he stared at Malcolm who started whimpering like a baby. He mumbled helplessly as Dylan's anger recoiled. He looked at me, questioning with his eyes. I shrugged. "I like him like that," he laughed.

"Me too," I replied. "Mr. Joiner confirmed your suspicions."

"About Stephanie?"

"Yep," I replied. "It seems she tried to enlist both of them knowing they were solid allies on my side. Malcolm, the incubus, seems to have fallen prey to a bigger fish. And by fish, I mean twat."

Troy snorted. "Why is she doing this? To tear you and Dylan apart?"

"I think that's just the flower on a long-rooted dandelion," I replied.

"If she can come between us, it's one thing. However, driving doubt into the fairies, because I chose Dylan instead of a fairy. Or that I can't control the craziness that ensues like these two yokels fighting. She's digging deep," I replied. "What did she want you to do, Caleb?"

Caleb turned green like a granny smith apple. "Answer her," Dylan prompted.

"She wanted me to go after Kady Rayburn, but Kady and Levi were already broken up. I didn't have to bother," he said, as the mute started pitching a mumbling fit. I waved my hand and released his bond.

"You fucking liar!" Malcolm yelled at him. "She's in his bedroom now!"

"What?!" Dylan and I said at the same time.

"Kadence Rayburn! Get in here right now!" I yelled.

She walked into the room with us wearing a man's button-up flannel shirt. I glared at her, but she held her chin high. "Levi and I were done. You know it."

"You most definitely are now," I replied. Levi said he was done with her, but Levi's heart was big. He would have welcomed her back. Not now. "You stay away from him. Do you understand me?"

"You can't have both of them," she spouted at me.

"Looks like I do," I countered.

"It's true. I couldn't get to her because Levi interrupted. She's actually the whore fucking two different men," Malcolm offered. I waved my hand to mute him again. He moaned.

Sucking in a deep breath to keep from blasting all three of them for being pawns to the snake, I looked to Dylan for guidance. He motioned to the door. He didn't want to burn them both to the ground, so he opted for escape. I followed him outside to the lawn. Despite the warmth of the day, the night was chilly as a breeze blew through the tall pines around the house. They swayed in the darkness, swishing branches together.

"I'm done in there," he said.

"What do I do with this mess?" I asked.

"I think you leave this one alone. Let them fight it out. Tell Levi about Kady and be done with it. No need to play her game," he said.

"I like that," I replied. "I just hate I had to get out of bed with you to do nothing."

"Beyond that, you need to quit sleeping with your bard," he teased.

"I mean, I knew people thought that, but damn, I didn't expect to hear it," I replied. "As long as you know that I'm not."

He put his hands on his hips. "You do swap gravy with him," he grinned.

"It's been a while," I replied.

"Keep it that way," he teased, but the tone of his voice meant it in a small way. "Go tell them your verdict and let's go home."

Going back in the house, everyone seemed calm. "Troy, I believe we are done here. Thank you for keeping them from beating the hell out of each other. Kady, I never want to see you in either of my homes again. Do you understand?"

"Not that I would ever want to be in either one of them. By the way, I'm voting for her," she stomped off back to wherever she came from in the first place.

"Caleb, thank you for trying to defend my honor. I consider both of you friends. I don't care if you fuck Kady. Do it because you want to do it. Not because Stephanie said to do it," I replied.

"She's good in bed," he laughed.

"La, la, la, la, la," I said putting my fingers in my ears. "I don't care to know. Git." I pointed in the direction that she stalked off.

"I'll get her to vote for you," he said.

"Good luck," I said to his back, as he ran down the hall after Kady.

Looking back to Dylan who stood in the doorway, I released the power I held back tied to the Unseelie realm. My eyes flickered to turquoise. Dylan smiled, knowing that I was about to give Malcolm a lesson in seduction. Letting go of the restraints holding back my power, the entire room iced over instantly. Snow fell inside. I opted for the short silver dress that barely covered my bits. I winked at Dylan who mouthed, "Wow!"

Stalking over to the mute incubus, I leaned down over him as I ran a frosty nail down his cheek. "Dear Malcolm, we need to have a discussion. Seductress to seducer," I said, as he shuddered. I traced my finger down his t-shirt over tight chest muscles. He shivered, but I didn't think it was from the cold. I stopped just above the waistband of his pants. He bucked his hips forward begging for me to continue. "Sweetheart, I play this game much better than you do. I suggest you keep your little talent buttoned up in those tight jeans. Or I will freeze that hard-on in place for the rest of your life. You've seen those commercials about the damage that can happen if you keep it up too long. I'd hate for you to have an accident."

A long, painful groan vibrated out of his closed mouth. With a simple flick of my finger, the magic released him as he gasped for breath. "Grace, I'm sorry. It won't happen again. I swear."

"Dylan tells me they ran the last incubus out of Shady Grove. I won't be so kind," I replied. "I'd really like us to be friends again. What do you say?"

"Yes, of course. I was voting for you, anyway. Stephanie is bad. Super bad," he stumbled over his words.

"She has nothing on me," I said narrowing my eyes on him. He winced, closing his eyes tightly. I snapped my finger. The snow and ice disappeared, and I stood before him in as my regular old self. "Glad we had this talk. Leave Caleb alone."

I turned to walk out the door with Dylan who couldn't suppress his laughter. Marching to the truck, he grabbed my arm and pulled me to him. "You are so damn hot," he said.

"Um, I think you have me mixed up. I'm the cold one," I said.

"Please wear that dress for me," he said. Troy and Amanda stood at their cruiser, but the other cops had gone. Just for Dylan, I released the power again. "Shit, you can see all the way down that thing!"

"It's identical to the black one, Dylan," I replied, reminding him of the dress I wore to the bar the night we played pool. The first time.

"I like them both," he sighed. He looked over to Troy who was laughing at us. "I'm the luckiest son of a bitch in the whole world."

"No, you ain't," Troy said as he dipped Amanda down for a kiss. She swatted him on the arm.

I eyed Dylan. "Don't you dare!" My warning didn't stop him.

CHAPTER ELEVEN

"She's such a whore," Levi said after we told him about Kady. He was sitting at Dylan's house on the couch. He'd built a fire saying that he couldn't sleep.

Dylan sipped coffee in the kitchen as I sat next to Levi on the couch. It was almost daylight, and no real reason to try to sleep. Although I was sure Dylan had plans other than sitting to have a chat with Levi.

"Now. Move on from her. There are plenty of fairy girls out there that will make you feel much better than her," I replied.

"I'm not sure I'm ready for a fairy relationship," he said.

"Huh? You dated her because she was a human?" I asked.

"I am half human, Grace," he said.

"Trust me. I know that, Dublin," I replied, knowing that had he been full-blooded I'd have already banged him by now. My resistance on that matter would have been more than I could take. He didn't understand what I meant by it. Probably best that way. "You need a fairy girl or boy, whichever."

"Girl. Woman," he smirked. "I'm going to bed." He reached over to squeeze my hand sending a ripple through me.

"Good night, Levi," Dylan said.

"Night," Levi groaned as he climbed the stairs to the bedroom he'd claimed in Dylan's house. When Winnie got up, I'd let her go in there to wake him up. It would make him feel better.

"There goes my brooding bard," I said.

"There would be something wrong if he weren't upset about something," Dylan said. "He will figure it all out, eventually. All of this is still new to him. He's actually adapted pretty well."

"I suppose," I said.

"Now, where is that dress?" Dylan asked.

"We have church today," I said.

"So?"

"So, I can't wear that," I replied.

"I don't want you to wear it to church. I want you to wear it to bed," he said.

"Do you ever stop?" I asked.

"Hell, no. The way I see it, I'm about five years behind on lovin'," he smiled.

I couldn't argue with him there. After Stephanie being in town for just a few days, I already considered her one of the most heartless beings I'd ever met. It still blew me away that Dylan even took the time with her.

"You want just the dress, or the whole queen?" I asked.

"Hmm, since we are playing dress up, why not go all the way," he said.

"As you wish, Darlin'," I purred.

"Tell me," I said.

"Why? I don't want to talk about it," Dylan whined. I knew we had to get up soon to go to church. Asking him to tell me more about Stephanie started off the day wrong. Forbid it that I might want to try to get the upper hand. The day got worse from there.

We dropped Winnie off at the Church of God because she continued to insist that Jesus would be disappointed if she didn't go to her church. It prolonged the talk about fairies because she hadn't seen the wonders inside our church. Dylan was quiet the whole ride to the Shady Grove Baptist Church. As we approached the front doors, he stopped, putting his hands on his hips. I didn't say anything because I wasn't sure what crawled up his ass. Best not dig an additional hole. He reached out to grab my hand. My impulse was to pull it away, but I didn't. We needed to walk in there united.

As the portal opened, we stepped into the grove of tall trees. The place where we held services didn't exist on this earth. It was another realm filled with beauty. The tall trees circled the wide expanse where we all gathered. Fairy lights hung from poles covered with vines. The place existed in a constant state of twilight. Some fairies attending wore their true faces, instead of their human glamours. Sprites, sylphs and other pixies never got to be themselves in the real world for fear of discovery, but here, in the Grove, they could be as they were meant to be.

It made me sad to watch them sometimes, knowing they could not return to the Otherworld. Shady Grove was my home, and I never intended to leave it. However, there were some here who might want to return to the Otherworld, but their banishment prohibited it. This place, The Grove, was like their Garden of Eden. Standing right in the center of it, Stephanie Davis talked to a group of fairies with Sergio Krykos, silently at her side. I wasn't sure about him, but I was positive she was Satan, especially if Satan wore a navy suit dress with tall heels. Even the long, shimmering black hair was demonic.

She hugged and talked to them as if she were deeply interested in what they were saying to her. I knew better. Nestor and Mable stood off to one side talking to Matthew Rayburn, the head druid. Dylan started walking that way, but I pulled back on his arm.

"What is it, Grace?"

"My anxiety goes nuts when it's like this between us. I can't stand it," I said.

"We will talk about it later," Dylan replied.

I didn't bother to respond. He put on a fake smile, speaking to Matthew. I didn't see Kady anywhere or Levi for that matter. I closed my eyes for a moment to reach out to my bard. He was on the way. Running late. The chill of power ran through me after reaching out to him. I opened my eyes to find Dylan staring at me.

"What was that?" he asked.

"We will talk about it later," I countered.

He ground his teeth together. "Fine," he said.

"Don't blame me. You started this. I'm not sure why you want to fight today," I replied.

"Grace, enough. Do you see this place? She has sucked them all in. None of them see her for what she truly is," he growled.

Coming today was a mistake. Believe it or not, I think I could keep my calm when he couldn't. "Maybe we should go," I suggested.

"It's too late now," he said, releasing my hand. So much for the united front. The entire service I was distracted. Speaking to as many people as possible afterward, I avoided any contact with Stephanie Davis. Levi, who finally showed up, and I talked with Nestor and Mable about what happened at Caleb Joiner's place, when I saw Nestor's eyes flare. I turned to look and Stephanie had hooked her arm through Dylan's as he talked to Matthew Rayburn.

"Please tell me not to lose my shit right now," I muttered.

"Grace, calm down. You know she laid the sneak attack on him. He probably didn't see her coming," Levi said. Who knew that my bard would be the voice of reason?

Nestor watched them without saying a word.

"He's not moving away from her," Mable said.

"She's trying to provoke me. I am not falling for it," I said as every bone in my body shook with anxiety. "Y'all. I can't do this." I breathed heavily. Levi touched my elbow. The skin to skin contact released a wave of calm through me.

"Calm down," he said lightly. Mable's gaze turned to Levi. She must have felt the power move.

"What did you just do to her?" Mable asked.

"It's okay. He's trying to help," I replied.

"How is he able to do that to you?" she pried.

"I allow him to do it, because I trust him," I said, daring to peek behind me. I saw Dylan shift his weight, but it wasn't to move away from her. He leaned into her ear, speaking quietly. Only seeing her profile, her eyes lit up. A smile crossed her face as she reached up to touch his cheek. "Okay, that's it. I can't handle it."

"Grace, don't," Levi said, but it was too late.

"Hey Stud," I yelled over to Dylan. He looked up to me with fire in his eyes. "I'm heading out. Levi's taking me to the trailer."

His nostrils flared. I'd pissed him off. Good.

"Damn it, Grace," Levi muttered.

"Let's go," I said.

"I'm on the bike," he replied.

"I don't fucking care," I said, grabbing his hand to drag him out of the Grove. It was all falling apart. I knew she would make more moves. That she wasn't done yet. When we got to the motorcycle, I looked up at Levi, "He could have walked away from her, right?"

"He should have," Levi said.

I motioned toward the bike. He put his helmet on me, then climbed on. As I got on the bike behind him, I wrapped my arms around his waist. Dylan ran out of the church.

"Go!" I urged Levi. He fired up the hog, and we sped away.

I hated motorcycles. Up until this point, I'd refused to ride it with Levi, so I held on for dear life. The wind blew in his hair as he concentrated on the road. The ride to the trailer was uneventful. When we got there, we hurried inside.

"You know he will come here," he said.

"That's fine. I'd rather fight here than at his house or in public," I said. My breaths were quick, and my heart ached. Levi looked pained.

"Honey, this isn't your fault. Everything will be fine. We always work it out," I said.

"I just hate seeing you so upset. This election is bad. Bad enough to quit. I know everyone keeps telling you to push through it. I know you don't want to give up on it because you are determined. You hate to lose, but Grace, if it keeps tearing you up like this, it's not worth it. If it tears you and Dylan apart, is it worth it?"

"It shouldn't tear us apart. We should be together on it. I'm not sure what happened today. I said something about them this morning, trying to get information about her. He told me just a few days ago that he had plenty of dirt on her, but when I asked, he clammed up. He's been acting weird ever since," I admitted to Levi. The brooding young changeling became the one person on this earth that I could bear my soul to without worrying about his loyalty. Dylan should be that person.

Levi sank into the couch. It was then that I realized that the furniture that Dylan bought had arrived. I opened the door to my bedroom to find a tasteful king size bed. It already had linens on it and a ton of pillows. Looking back at Levi, he smiled. "It's nice stuff."

"Yes, it is," I said. "It came with bedding and stuff?"

"No, Tabitha brought it all over yesterday. She said that Dylan called her, asking her to pick out some things that she thought you might like and buy them," he said.

Refusing to hold back any more, my eyes poured like a summer gully washer. How did we go from buying nice things for my trailer to surprise me to whispering in his ex-girlfriend's ear? I fought back the naughty things that he might have said to her and tried to focus on possibilities like maybe he threatened her. Her smile and flirt were diffusers. I leaned against the door to my bedroom. Levi's denim blue eyes watched me. I realized then that he was holding back.

"What are you holding back?" I asked.

"Grace, I want nothing more than to wrap you up and just let you cry on my shoulder, but I know that the moment that I do, he will bust through that door. It would make things worse. So, I'll sit over here and just hug you with my eyes," he said.

I laughed and cried at the same time. "I should call Jeremiah and thank him for dropping you off in my lap."

"I *really* shouldn't be in your lap," he smiled.

"Or me in yours," I added.

"Yeah, that," he laughed.

"So, you sit over there hugging me with your eyes, and I'll sit over here wishing I'd bought a smaller trailer with only one bathroom." The blush that ran over his face was worth every minute of anxiety that I'd had in the last hour. "Damn, you are so adorable when you do that."

"What?" he asked.

"I don't guess I've ever said that out loud," I admitted.

"You like embarrassing me?" he asked.

"Yes, because when the blush washes over your cheeks, it makes that crazy fairy part of me flare up," I said.

"You are welcome to embarrass me whenever you want," he said. "If you keep talking like that, Dylan can go to hell, because I'll do more…"

He didn't finish the sentence when Dylan ran in the door, pouring sweat. He looked at both of us. Levi hung his head, refusing to look at either of us.

"Did I interrupt something?" Dylan asked instinctively.

"We were having a discussion, but you aren't interrupting," I replied coldly.

"That's my cue to go watch some television in my room," Levi said, looking at me one last time. There was so much in just one look. He had my back, and with one word, he would be by my side again. If he'd meant more than that, I didn't want to know.

"Did you have to drive off with her?" Dylan asked him as Levi walked past.

"Yeah, I did, and unless you want to argue with me too, I suggest you leave it alone," Levi said standing up to Dylan. Oh shit. I did not want the two of them fighting. Especially about me.

"Get out of my face right now," Dylan growled at him. Levi calmly walked by, entering his bedroom, but he left the door open. "Seriously, what were you running from?"

"You. Arm in arm, whispering in her ear," I said.

"It wasn't what it looked like," he said.

"That's just it, Dylan. I know what it looked like to me. Imagine what it looked like to everyone else in that room. I don't care if you told her to go eat shit. Everyone in that room saw her smile and flirt with you. It looked very intimate," I said.

"No worse than you climbing on the back of a motorcycle which

I know you hate with a passion and driving off hugging Levi?" he spouted.

"I was scared of the bike, so I hugged Levi not to fall off of it. I would have gladly left with my fiancé but he was too busy whispering in the woman's ear who has determined to ruin my whole damn life!" I screamed. I had no more patience. "You should have just walked away from her! Why didn't you just walk away?"

"I didn't want to make a scene," he said.

"I know you don't like to draw attention, but damn it, Dylan, there are times when pitching a hissy fit is entirely appropriate. When someone you loathe wraps their arm into yours to provoke the woman you claim to love, it is a good damn time to make a fucking scene," I continued to yell.

He stared at me as if he had nothing else to say. "You are right," he said.

"What?"

"You are right. I should have shoved her away. Maybe she would have even fallen on the ground where someone else could rush up to help her make me look like the bad guy. Perhaps, I could have called her whore and cunt right there in church. I'm sure everyone would have loved that. But instead, I threatened her very quietly. I told her if she didn't leave me and you alone that I would air her dirty laundry up and down Main Street. I didn't expect her to smile or kiss me on the cheek. She played me," he said.

"She kissed you on the cheek?" I asked, because it's a good damn thing I didn't see that little tidbit.

"Yes, after you ran out with Levi," he said. "I could have handled it better, but I couldn't think of the best way to get her off of me! Grace! You know I hate that woman! You know I do," he said.

"So, I'm supposed to stand by and let you play a game with her that makes it look like she already has you wrapped around her slimy tail. To everyone in that room that's what it looked like. Even Mable, who adores you, stood there and said that you weren't pulling away from her. That's when I looked again, and you actually moved into her. Not away. Everything inside of me broke. It took everything I had just to walk away. Do you understand that?" I asked him. The anger that seethed through his eyes faded. "You own my heart, Dylan. It's not as strong as I'd like it to be. It doesn't matter how many times we make love or if there is a ring on my finger, this is a first time for me. I've never given my heart to anyone. I didn't know it would hurt so much."

Tears made tracks down my face, and I refused to look at him. I knew he wouldn't stay on the other side of the room much longer. He took his leather jacket off like he used to in the old trailer, laying it on the back of the couch. The memories of the last few months flooded over me. Instead of warming my heart, it made me ache more knowing that I'd given a part of myself to him. The strength and independence that I once held so dear I'd forfeited to love Dylan Riggs. Right now, the trade off didn't seem worth it.

My heart pounded with every footstep as he drew nearer. My emotions battled back and forth. To push him away or allow him to draw me back in.

Leaning on the door frame across from me, I felt the heat radiating off of his body. The thought crossed my mind that perhaps I should allow the winter queen to handle this. Asking myself what I'd do if I went that direction. The answer appalled me. I could lure him back, fuck him one last time, then kick him to the curb for this bullshit, because I didn't need it or him. I decided that whatever I did, it wouldn't be that. I hated that part of myself.

For a moment, he watched my internal struggle. "What have you decided?" he asked quietly.

I swallowed, not trusting my voice. "This wouldn't be so bad, if I wasn't already confused."

"Confused about what?" he demanded. I didn't like his tone.

"This morning. You shut me out when I asked about her. It wasn't so long ago that you said you could destroy her with the information you had on her. Forgive me for wanting to know my opponent. I don't want to know the intimate details of your life with her. I just thought there might be something useful going forward. However, you built a wall between us. When we went into the grove, it was still up. When you stood with her on your arm, it was still fucking up!"

"My relationship with her was fucked up, Grace. Forgive me if I don't want to discuss it with anyone," he said.

"Not fucked up enough to push her away," I spouted at him.

"What do you want me to say? What do you want to know? Details? I'll tell you all of it, if you will just stop pushing me away!" he yelled back at me.

"Dylan, I don't want details. I just don't understand how you can stay with someone for five damn years while she fucked every other man in this town, and everyone knew it. I didn't, because I'm blind to everything. I've never felt more insecure in my entire life. I've given everything to you. My heart. My independence. I just don't know how much more I can take," I said.

"I was with her, because after hundreds of years of fucking around, I thought I couldn't do any better," he said through gritted teeth. "I got what I deserved."

My heart really broke with his words. Not for me. I'd never seen Dylan as anything other than the most honorable man I knew. His past didn't even register with me because I had the same past. Even now, I thought inside myself I'd fucked this up. That I was the one that didn't trust him. Neither of us knew how to have a relationship. We both sucked at it.

"I've been waiting for the day for this to fall apart. I guess that day is today, because I knew I didn't deserve you either," he muttered. His shoulders slumped. Any fight he had left in him was gone.

"You are giving up on us?" I asked.

"It seems I have no choice," he said.

"Fuck that," I said.

"What?"

"Fuck that. I'm not going to let you stand there and pretend that you deserve to go through hell. That's ridiculous horse manure, and I won't let you do it. You've been everything this town has needed for years. You spent long hours hunting for missing kids and cows. You've gone to people's houses to give them bad news, then stuck around to share their grief. Just because your relationships aren't peachy keen doesn't mean you aren't a good man. There's a little girl out there that thinks you're good enough to be her Daddy," I said. "We don't ever have to mention Stephanie's name again, but I'm not giving up on us even if you do." Crossing my arms, I stood and watched him. One thing I did know about men was that sometimes they need a little ego boost. For whatever reason, Dylan needed that right now. I pushed away my worries and doubts, giving him what he needed.

However, his body remained motionless. With his head pointed to the ground, he focused on the carpet. He made no motions to move toward me or move away. I sighed. It was going to have to be on me. I wasn't giving him up. With two steps forward, I stood in his personal space. The way he leaned on the door, our legs touched. Still, he did not move. I suppressed the need to be pissed. He should be coming to me, not the other way around. However, I guessed that sometimes in relationships you have to do things you didn't want to do. Tracing my fingers down the side of his face, I felt him shudder. He leaned into my hand as I cupped his cheek. He groaned as I pressed my body to his. His hands grabbed my waist as the heat in them passed from him to me.

"I'm sorry, Grace. I'm so sorry," he muttered.

"That's what I wanna hear," I purred, kissing him on his neck.

"Keep doing that, and I'll say it again," he said. Instead of continuing, I pulled back to look him in the eye.

"I don't want you to say it again. I just want you to love me. To understand the things, I gave up and the things that scare the shit out of me," I said. "I want you to teach me those things about you too. No more walls."

"What scares you?"

"Losing you. Losing Winnie. Being forced to leave our lives here. Lots of things," I said.

"Losing you is one of mine, too. But I could leave Shady Grove in a heartbeat as long as my family went with me," he said. "You and Winnie. Fuck Levi."

I laughed. "At least you admit you want to swap gravy with him," I said.

"That is not what I said Grace Ann Bryant," he said as the glint of life returned to his eye.

"Don't use my whole name, Dylan whatever-your-middle-name-is Riggs," I replied.

"I don't have one," he replied.

"Really?"

"Didn't see the need," he said.

"I'll make up one," I said.

"No, I've heard your list of name choices," he laughed remembering our Christmas game of pool which I let him win. Or rather, I lost on purpose. His laugh meant that everything was going to be okay for now. I liked it better when our fights weren't real. Relationships suck.

CHAPTER TWELVE

PASTOR ZEKE CALLED SAYING THAT WINNIE WANTED TO SPEND THE afternoon with his daughter playing. Winnie did that frequently on Sundays when her mother was still alive. It was fine with us for her to have play time with her friends.

I made some lunch for us. Dylan talked to Levi, and they seemed to be okay. My thoughts drifted back to what Levi was about to say when Dylan walked in. It's probably a good thing he didn't finish the sentence. We both were a little high-strung, and I would hate for either of us say something we would regret later on.

As we ate, Dylan and Levi watched football on television in an awkward silence until the buzzing of Dylan's phone interrupted.

"Riggs," he answered which was his typical answer when he didn't know the caller.

Pause. I heard a female voice on the other end.

"She what?" he asked with alarm.

He paused to listen again. Levi and I stared at him.

"No, I'm not the father. Where is she?" he asked.

"Who is that?" I asked.

Dylan put his hand over the phone and said, "The med center. Misaki is there."

"Oh hell," I muttered.

"No, I'm not coming down there. In labor? How is that possible?" he asked.

The woman on the end of the line sounded stern. She must have hung up on him because he just stared at the phone.

"In labor?" I asked.

"Fucking fairies," he grumbled to which Levi and I laughed. A smile crossed his face. "Apparently, a kitsune can get pregnant and reach full gestation within just a few days, and it's a shame that the deadbeat worthless father can't even show up to the birth of his child."

"She's going to put you on the birth certificate!" I concluded.

He pitched the bridge of his nose. "I don't know."

"They want you to go down there?" I asked.

"Yes, but I'm not going down there," he said.

"I'm not going to sit by and have that woman put your name on a child that isn't yours!"

Levi and Dylan both stared at me. "What do you want to do?"

"I'm going down there," I replied. "You can stay or go. I don't care."

"Fucking fairies," Levi said. They fist bumped.

"Hey! You are one too!" I pointed at Levi.

"Half. It means I at least have some sense," he laughed.

"I'm going to jerk a knot in you," I said.

"Jerk what?" Dylan asked.

I opened my mouth to continue the banter, but I blushed. I stuttered, "Qu-quit! Let's go!"

As I stomped out the front door in my faux rage, I heard Levi behind me, "Now you know how to get her to shut up."

"I can get her to shut up better ways than that," Dylan implied.

"Enough! Like I can't hear you both," I said, climbing into the truck. I shut the door, giving them both the go to hell look. This was the kind of fighting I liked. Less heartbreak and angst. Sometimes I felt like I was on a damn soap opera with the mess that goes on around here. The Days of Our Fairy Lives. The Forever Young and Restless. One Long Life to Live. Now we were off to Fairy Hospital.

The drive to the med center only took five minutes, but we spent five minutes bantering back and forth about women, fairies, and ways to get people to shut up. When we arrived, Dr. Tabitha Mistborne was waiting on us.

"Hiya Dylan, congratulations are in order, it's a boy," she said.

"Stuff it, Tab," he said.

"Where is she?" I asked.

"Down the hall in room 156," she said.

"Can I visit the mother and child?" I asked.

"Well, of course, you are here with the father," she teased. I scowled at her to which she laughed her head off. Friends.

"Come on, big Daddy," I replied.

Dylan and I sauntered in to a smiling Misaki holding a tiny little bundle.

"Oh, you come see you baby," Misaki said. "He is beautiful."

"Yes, he is," I replied. "Misaki, we need to talk."

"Oh, sure. I cannot thank you enough for allowing Dylan to save me."

"That's just it, Misaki. I know you are lying about Dylan being the father. We came down here to clear up any misunderstanding," I said.

"No, he is the father. He gave me his sex, and I get pregnant," she said.

"Is it just me or is her English worse today?" I asked Dylan. He shrugged.

"My English is bad all day," she replied.

"Yes, well, let's see if you understand this. You came into my town and asked for protection. Right?" I asked.

"Yes, you so generous to help me," she said smiling.

"Right. Under my protection, I require fairies to speak the truth regarding all things relating to that protection. Are you lying about Dylan being the father of this child?" I asked.

She paused and looked at me. Knowing what I was implying, she did not speak. I stared at her. "I do not understand," she muttered.

Sitting down on the edge of the bed, I pulled the blanket down and peered at the little face inside it. "I think you do, Misaki. If you break the terms of protection, I cannot protect you."

"I no need protection now. Demon does not want me," she said.

"Are you sure about that? I could have sworn there was a snake demon lurking around these parts," I replied. "She's tall with pale skin. Her hair is black like the feathers of a raven. You know this snake?"

Her eyes widened. "I do not know this snake."

"Misaki, you will not avoid my questions any longer. Please. Is Dylan the father of this child?" I asked.

She looked around to the exit. Levi appeared in the door, smiling at her. Dylan leaned back on the wall with his arms crossed. No one here was going to help her. "No, he is not," she mumbled. I smiled. Sometimes it was good to be Queen.

"Why don't you tell me everything?" I said to the fox.

What did the fox say? She shape-shifted into a devil creature with fangs and horns. The bundle in her lap which looked very real disappeared completely. Shoving me off the bed with one arm, I flew against the wall. Mid-flight I pushed power through my tattoo to absorb the impact, but it still hurt. My head went *ring-ding-ding-ding*. Dylan rushed at the demon as his arms ignited into flame. The demon faded into wisps of black smoke, then reappeared behind Dylan, shoving him against the opposite wall with a *wa-pa-pow*.

I felt Levi pull power. The surrounding forces that I could see through fairy eyes sucked to Levi's arm, and his tattoo pulsed under his shirt. "Cease," he said. His voice rumbled the walls several octaves lower than his normal speaking voice. Holy shit, he was learning too fast.

The demon froze in place staring at the bard. Standing up I pointed my finger at the demon and said, "*Chacha-chow!*"

"You okay?" Levi asked. Dylan stood up behind the demon. His eyes flicked back and forth to us.

"Never heard that song?" I asked.

"What song?" Levi replied.

"Nevermind. How long can you hold him?" I asked.

"Not much longer. He's fighting it," Levi grunted.

Releasing the icy power inside of me, my tattoo turned silver and blue. Silvery swirls ran up my arm and around my neck. My glamour dropped as I reached out to touch the demon. When my fingers brushed his neck, ice covered his body from tip to toe. Horn tip to hoof actually. "I've got him, Levi."

Levi groaned as he released his spell. The dancing lights of power returned to my vision as I examined the horned demon before me. "Oni," Levi said.

"Still curious that such a creature would be so far from its native area," I said. "Demon, were you brought here by Stephanie Davis?"

"He can't talk. You have him frozen," Levi said.

"Seriously, you think I didn't know that?" I said. I heard Dylan chuckle.

"She did not," a deep voice reverberated in the room.

"What the hell?" Levi said.

"Demons aren't of this world. They don't need lips to speak. His life force is trapped in that body, but his being is not," I replied. "I did assume this was the case even for a Japanese demon."

"Why do you know more about demons than fairies?" Dylan asked.

"Ugh. Long story. I'll tell you when we are done here," I said. "Who summoned you?" The thing about demons, that I had found, was that they hated to be bound. This could go several ways, but I was hoping that the demon would give me the information I needed, then skidaddle.

"I cannot say," the demon replied.

"Hope you like life as an Onicicle," I replied. "Come on guys. Load him up in the truck. He will make a great lawn ornament for the trailer."

"Krykos," he replied.

The Greek fiancé of Stephanie Davis summoned a Japanese demon to pretend to have a child by Dylan Riggs. It was the most creative plot I'd ever heard, but it seemed like there was a piece missing.

"Why?" I asked.

A low rumble rattled the walls. "I told you the name. Now release me," he said.

"Why?" I cooed.

"Let. Me. Go." He protested making the walls shake. I was sure that the Sheriff had already been called.

"Wrong answer," I replied.

A noise I can only describe as sandpaper grinding on sandpaper filled the room. The demon was grinding his teeth. "I owed him a favor," he replied.

"You owed a fairy a favor?" I asked.

"He is no ordinary fairy," he provided.

"What is he?" I asked.

The demon's laughter filled the room. "Time to let him go, Grace," Dylan said.

"Why?" I asked, as I heard the sirens outside. "Oh. Yes, well, Mr. Oni, you are no longer welcome in Shady Grove. If you leave now, there will be no repercussions of your actions here. However, if I ever see your face again," I said, lifting my hand towards the glass of water on the bedside tray. It froze instantly. With a jerk, I made a fist, and the solid ice block of glass and water shattered into a thousand tiny specks of water.

"Agreed. I never want to see this hell hole again," he said.

"It may be a hell hole, but it's my hell hole," I replied, waving my hand to release him. His laughter rumbled the walls as he turned to swirling black smoke and dissipated into nothing. "Sorry, Darlin', no more kiddos for you today."

"Winnie is enough," he smiled. "For now."

"I wonder what else stupid could happen today?" I asked.

Famous last words.

CHAPTER THIRTEEN

BITING DOWN ON THE APPLE, I PAUSED TO THINK ABOUT THE STORIES of Snow White. Not that I was a princess, hiding with a bunch of little people, trying to find my prince, but the thought crossed my mind that Stephanie might try to poison me. "Where did you get these apples?" I asked Levi out of paranoia. We had picked up Winnie on the way back to the trailer, and they were coloring at the new kitchen table.

"At the Food Mart," Levi said. "I went to the store and picked up a few things yesterday since you haven't done any shopping."

"Sorry," I replied.

"What's wrong with the apple?" he asked.

I leaned on the counter, lolling my head around like I was going to faint. As I rolled my eyes back in my head, Levi jumped up. Dylan smirked, then Levi realized I was pretending. "Thanks a lot, Dylan."

"Just keeping you honest," he replied as he returned to his newspaper.

"You must tell the truth, Aunt Grace. We learned that in Sunday School," Winnie supplied.

"You are right, Winnie. I'm sorry," I said.

"Don't apologize to me," she said. "You have to apologize to Jesus."

Dylan muffled a laugh, and Levi looked away from my gaze. "I'm sorry, Jesus."

"No, Aunt Grace, you have to pray and ask forgiveness," she said.

"Oh, my bad, well, I can do that when I go to bed tonight," I replied.

"Where is Rufus?" she asked.

"He's at Dylan's house," I said. "We need to go let him out."

"I'll go do it," Levi said. "I need to run a quick errand, anyway."

"What kind of errand?" I asked, chomping down on the apple.

"None-ya," he replied, meaning it was none of my business.

I rolled my eyes. "Alright. You coming back here?" I asked.

"Yeah, probably," he replied, as he took off in a hurry.

I wondered what got into him. Looking out the window as he left, I saw Cletus and Tater working on that hunk of junk they called a car. It was a 1987 Cutlass Supreme. It was silver, but the hood was brown covered in duct tape. It was their way of "Rednecking it up" they told me. If that meant looking ridiculous, they hit the nail on the head.

"Can I watch cartoons?" Winnie asked.

"Sure," Dylan said, as he clicked the television to one of those all-day cartoon channels. He got up from his spot to stand with me in the kitchen. I offered him a bite of the apple. "Why would I want a poisonous apple?"

"Because I offered it," I said.

"The last time mankind did that they got themselves in a hell of a lot of trouble," he said.

"Good thing you aren't human," I replied.

He took a huge bite out of the apple, leaving very little for me. He wrapped one arm around my waist, pulling me to him. When his lips met mine, the tart juice of the green apple combined with the heat of his mouth sent my hormones into overdrive. Hungry for him, I pressed myself to him harder trying not to moan as his lips worked with mine. When he released my lips, he said, "You taste like sin."

"Keep it up and we will both need to ask Jesus for forgiveness," I smiled.

"I think we are past that point," he said.

"If not, we need to try harder," I said. For a moment, the blue fire of desire burned in his eyes. If it weren't for the child on the couch, we probably would have christened the kitchen counter. I looked back at Winnie who was enthralled by the television. "It's tough being parents."

Dylan released his grip on me allowing the cool air between us to quench the flame between us. "Now or later, doesn't matter. I will have you," he said. Shit. When he said things like that, I had no response. My brain melted, and I couldn't think of a witty remark. He knew it too. The devious light in his eyes betrayed him. Instead, I settled for poking him in the ribs. He caught my hand before I could do it, bringing it to his mouth he sucked my finger. My mind flashed back to Malcolm using the same gesture. Dylan did it so much better.

"Oh, shit, you gotta stop," I managed to whisper while fighting back the driving need to *let* him have me.

As I made the move to the bedroom to give in to Dylan, Levi pulled back up outside. He hadn't been gone long enough to go feed and let Rufus out. He surged in the front door out of breath.

"What's wrong?" Dylan asked. Winnie stared at him with wide eyes. He looked positively wild.

"You have to go to the town square. Right now," he said.

"What is it?" I asked.

"They are going to burn it," he said.

"Burning the town square?" Dylan asked.

"No. You," he said looking straight at me.

Dylan clamped down on my hand, pulling toward the door. "Winnie, we will be right back," I said to her.

"Go! I've got her," Levi said with fear in his eyes.

We jumped in the Camaro. Dylan drove like a maniac. I gripped the door, trying to breathe. As we approached the town square, it looked like someone had started a bonfire near the gazebo in the center of town. Dylan parked a half block away. "Stay with me," he ordered me with a gruff tone.

He locked hands with me. We approached the flames to see that it wasn't a bonfire. It was an effigy of a woman with long blonde hair. The image was made of straw, and it burned quickly. It looked like the hair was made of yarn. Clearly, it was me. There were a few people standing at a distance as we approached the flames. I heard sirens in the distance. The fire spread across the dead grass heading toward the gazebo. Pulling power from my tattoo, I thrust my hands toward the flames. The fire extinguished leaving a blackened carcass. A charred sign sat at the base of the image.

Dylan squatted down, wiping across it with his hand. Soot brushed away to reveal a shocking message. "Death to the Queen."

"Fuck," I muttered. The square filled with sirens, and the on-lookers dispersed. Dylan looked at me with pure fear in his eyes. "It's a joke. Not a big deal."

"This isn't a joke, Grace," he said, rising to face me. "This is going too far. Even if she didn't do this directly, she's got people in this town thinking about killing you."

"I'm like you. Not so easy to kill," I said.

"You can be though, and if anyone knows how to do it, it's her," he snarled as Sheriff Troy Maynard approached us.

"Jesus," he said, looking at the sign. "Grace, you need to go back home."

"I'm not running from this," I said defiantly.

"How did you know about it?" he asked.

"Levi came home in a tizzy. Talk to him to find out what he saw," I said.

"I'll talk to him, and call you," Dylan told Troy.

"Thanks, man," he said. "We will get this cleaned up. Who put out the fire?"

"I did," I replied. "It was getting close to the gazebo. It's not a big deal." I tried shrugging it off, but inside me, a fear grew quickly. I looked around the square to the firefighters who had arrived, along with the cops. Meeting each set of eyes, I saw fear. The fear in me reflected in them. I couldn't let this consume me. People looked to me for guidance, and if I was afraid, they would be too.

Dylan tugged on my hand to get my attention. "We need to go," he said softly.

"Look at them. They are afraid," I said.

"They should be. This is serious. You should be, too," he said. The strong façade I'd tried to present was working. No one could see my fear. Not even Dylan who pleaded with me to leave. "Let's go home. Troy can handle this."

I nodded looking back at the firefighters who jumped to work once we started moving away. Troy retrieved a camera from his cruiser. As I lowered myself into Dylan's car, Troy started taking pictures of the remains. Dylan climbed in with worried eyes. "It's okay," I said.

"No, it isn't, Grace," he muttered, cranking up the car to rush us back to the trailer.

When we got there, Levi had put Winnie to bed in her new room. He shoved his hands in his jeans. "Well?"

"It was burning when we got there," I said.

"Who did it?" he asked.

"Doesn't matter. It all leads back to her," Dylan growled. "What did you see?"

"A couple of people in masks. When I saw the sign, I didn't care about what was going on there. I turned around to come back here as soon as possible," he said.

"Do you still need to go run your errand?" I asked.

"Doesn't matter now. But I'll go get Rufus," he said, grabbing his jacket.

"Keep an eye out, Levi," Dylan said.

"They aren't after me. They are after her," he said.

"And if something happened to you, do you think it wouldn't bother her?" Dylan asked.

"Hey, I'm right here," I said. Dylan turned to me with fire in his eyes. I backed down. The fight in me was gone. The tension in the room sucked the air out making it hard to breathe.

"Go and come right back. Take the truck," Dylan said.

Levi nodded, then headed out the door.

"This is serious, Grace," Dylan turned on me.

I dropped my head. His warm hands cupped my cheeks dragging my gaze back to him. I swallowed at the fear in his eyes. "I know," I muttered.

"I see it now. You are afraid," he said. "You hid it very well."

"Yes," I gulped.

Opening the door to the bedroom, he guided me inside. "She will stop at nothing. I've seen it before. She's destroyed people over nothing. Maybe there is more to this than just trying to break us up. I need to do some more digging."

"She can't be allowed to win," I said.

"What do we do though? It's not worth me losing you. Shady Grove can go to hell as long as I have you," he said.

I made a promise to the people here. Abandoning them now wasn't an option. I couldn't turn tail and run. Looking into Dylan's eyes, he knew the struggle inside me. "You have me forever," I said. He groaned pushing me back against the wall. His kiss devoured my mouth. It was hot and forceful. Hot hands traveled up my sides lifting my shirt over my head. His lips traced a line from my mouth to my neck to my shoulder. I looped a finger through his belt to pull him closer to me.

He stopped the barrage of kisses to pull his shirt off over his head. Then his mouth collided with mine as if his kisses could keep us safe forever. Considering the fervor of his efforts, I could believe in that safety. The sweat of his bare skin pressed against mine. Warm and wet. This wasn't angry sex or postponed desire. He held on to me with uncertainty as the driving force. For me, I knew he was my forever, even if that meant only a few more hours to my long life. For him, I was his right now with a maybe of forever. Not because he didn't want me for that long, but because sometimes life doesn't give us the time we want.

With smooth movements, he had my jeans unbuttoned and down in an instant. "I won't let you go," he whispered in my ear. "Even if I have to take you away from here. Grace, I can't live without you now."

"Nothing is going to happen to me," I said, looking into his eyes. He grimaced as if I didn't understand his desperation. I did understand it, but he managed to prove his concern by the heat of his love making.

❦

"I'm postponing my stuff in Montgomery tomorrow. I'll finish the paperwork later," he said, laying next to me after he had made desperate love to me.

"Levi will stay with me. It will be fine," I said. "You've wanted this for so long. Please don't let me be the reason you don't get what you want."

"I don't trust Levi to keep you safe," he said.

"Trust me to keep me safe. Levi is back-up," I smiled. He didn't. "How long will you be gone?"

"Most of the day. It can wait," he said.

"No, you are going," I said.

"Grace," he protested.

"No more sex until you go to Montgomery. So, if that's tomorrow, great. If not, guess you will be waiting a while," I teased.

He groaned, putting his forearm over his eyes. I didn't realize the threat would be so painful. I didn't even mean it as a real threat, but he took it like that.

"Don't do this to me," he begged.

"I was joking," I said. He lifted his arm, and I saw the light in his eye. He knew I was joking. "Asshole."

"Yes, but I'm your asshole," he said.

"No thanks, I've already got one," I replied. He laughed loudly. I placed a finger over his lips. "You will wake the child." I climbed over on top of his body looking down at him as I shifted my hips grinding down on him. He latched his hands on my hips.

"Good god, woman," he moaned.

"You are going to Montgomery," I said as I ran a fingernail down his chest.

"Yes, whatever you say," he gave in easily.

Leaning down over him, I kissed him. "You didn't fight me," I whispered, kissing his neck.

"There's no need. You are too damn stubborn, plus I can't handle you naked on top of me teasing like that. Now you know my weakness," he said, as I kissed lower and lower on his chest to his navel.

I looked back to him meeting his eyes. "I already knew your weakness," I said, moving down between his legs.

"Oh, God bless me," he moaned.

My life would never be the same because of Dylan Riggs. He awoke feelings inside me that I didn't know existed. From the earliest flirts between us, I told him I didn't have a heart. With every kiss, every touch and every time we made love, he proved to me how wrong I was. Nothing could break me. Nothing, but him.

CHAPTER FOURTEEN

I SHOULD HAVE KNOWN THAT SHE WOULD TRY SOMETHING ELSE. Dylan's insistence had driven home the idea that Stephanie was a determined individual. She would stop at nothing to get what she wanted. The question was, what did she want? I stared at her across the room as I walked into Dylan's house.

"I don't mean to be rude, but this was my house once," Stephanie said.

"You need to leave," I quickly responded.

She laughed. "How do you think I got in here?"

"I don't know. I don't care. Just leave," I said exasperated. She'd tried every way she could think of to separate Dylan and I. Finding her in our home pissed me off to no end. She had no boundaries. No reservations about ruining our lives. I had no idea what her hidden agenda was, but I seriously doubted at this point it was because she wanted to be Queen of the Exiles. As good as Dylan was in bed, I could almost believe it was just a ploy to get him back, but even then, I really felt there was more to the story. Perhaps it was the more to their life that Dylan refused to tell me. The moments it was mentioned he flared with anger, shoving off all my inquires. There was more to this. There had to be.

"He let me in," she said.

Dylan left early this morning for Montgomery to finish his private investigator registration because I insisted that he go. I knew he didn't have time to let her in. "Dylan is out of town. So, you are a liar," I responded.

"Grace, I can be very persuasive. Perhaps you aren't giving him what he needs, but he knew I could. I hope you don't mind that we used your bed," she cooed.

"I trust him. He would never," I replied.

She shook her head and walked up the stairs. Following her, I feared what she intended to show me. His shirt that she wore brushed the back of her butt cheeks as she climbed the stairs. She wasn't wearing underwear. It was the shirt he was wearing when he left the trailer this morning or at least one very similar. Her clothes made a trail from the top of the steps to the bedroom. Waltzing into our room like it was her own, she revealed the mess of the bed.

Laying down in the middle of it, her ebony hair contrasted with the white sheets. She moaned. "It was so good to be with him again. I'm sure he missed me," she laughed. "It's time you moved on, Grace. Dylan and Shady Grove are mine. You were a temporary distraction."

The last few days I'd fought her tooth and nail. My resolve wavered as my heart pounded in my chest. A cold chill passed through me hardening my heart. All of this was too much. Staring at her writhing like a whore on my bed, I seethed in anger and disgust. Even if she was lying, seeing her there sickened me. Nausea overwhelmed my senses as my cheeks turned hot with fury. Without another word, I turned from the room. I grabbed a few things in Winnie's room and threw them into a pink travel case she kept in the closet.

Slowly, I lurked through the house. I felt like the ex-fiancée in a foreign world when that was the way *she* should have felt. Slipping the diamond ring off my finger, I laid it gently on the black marble countertop in the kitchen. The ring he had made just for us. The symbols and power in it bound us together. For me it was forever. I knew what she was, but so did he. If he did this, it wasn't because she seduced him. It was because he wanted it. Either way, something happened here. The house smelled like sex. Musty, dank sex.

She shadowed behind me without saying a word. I desperately wanted to get to the truck before the tears started to fall. With my back to her, I said, "You win." A mocking laugh escaped her as I went through the garage to the truck.

Driving at a normal speed, I took in the magnificent land and home I'd lived in for such a short time. The memories here would be good ones, except for the last few moments. I said my goodbye silently and hit the main road back to town like a bat out of hell.

Pulling my cell phone out of my pocket, I dialed Levi.

"What's up, Grace?" Levi answered.

"Levi, can you pick up Winnie at school?" I asked.

"No, tell me what's wrong," he said immediately. My bard and his damn intuitive self could hear the tears although they were silent.

"Stephanie was in the house. In the shirt he wore today, and nothing else. His clothes were all over the house, and the bed was a wreck. He didn't go straight to Montgomery this morning," I muttered.

"Where are you?" he said anxiously.

"On the way to the trailer. I picked up a few of Winnie's favorite things from her room. We will have to get rest later. If you talk to him, tell him I left the ring on the counter," I said.

"Grace, this is messed up! You know he didn't do this," Levi said, defending Dylan once again. I wasn't sure why he was hell bent on being on Dylan's side.

"Levi, I'm tired of fighting. I'm tired of politics. I'm tired of Shady Grove. If I leave, are you going with me?" I asked choking back sobs.

"Wherever you go, I go, but you can't leave without talking to him, even if it is to tell him to fuck himself," Levi said, as his anger grew.

The tears flowed freely, and my vision blurred. I concentrated to keep my eyes on the road. The wind picked up outside blowing the truck. Gripping the steering wheel, I cried to Levi, "I can't do that. I love him too much to say it."

"Grace. Come to me," he said. The command was subtle and loving. It washed over me, and all I wanted to do was to go home to my bard. There was nothing romantic in it, but I knew his loyalty was solid. Nothing could separate us. Through the command, I felt the strength of his arms that had wrestled me from attending to a dying Dylan on the steps of the courthouse last year. I craved those strong arms through the command. A safety that right now, I couldn't find anywhere else in the world.

Resolving to get home, I kept my eyes on the road. "I'm on my way," I replied. My *give a shit* was broken, but perhaps if I got home, then it could be repaired.

"Don't hang up. I need to know you are safe. A storm is moving in," he warned.

"Okay," I said. The wind blew the truck harder, and at the last moment, I saw the child. She stood in the middle of the road bending over to pick up a doll. I swerved hard crossing the middle line into the other lane of traffic. The wind gusted again. I lost all control as the truck exited the road on the opposite side. "Oh, no. Levi!" I screamed as the vehicle launched over the edge of the road into a drop-off. Holding the steering wheel, I continued to scream in panic. The truck barreled toward a tree. Pulling power from my tattoo, I tried to shield myself, but the impact into the tree just threw me into my icy shield doing as much damage as the tree would have. Glass shattered all around me grazing my skin in a thousand tiny cuts. My hands thrust out in front of me hit the shield, and my right wrist cracked. The bone stuck out of the skin as I bled. My chest hit the airbag with force. Gasping for breath, I searched for my cell phone.

Weakly, I heard Levi screaming my name, "Grace! Answer me! Grace! Where are you? What happened? I'm on my way!"

The world swirled around me. The mocking laugh from Stephanie's lips haunted me as my chest heaved once more. My heart stopped, and my blood ran cold. I felt the power of Gloriana wash over me. No heartbeat. No blood flow. Ice in my veins.

However, because I'd lost the will to fight, not even the power of the winter queen could sustain me. I greeted the darkness happily and the last word on my dying lips was "Winnie."

My body moved painfully as a distinctly male voice cussed the stormy air around us. The wind and rain whipped through the destroyed cab of the truck. Without ceremony, my body hit the wet forest floor. Still no breath nor a heartbeat, but I knew I was still alive somehow. Dragged through the forest by my left arm, I groaned in pain.

"Shut up, wench," the voice growled. A deep, male voice with the hint of exotic.

"Help," I whimpered.

The male laughed jerking on my arm. As pain shot through my chest, darkness consumed me once again.

CHAPTER FIFTEEN

"As my broken body was being dragged through the forest, my bard was taking his damn sweet time trying to find me," Grace said.

"Hey, you can't tell this part. You were unconscious," I reminded her.

"You shut-up, Levi Rearden. This is my story, is it not?" she asked.

She'd been telling the story while pacing the living room. I hated typing as she talked, because a lot of the times, I missed what she was saying. She hated to repeat things, but I was the bard, and she was the queen. She reminded me daily. A smile crossed my lips as I stared at her. She rolled her eyes turning her back on me. "It is your story, of course, but most of it, I'm telling it my way."

"What have you typed there that I can't see?" she said pacing over to the laptop. I closed it quickly. The truth was, we'd just started recording her tales, but I had thrown in bits that I knew to be true even if she didn't admit to it. The turquoise in her eyes flared at me.

"It may be your story, but I'm telling it," I said. "And the parts that you weren't in, I get to tell from my perspective."

"I will jerk a knot in you so fast," she threatened.

I laughed at her. Grace was infuriating and beautiful all at once. I'd come to appreciate the dangerous combination over the years. "I'm telling this part," I leveled a powerful, but small command. She grimaced as it rolled over her.

"Oh, you are so going to get it," she played. I knew my limits. For now, I hadn't reached them. "Go ahead, Dublin. Write it your way. See what happens." I grinned from ear to ear. I actually won the argument. Nevermind that I cheated by throwing some persuasive power behind it. The truth was no matter how much power I put behind it, I was never truly convinced that she didn't just let me get my way sometimes. Except that first night when I sang to her. That night, I won. My life depended on it. Her life depended on it. If I'd let her take me, as I so desperately wanted out of sheer hormonal desire, she would have lost herself. I would have lost myself in her, and a dangerous future it would have been for both of us. That one defining moment sealed our friendship and her complete trust in my abilities. Even then, I wasn't completely sure of what all I could do, but I trusted her to teach me. Grace, my best friend, my Queen. The woman who ruled my life. I loved every minute of it.

"I don't have to have your permission now," I smarted off to her.

"Despite your power, Levi Rearden, you fell off the

turnip truck if you think I'll let you get away with this. Eventually, you will pay," she threatened. I was sure that I would. I hoped that I would.

ॐ

HEARING HER SCREAMS THROUGH THE PHONE SENT ME INTO A PANIC. I grabbed the keys to the motorcycle and my helmet. I only had on jeans and a t-shirt. I stuffed my gun into the front of my pants where she hated. She always said I'd shoot myself doing that, so I moved it from the front to the back. She was right. I didn't want to damage the goods, perhaps I'd need them again one day. The rain had already started to fall, but I knew something was very wrong. I had to get to her as soon as possible.

The crunching of metal assaulted my ears through the phone, then went quiet. "Grace! Answer me! What's happening!"

No answer. Only silence.

"Shit!" I yelled into the phone.

Calming myself as I mounted the bike, I heard her faint voice once more, "Winnie."

Fuck!

I dialed Dylan. No answer. I swore to God that if he did this to her after everything we'd gone through over the last few days, I'd kill him myself. I dialed Nestor.

"Hot Tin Roof," he answered.

"Nestor. I was just on the phone with Grace. She wrecked. She was upset. I don't know what happened. Stephanie was at the house. I've got to find her. Can you get Winnie from school?" I asked.

"Slow down, Boy. Where is Grace?"

"I don't know. The truck crashed. I could hear it. She said she was on the road from Dylan's house to the trailer. She can't be too far out of town," I said.

"What's this about Stephanie?" he asked.

"Grace went home to get things ready for Dylan's homecoming today. His paperwork was going to be done today. She was going to

131

bake a cake to celebrate with him. Stephanie was there. She said Dylan and she…" my voice trailed off in anger. Fucking Dylan.

"Alright. We can't do anything about that right now. I'll call the school to send Winnie home on the bus. Wait right there. I'm bringing my truck. You can't go out in this on that bike," he insisted.

"I don't have time. She could be dying," I said desperately.

"No, Son. She might be hurt, but she won't die," he said.

"Nestor, I have to find her," I said desperately. All I could think about was getting to her before someone else did. I focused on her to feel her like I knew that I could. She was hurt, but I didn't know where or how badly. Damn Grace. Hang in there.

"I'm walking out the door. Wait there," he said, hanging up. I knew he was right, but I also knew I needed to get to her fast.

While I waited, I walked back inside and called Troy Maynard.

"Maynard," he answered.

"Troy, I was on the phone with Grace when it sounded like she had a wreck. I'm going out to find her. Can you spare any help?" I asked.

"Yeah, sure. I can come myself. Where was she?" he asked calmly.

"She'd left Dylan's place and was heading here," I said. I left out the details. He didn't need to know. Hopefully, all of this was just a bad dream. The whole last week had been a nightmare. Why not this too?

"Okay, I'm heading that way. Don't get on that bike in this weather," he said.

"I'm not. Nestor is bringing his truck," I said.

"See you out there," he said.

Nestor's short drive from the bar to here put him in the driveway the moment I hung up with Troy. I met him outside. "Listen to me, Levi. You be safe. She would die if something happened to you, too. If Dylan has done this, and she's hurt, Winnie will need you. You got me?"

"Yes, sir," I responded as he handed me the keys.

"You go find her," he said. "You got something of hers?"

"I don't need it. I've felt her power flow through me when we swap power. I can track her like that," I admitted to him. It was a secret that she and I had kept for a long time. She felt me, and I could feel her through the power we'd shared. We both agreed that no one needed to know about it. It wasn't a secret that hid anything intimate between us or anything like that, but it very well could be construed as something that it wasn't. It was bad enough that we both nearly orgasmed every time we did it. The last thing we needed was our significant others realizing how close we really were. Although, I was currently without a significant anything. I badly needed to get laid. Stupid fairy hormones. I was fine until I realized what it was. Awareness drove me over the edge. However, I wasn't desperate enough to call Kady. No more Kadence Rayburn. Ever.

Nestor didn't seem to be surprised by this. He was damn observant and probably already knew. "Be careful," he said as I cranked up the little pickup. Backing out of the drive, I looked at the storm clouds growing. Reaching out to feel her power, it returned to me faint and cold. Freezing like the day she died just before Christmas. I gripped the steering wheel and cussed Dylan for this bullshit. This was the worst day in the world to go to Montgomery. His selfish quest to be a private investigator after getting Grace into this Queen business in the first place pissed me off.

I'd always wanted her to forgive him right after I met them both. They were great together, but to be honest, I wasn't sure that Misaki's child wasn't his until Misaki turned out to be a Japanese demon, but that didn't mean Dylan didn't hit that. I'd read up on his ancestors. The stories were as promiscuous as if he were an incubus. The Phoenix were known as lechers. Dylan seemed devoted to Grace, but lately, there were too many questions. Even Kady accused him of coming on to her after she inquired about his male parts. To be honest, I was glad Grace punched her for that bullshit. I didn't believe her when she said that Dylan came on to her one night when Grace was attending a PTA meeting at the school for Winnie. Now, I wasn't so sure. Grace assured me that he would never do such a thing, and that Kady was being an immature brat. I hoped for Grace's sake that she was right.

I drove as fast as the little truck would take me. However, driving to Dylan's place, I never saw her truck. As I approached, the drive leading to Dylan's house I turned around heading back toward town. Troy's cruiser approached with his lights flashing. He didn't have his siren on, but he stopped as I drove up next to him.

"I don't see anything," he said. "You sure she came this way?"

"Yes, I need to get out of the truck. I can track her," I said.

"You got something I can smell?" he asked.

"No, it's different," I replied. It hadn't occurred to me that if tracking her by magic didn't work that Troy's werewolf senses would be our best option.

I pulled over on the side of the road, stepping out into the rain. It was steady, but not a torrent. Concentrating on the tattoo on my shoulder, I immersed myself in the memory of the touch of her cold hand on it. Feeling the power we shared well up inside me, I released it out of my hand. A wave of cold energy floated into the surrounding air. I felt it pulling me back toward town.

"I need you to drive," I said to him.

"Get in," he said. Climbing in the passenger side, I held my hand out in the rain.

"Sorry about the rain," I muttered.

"Just find her," he said.

Concentrating on Grace in her truest form, I imagined her lovely turquoise eyes glittering with power. Long locks of platinum tresses that flowed down her back. The delicate twist in her speech patterns when she fully released the trailer park façade. All of these things flowed through my hand connecting our powers. In truth, Grace was not my patron. Gloriana was, so that's who I was tracking. I also knew that if she were near death, that the winter queen would sustain her for as long as she could. The connection drew me to her, but as I got closer, it waned. She was dying. "Grace," I muttered. "Please hang on." Troy glanced at me worried. He admired Grace for taking the position that she did. He and I had talked about it around the holidays after all the craziness with the Yule Lads. He knew the restraint it took to give Amanda a reprieve that she didn't deserve. He told me that he'd known a lot of fairy queens over the years, and none of them were like Grace. She had a heart. She claimed that she didn't, but those of us that knew her, knew she had a heart of gold.

We drove at least two miles when the power overwhelmed me, and I jerked on the door handle as Troy drove slowly. The door was locked. "Hold up, Levi!" he said unlocking the door. I barreled out of the door twisting to feel the connection. Walking over to the opposite side of the street, I looked down the embankment. My heart dropped.

"Grace!" I yelled as Troy came up next to me.

We both started down the hill sliding on the wet pine needles that covered the ground. The truck smoldered as the front cab had been split in two by a tall pine. The driver's door hung open. The crimson sheen of blood coated the window and door.

"Blood. Lots of it!" Troy cried out. He clicked the mic on his walkie. "Dispatch. This is officer 001. I've got a 10-50 PI on state highway 219, two miles from Shady Grove city limit. My cruiser is alongside the road. 10-33. 10-52."

"Officer 001, 10-4," a woman replied.

"Amanda, it's Grace. Get out here," he said skipping protocol.

"10-4" she responded.

As we reached the truck, I realized she wasn't inside. Frantically, I searched around us. The power led to right here. I didn't feel her beyond this.

"Levi, what's wrong?"

"Something is blocking me. This is as far as I can feel her," I said.

He looked around us. We noticed the drag marks. "I can track her with the blood, but I'm not going in the woods without back up. Amanda will be here in a minute with help."

"I'm not waiting on Amanda," I said as my phone rang.

"What?!" I yelled into the phone seeing the caller I.D.

Dylan's voice came through the phone. "What's going on?"

"Stephanie is at your house practically naked walking around in your shirt. Grace found her," I said. Stopping as he tried to interrupt, I pulled power. "Shut the fuck up."

I was greeted with silence. "You have done too much now,

Dylan. None of it matters. The truck is down a ravine. There is blood everywhere, and someone is blocking power so I can't find her. You did this! I swear to God. I'm going to kill you." My anger toward him seethed. The man that was supposed to protect her left her open to an attack by his ex-girlfriend. If he fucked Stephanie after all of this, after being with Grace last night, I would rip his lungs out of his chest just to watch him turn to ash. I'd do it over and over until it took.

"Where?" he said.

"Fucking figure it out yourself," I said hanging up. The phone rang again. "Fuck off, Dylan!"

"Levi, where is Grace?" Remy's smooth voice came through the line. Just what I needed was *this* one on the line, too. I knew his idle flirtations. Remington Blake was waiting for his moment. The moment that Dylan fucked up, and Grace lost sight of her future with him. Remy would swoop in with his New Orleans accent and take her away. Fuck him, too.

"Why?" I growled. Hearing sirens, I knew Amanda and help was arriving.

"I just got a text with a link. It's a video auction. Someone is trying to sell her. She looks bad," he said. "What's going on?"

"We just found her truck wrecked. Sell her? What do you mean?"

"Fairies are big business on the black market. Nothing is worth more than a fairy queen," he said.

"Why do you have the link?"

"I'm not sure. Perhaps someone knows I love her. Maybe they thought I'd pay to get her back," he suggested. "Either way, I'm watching her now. Half dead on a concrete floor as someone is shooting iron nails into her calves."

"What!"

"She's mostly immune to iron, because she's lived here so long, but a direct insertion will eventually poison her," he murmured. "You gotta find her quick. I'm bidding now, but it's almost outside my pay range."

My heart throbbed. Poisoning her. Fuck all this shit. I had to find her. "No. Please no," I muttered. Troy looked at me questioning. "Someone is auctioning her off. They are torturing her."

"Fuck. Fairy trafficking," he said.

After I hit the speaker button on the phone, I asked, "How did I not know this was a thing?"

"We don't talk about it, but it happens. We need to find her before they kill her or someone buys her," Troy said.

"Remy is bidding," I supplied.

"Yeah, but I'm running out of money!" he exclaimed.

"Keep bidding. I'll cover it," Dylan's voice rang out behind me. Spinning around on him, I threw a punch to his jaw. Hitting him square, he dropped to one knee as blood rolled out of his mouth. Troy restrained me from hitting him again.

"Levi, stop! This won't get her back," he said.

"How did you get here?" I asked.

"I flew. You idiot," he growled, looking horrified at the blood behind me dripping down the door as the rain thinned it out. It puddled on the ground. Grace's blood. "What the fuck are we waiting on?"

"My idea. I didn't want to go in with just the two of us," Troy said.

"I'm not waiting," Dylan said wiping the blood off his mouth. He squared to me. "You want another shot, Levi? I can take them all day, or we can go find her."

Turning away from him, I ran toward the drag marks. I heard their footfalls behind us as I hung up on Remy. There was nothing he could do for her, but watch. The rain continued its steady fall as we ran through the woods. The trail was clear. Amanda caught up with us as a gray wolf. She ran ahead of me slightly, but not at full pace. I kept reaching out to feel Grace, but I couldn't. Every part of me hurt like a case of the flu, but I kept running. Amanda slowed as we approached a clearing. She whined.

Troy ran up behind me with Dylan. "She says she's in there," Troy said. Grace once told me that if two wolves, even those without a pack, bonded, then they could speak to each other in either form. Amanda and Troy definitely moved past the mess that happened last year. They were in tune with each other. I knew that feeling, but Grace wasn't mine. She would never be mine.

Through the trees, we could see the remnants of an old wooden cottage. The roof caved in partially on one side, and the forest grew up around it. "Let's look around before we go in," Dylan said.

"Fuck that," I replied marching out of the woods toward the house. I didn't care what was waiting on me. Nothing was going to stop me.

"Levi, wait," Dylan said, grabbing my arm. "I know you've heard this before, but I can explain all of this. I know you think I'm cheating on her, but I swear to you on my life, I am not. She is everything to me. Please don't rush in there. She loves you. She would never forgive me if I let something happen to you."

"I am not a child, Dylan Riggs. I'm sick of your excuses. You had a good story when I told you about Kady. You skirted around the thing with Misaki, but Stephanie, in your house, in your shirt, in your bed! Even if you didn't, you have dirt on that snake that you won't divulge, because you are too scared. You are a coward, and I hate the day she finally gave into you. You can't explain everything away. Not anymore. She is in there. I'm going after her," I said to him.

"Fine. Let's go in," Dylan said, waving toward the house. It felt like he gave in too easily, but there was very little he could say to get me to believe him. I didn't want to believe him that all of this was just an unfortunate stack of circumstances. It felt like the twelfth round of Jenga, and the tower teetered on the word of the honorable Dylan Riggs.

"We will go around back," Troy said following Amanda around the side of the carcass of the house.

Slowly we walked over the rotting boards of the porch trying not to make too much noise. I knew I'd raised my voice. Whoever was in there with her probably knew we were coming. Once inside, the house didn't look as bad as it did from the outside. In fact, the roof was solid.

"Glamour," Dylan whispered.

I nodded. He pointed to stairs leading up. As he walked that way, I turned into a kitchen with a small satellite link up sitting on the counter. I'd seen something like it at the house of one of my card playing buddies. He said he lived so far out he couldn't get the internet, but he could link to a satellite. Even though the connection was slow, he could get pretty good reception. I jerked the power cord out of the wall, hoping to stop the feed. The lights on the contraption died out. Behind me, I heard the creak of a board.

Spinning around toward the noise, I saw nothing. However, another door opened up to the darkness beyond. I approached it slowly. Looking past the door, wooden steps led downward. A faint light flickered at the bottom like a dying florescent bulb. I reached in my waistband and pulled out my gun. Slowly, I went down the stairs pressing my back to the solid wall looking into the room below. It was a stark empty room with concrete floors. A streak of blood trailed through another door. Following the trail, I walked into another room. A camera sat on a stand facing down to the limp body of Grace. Quickly, I looked around the room with my sight. Seeing nothing, I tucked the gun away as I rushed to her side.

"Alright, that's far enough, Bard," she said.

"Aw, come on. You don't remember all of this," I complained.

"I remember enough to tell the story. I'm on to you now, Levi. No matter what I say, you are typing what you want anyway. So, you might as well let me tell the rest, so you can twist my words," she reasoned.

"What was the first thing you remember?" I asked, knowing the answer.

"You," she smiled.

"That's right! Me. Not Dylan," I said.

"The two of you eventually worked it out," she
    warned me.

"I know! I know, but it's the truth. I found you," I
    proclaimed with pride.

"You did," she conceded. "Now hush your mouth."

"Yes, ma'am," I replied.

CHAPTER SIXTEEN

Despite what everyone told me later about the incident, including my bard who was quite pleased with himself, I did remember a lot about what happened in that basement.

I first recalled waking up as my body hit the cold floor with a thump. The lights in the room blinded me. The man who dragged me through the forest breathed heavily. It wasn't that I was fat, but he made it sound like I was a few inches short of being round.

"Just smile for the camera," he chuckled. Through the blood, I could see the blinking red light of a camera.

"You bastard," I said. The power I had remaining kept me alive. I couldn't take the chance of using it for anything else like disrupting the electronics in the camera. I knew that Levi would come for me. Normally, I'd rely on Dylan, but at the moment, I didn't know where Dylan and I stood.

The man's haughty laugh echoed through the room. It sounded familiar in a way, but I couldn't place it. The lights impaired my vision to the point I couldn't make out any of his features as he moved around the room. When he moved closer, his shadow blurred my vision. Quickly, the pain overcame me again. I slept.

୧ଈ

When I awoke again, the cold floor touched my bare skin. Shivering, I winced at the bright lights. The red blink continued. My clothes lay in a pile under the camera. My broken and bloody body lay bare to whoever watched beyond the lens.

Speaking with confidence the man said, "Now I will prove that she is the fairy queen known as Gloriana."

"What the hell?" I muttered.

A sound I could only describe as a *swish* then a *chuck, chuck* pierced the air as red-hot pain shot through my left calf muscle. I screamed in pain, but my throat raw from the cold released no noise. *Swish. Chuck, chuck.* The searing pain ripped through me again. Dark tendrils of heat spread through my leg up to my thigh.

The man leaned over, whispering in my ear, "Even you aren't immune to iron, my Queen."

I groaned as the poison spread through my body. He'd fired two iron nails into my calf causing my remaining blood to curdle into black ichor killing me inch by inch. If the ichor reached my brain, there would be no reversing it. Even now, I had very little chance to survive.

"Let the bidding begin," he muttered, kicking me in the head. Nothingness consumed me again.

୧ଈ

"Grace, can you hear me?" Levi said. The tingle of his touch rushed through his hand into my cheek. His handsome face taut with concern looked down upon me blocking the bright lights.

"Levi, don't touch me. It can spread to you," I muttered. The poison would pass from me to him if we shared power.

"Let me give you a little to help," he said quietly rolling up his sleeve.

"No, Dublin. It will spread through the power swap. You need to take me to my father," I replied.

He grimaced. "Are you sure?" he asked. He knew very well that going to my father's home would be a last resort. I didn't know how long I'd lain in that basement dying. It was beyond any fairy medicine that Dr. Mistborne could perform.

"Yes," I muttered.

"Fuck," he said. "Dylan!"

My body tensed as he called out Dylan's name. "What?" my voice shook with the realization that not only had Levi come for me, Dylan had as well.

"He's here. Just lay still. He needs to know I'm taking you so he doesn't kill me," Levi said.

"No, I don't want him here," I muttered. It was too late. I heard the banging of heavy footsteps on a wooden stair.

"Levi!" he called out.

"Back here," Levi said stroking my cheek. "We do this right, Grace. I promise to take you as soon as he sees you."

"Grace!" Dylan cried out pushing Levi out of the way. His warm arms enveloped me.

I cried out in pain as he squeezed too hard. Releasing his grip, he apologized softly. "Oh, Grace. What have they done to you? It's okay. I'm here now. Please just stay with me."

"Levi is taking me to Father," I said as firm as my weak body would allow.

His eyes darkened, and his body went rigid. "That's fine, but I'm going, too."

"I don't want you to go with us," I muttered. I felt the rush of pain move through my leg into my stomach.

"Grace, I'm going," he said stroking my platinum hair. "Levi, what do we need to do?"

"Pick her up, and I'll shift us through the closest oak," Levi replied.

Dylan looked at Levi begging him, "Give me one moment."

"No," Levi protested. "She's dying!"

"Fine. Grace, look at me," he said sending warm pulses through my skin. He kissed my forehead gently laying me back on the cold floor. Unbuttoning his shirt, he slipped it off his shoulders. Levi leaned me up as Dylan threaded my arms through the shirt careful

143

not to damage the broken bone in my right wrist any further. One by one, he buttoned his shirt around me. "I did not, nor would I ever sleep with Stephanie Davis. She tried to pull some crap, probably to upset you, putting us all in this position. She's a deceitful bitch. I curse the day I begged her to move in with me. I swear on my life that I did not sleep with her. If you don't believe me, I understand. All of this is too overwhelming for all of us. My only concern right now is getting you to your father. Whatever you decide, I will do." His hands slid down the backs of my arms sending the warmth though them. I'd stopped feeling them a long time ago, but his warmth surged past that numbness. As he reached my left hand, his finger traced over my ring finger. His face filled with alarm.

"She said she left it on the counter at your house," Levi said for me.

"Okay," he muttered sounding defeated. "I'm going to do my best not to hurt you when I pick you up."

I shook my head knowing that pain would wrack my body when he lifted me. "Doesn't matter," my voice shook hopelessly.

Levi gave instructions to Troy to call Nestor. As Dylan lifted me, the pain I anticipated turned out to be more than I could bear. This time the darkness found me without hope. Dylan's speech didn't sway me. The same old story. Swearing on his life must not mean anything for someone who readily came back to life. It didn't matter. I didn't expect to survive.

CHAPTER SEVENTEEN

"Go ahead," Grace said, looking at me.

"Oh! So, now you agree that I should tell the parts
where you were passed out," I said.

Staring at me she didn't answer. However, I saw the
light of amusement in her eyes. She couldn't hide
it from me. I'd known her for too long. I knew
everything about her now. Back then, I didn't. It
took her many years to agree to allow me to write
her story even though I begged. It was what I was
made for, I was sure of it. I had musical talents
before I met Grace, but she molded them into the
bard that I became. She made me. Now it was
time for me to make her a legend. Not that I had
the confidence in myself to do it, but to me, she
already was. I just had to make sure the rest of
the world knew it.

"Do you really want to test me right now?" she
asked.

"I want to test you constantly. You are sexy as hell
when you are mad," I said.

"Levi!"

"See," I smiled.

"Just fucking tell your part of the story," she said.

When I found her, the striking state of her body scared the crap out of me. Black lines coursed over her body where her veins usually pumped blood. When she opened her eyes to look at me, even the veins in her eyes were ebony strands of ichor. All of it too close to her brain. Even if she survived, I worried that it was doing permanent damage to the woman she had become. Absent from her eyes was the blue sparkle that I expected to see. Even her platinum locks looked dull. I was losing her. We were losing her. I decided against my best judgment to call Dylan who immediately took her from me. There was nothing I could do, but stand by and watch him lie to her again.

Her pale skin shimmered translucent popping the black veins out to the surface of her skin. If I didn't know her heart, she looked like the evilest being I'd ever seen.

After putting his shirt on her while swearing on his life, he decided it was time to go. I spoke to Troy instructing him to call Nestor letting him know where we were taking her. Troy said he would spare him the details. I told him not to. Nestor needed to know the terrible condition in which we found her. I also told him to call Remington. I don't know why other than he was her lawyer and might need to know for election purposes. The vote was in three days. If we couldn't get her back before then, perhaps he could do something to delay the vote.

When Dylan lifted her, she winced in pain. Her head sank limply into his arm. I hurried up the steps with him right behind me. Walking out of the house, I headed for the first large oak tree I saw. Dylan paced on my heels.

"She's so light like all the life is gone out of her. I can't feel her heartbeat," he said.

"That's because it isn't beating. Gloriana is keeping her alive. We've been through this before with her," I reminded him.

"Yes," he muttered.

Placing my hand on the tree, I thought of the underground hallway that I once stood in with her which seemed like ages ago even though it was only a few months. The tree responded by sucking us into the Otherworld to the exact spot that I imagined.

"Don't provoke anyone here," I said. "They won't be happy to see us. Especially bringing iron into the realm. The first guards we come across we will beg to take us to Oberon."

"No need," Oberon's voice reverberated through the dank hallway. He walked up to her brushing her hair out of her face. "She's almost gone." A sadness passed over his face and into his cold dark eyes that I didn't think was possible for the Wild King of the Fairies.

"My King," I bowed to him. "Can you save her?"

"I cannot, but there are healers here. Bring her quickly," he said, as he turned the whole room shifted to a corridor with stone walls and brightly lit torches. They burned with an orange light. Dylan and I were both disoriented by the shift. Oberon's power to move about his realm allowed him to move us as well.

He turned into a large room with a giant bed in the center. Pillows covered every corner of the bed cascading into the floor. Grace told me once about her bedroom in the Otherworld. She was quite proud of the swimming pool sized bathtub. However, she assured me that she wouldn't trade her new garden tub in the trailer for it. The giant bath meant she would be isolated to this damp, musty world. The whole place smelled like wet soil. I'd worked on a farm my whole life. Sometimes you couldn't get the stink of wet soil out of your clothes not matter how much you washed them. There was no way I could live here.

Dylan gently laid her on the bed. Two women with exaggerated features entered the room. Their feline eyes traced my body seductively. Dylan didn't look up from Grace's face to notice. I was going on over a week without sex, so I noticed. Man, did I notice.

"Really? You are putting that in there?" she asked.

"Really. Shut-up," I replied with a little magic. The look in her eye told me I'd reached my limit. I just grinned deviously. She couldn't stop me even if she wanted to stop me. The good thing was, I knew she had no intentions of stopping me. Ever.

The women took Dylan's shirt off, washing her body to remove the dried blood and mud from her skin. They worked around Dylan, so he did not have to move. Carefully they avoided her leg with the iron in it. As they exited, Oberon returned with another woman. My voice caught in my throat. She was the spitting image of Grace's glamour. It hit me that this was her mother, Ellessa.

"Gloriana!" she cried out rushing to her side. She practically shoved Dylan away. He stood at the edge of the bed watching her mother stroke her face. "Oh, my dear child, what have they done to you?"

"Careful of her leg, my dear," Oberon warned.

"I don't care. It's been so long. Where is the healer?" she asked.

"She has been summoned," he replied.

At the door, a woman stood with illuminated skin. Her hair was black as night, and her eyes pastel blue. As she walked into the room, Ellessa backed away from Grace. Dylan tried to lean in, but her mother jerked him back.

"Dylan Riggs, we have allowed you to continue this relationship with her, but it seems that it's come to a point where it's too detrimental to continue," she said.

"I understand that she is upset with me, but I'm sure once she is well that we can work it out," Dylan replied.

"Do not speak to me as if I do not know who you are, Phoenix. So many names over the years. Serafino Taranis. Keme Rowtag. Kenneth Alderbrand. Dylan Riggs. A man who crossed the world fucking every being he could for a time. What makes you think we trust you now?" she spouted at him. "You are not different, despite your protests to the contrary."

"Yes, I've had many names. Many conquests. As has Gloriana. Now, it's just us. No one else," he said.

She paced forward to him, and although he stood a foot above her, he cowered at her advance. "I dare you to lie to me," she sang. Her voice tinkled out of her mouth in a melodic wave. My ears pricked at the power that she held through her voice. A siren. "Do I look like her to you?"

"Yes, my lady," he said, as he cringed away from her.

She hummed lightly. I concentrated on Grace's face as the woman who'd entered earlier began to place candles on stands around the bed. She pulled crystals that glowed out of her pockets placing different variations on each stand. The siren song permeated my skin. Forcing myself to look away, I heard Dylan whimper like a child under the strain of her power. "I assure you that I could provide you with an experience that you would never forget. My daughter may be a royal fairy, but she is no siren. My song will reverberate through your body pulsing climaxes like you've never felt." Her lips almost touching his cheek as she spoke.

"No, I love Grace. Please stop," he said, holding his resolve. I pitied him. I'd been in that position before with Grace. Thankfully, I resisted her in that moment of weakness for both of us. I wanted her badly then. Watching him resist her, I knew right then that he wasn't lying about sleeping with Stephanie. Whatever she had said was a lie. Dylan hadn't cheated on Grace. I should have known better. I didn't approve of him leaving during the middle of the election, but he hadn't lied. I knew better. My anger got the best of me. Grace had her moments of rash behavior, but sometimes mine was much worse. It was the damn hormones.

"Enough!" Oberon's command shook the room. The candles flickered, but the healer did not stop her set up.

Ellessa backed away from Dylan who groaned and turned away from all of us. I knew what he was hiding. Like I said, I'd been there.

"You must all leave the room," the healer demanded.

Oberon escorted Ellessa to the door. She shot one final look to Dylan. I thought it was going to be a final test, but instead, it was approval. He'd passed her test. Dylan looked undecided.

"I don't want to leave her. If these are her last moments, I want to be with her," he said.

"She will survive," Oberon said confidently. However, I saw the grave look on the healer's face. She didn't agree with his assessment. Dylan slowly walked past me to the door. I turned to follow him.

"Bard," the healer said. "Stay close to the door. I will need your help soon."

"Me?"

"I see no other bards," she smirked.

"Um, okay," I replied.

Dylan moved to the door, but leaned on the wall opposite keeping his eye on her.

I stepped outside of the door putting my back to the wall to the right of the door. Oberon and Ellessa walked away leaving us. I watched Dylan's eyes as the healer began to chant. It sounded a lot like some chants that Matthew Rayburn would do at services on Sundays.

"I'm sorry that I hit you," I said.

"Don't be. I shouldn't have left for Montgomery. I knew Stephine was up to something, but I thought I'd deterred it," he said.

"What do you mean?" I asked.

"When I left the trailer this morning, I realized I'd left one of the forms on my desk at home. It was on the way, so I stopped to get it. It was pouring, and the power was out at the house. I couldn't get in the garage, and I knew the alarm system would be down. The house is still warded, but the technology was off. Stephanie waited on the front porch. She ran around to meet me as I tried to slip in the side door leaving her out there, but she forced her way into the house behind me.

"She said she'd left something upstairs in the bedroom, and she wanted to get it back. I informed her that all of her things were in storage. I pulled the key to the storage unit out of a kitchen drawer.

Handing it to her, I opened the back door for her to leave. She made her move much like Ellessa did in there. Less powerful than the siren, but she still tried," he said.

"Did she get the same reaction as Ellessa?" I asked.

His eyes shot to mine for a moment, then returned his gaze to Grace. "Surprisingly, no. You know as well as I do that it takes very little sometimes to get aroused at a beautiful woman pawing on you, especially fairies. However, no one repulses me like Stephanie does. No movement at all. I hate her with a passion," he said.

I didn't believe him. He may have rebuffed her, but a man's body responds to stimulation. Even unwanted stimulation. "How did you get her to leave?"

"I grabbed her arm and shoved her out the door. She screamed and hollered like a banshee. It was ridiculous. Ignoring her, I went upstairs and changed into dry clothes. I was soaked from getting out of the car and wrestling her out the door. Grabbing the papers I needed from the office, I went back downstairs. I took a drink from the fridge and an umbrella from the garage. Waiting for a moment before I went out the door, I listened to see if I could hear Stephanie. As I opened the door, I noticed how much the rain had stopped. Without the umbrella out, I walked to the car looking all around me. I didn't see her anywhere. I went to Montgomery and didn't think anything else about it."

"You should have told her that you found her there. You are an idiot," I said.

"Yes, I am. I've tried splitting my focus on finishing this paper-work and the election. Grace needed me to focus just on her. I could re-file the paperwork. We didn't expect to be in this fight, anyway. It's been devastating. I shouldn't have left. I told myself it would be okay, since Grace insisted that I go," he said taking his eyes off her. Staring at the stone floor, he crouched down putting his face in his hands. "I've got to do more than swear to make this up to her, but I will. Whatever it takes."

"It might take time. You may have to step back and let her breathe," I said.

"Whatever it takes, Levi. I see the way you look at her. Trust me, I know that look. You would do the same," he said.

He was right. I'd do anything for her.

"Anything?" she asked.

"How many times are you going to interrupt me?" I asked.

"As many times as I want, Levi Rearden," she laughed.

We waited for hours as the healer chanted and paced the room. When I looked in, she circled the bed tracing shapes in the air with her fingers. As she traced, a fine white line would leave an impression in the air. They were runes. Grace told me I needed to start learning them. She knew them all, but of course, she didn't need to know them. Her power didn't need any enhancements. She thought mine did. I'd begun studying them recently, but I didn't know enough to understand what the healer was doing.

Oberon returned to our watch carrying a stringed instrument that looked much like a guitar. However, it had twelve strings with a rounded hollow back. The carving around the circle in the center depicted a large stag inland in the wood in mother-of-pearl. He handed it to me. "You need a proper instrument," he proclaimed.

Before taking it, I said, "My King, your gift honors me. However, I cannot accept such a gift for the price would be too high."

"My daughter has taught you well not to accept a gift from our people, however, because you have been a good companion to her, I give this with no recompense or payment required. I swear it."

I bowed taking the instrument from him. Feeling stupid, I was pretty sure the instrument was a lute, but I'd never actually seen one. "I'm not sure how to play it."

"You must figure it out. The healer will need to rest soon. Your music will sustain Gloriana until the healer can resume her work," Oberon explained.

Immediately, I sat down on the floor. Beginning at the top of the neck, I pressed the strings down strumming the instrument lightly. I picked around with it for a few minutes realizing the nuances of the lute. Before long, I could make a tune with it.

Dylan watched me, then Oberon, then Grace. "Forgive Ellessa. She worries about her. I'm sorry she tried to provoke you," Oberon said.

Dylan faced forward. "Your Majesty, while I have not been the perfect fiancé to Grace, I have not cheated on her. Nor will I ever. I can resist any woman. You know this to be true."

"Yes, you are the seducer in most cases," Oberon said.

I continued to play the strings lightly as they talked, but I listened.

"Yes, usually, but you must know that gets old after a while. When I met your daughter, she was something new and fresh. I was mesmerized. This is a stark reminder that even our lives can be stripped from us. Sometimes playing the long game doesn't pan out. The immediate, fleeting moments are just as important as a grand scheme," Dylan said.

"Indeed. You need not worry. She will forgive you in time. Besides, I approve of your relationship with her, if that matters at all," Oberon said.

Dylan stood and faced him. "It does matter. Thank you, your Majesty," he said bowing deeply to the King.

"I'll do what I can to help," Oberon said, looking into the room. "Okay, Mr. Rearden. Please step in the room and play a pleasant song. Peaceful and healing."

I nodded then walked into the room. As I sat in a chair across from Grace, I noticed that the color had returned to her skin leaving it a pale pink color. The tendrils of black were receding, but not completely gone.

As I began to play, the healer settled down in another chair in the room closing her eyes. Focusing on Grace, my fingers fell over the strings in ways that I didn't know was possible. I'd let go of my trained hand allowing the power of music to take over. It felt like I'd played lute all of my life. The sounds filled the room. Looking back to Dylan, I saw a sadness creep over his face. My fingers responded to my emotions watching him. He made me sad, too. Tearing my attention away from him, I focused on Grace.

When the healer stood again, I finished the song. I wasn't clear as to how long I'd actually played the instrument, but my fingers were raw. Grace looked peaceful, and I stepped out of the room.

"Well done, Levi," Dylan said.

"What was with the sad face?" I asked.

"If I hadn't gone after her in the woods with Lysander, perhaps if I hadn't returned after dying at the courthouse, she would be with you instead of me. Stephanie wouldn't be challenging her. No one would have hurt her like this," he said, staring into the room at her.

"Dylan, I don't think she would have been with me. She came after me once when she thought you were dead, but it was just like her mother did to you earlier. I resisted her because something inside of me told me it was wrong. I had to sing to her to get her to back down. She turned on full winter queen, but when I sang to her, she relented. The whole thing was awkward. Don't get me wrong, she's amazing, but she doesn't belong to me. I can't tell you how many times I've thought of that night and was thankful I resisted her. She loved you," I said.

He closed his eyes turning his head slowly away from me. "Why did she come after you like that?"

I laughed, "Because she was crying over your death. I felt her losing grip on the darkness inside of her. When I tried to remind her who I thought she was, she felt the need to prove to me that she was something else."

He chuckled, "Sounds like Grace."

"She failed," I smirked.

"Thank you," he said.

"Dylan, I'm not the man to give advice about relationships, but Dude, you gotta man up. If she really is everything to you, then prove it. Nothing else matters. Sometimes she needs someone to tell her no. You gotta be that person. She still thinks I'm a kid," I said.

"No, she knows what you are," he said. "She wouldn't have tried to seduce a child."

His word rang true. Grace didn't have a bone in her body that would allow her to hurt a child, contrary to all the beliefs about fairies stealing children and seducing anything. She saw me as a man, even then. "Maybe she saw me as an adult, but she definitely saw me as a threat."

"I wish I could order her around like you do. It's fucking hilarious," he laughed. He paused to look at her in the room. A distant look of memory crossed his face. It had to be something pleasant between the two of them because a smile flirted with the edges of his eyes. "She looks so much better now." He leaned hard on the entrance to the room. I saw the battle within himself to keep from going in to her knowing that the healer didn't need to be interrupted.

I looked around the corner, and he was right. She looked closer to normal than just hours ago when she looked like death warmed over. "You don't need my power to tell her what to do. She will do whatever you ask her to do. It's a mutual thing for the two of you. It will never be like that for us." Grace and I had a trusting friendship, but it wasn't the deep burning emotion that erupted between the bird of fire and the queen of ice.

That conversation with Dylan started a friendship that was more like brothers than anything I'd ever had. Our bond was Grace. He loved her more than anything in this world, and from that moment on, he set out to prove it to her. I was content to watch it all happen as long as he didn't hurt her anymore.

Oberon appeared out of nowhere startling both of us. "The healing is complete."

The healer exited the room. She looked at us. "She still needs rest, but she will live."

"The iron?" Oberon asked.

"The bard must remove it and return it to the human realm," she said.

"The nails are still in her?" Dylan asked.

"Yes, but their poison is blocked by magic. They must be removed immediately. A maid will come and aid with the blood. I must rest," she said walking away from us.

I turned green as my stomach churned. "I don't know if I can do that."

"Man up, Levi," Dylan smiled.

"Why don't you do it?" I asked.

"I'll probably have to hold her down," he said.

"I can do that," I said.

"Over my dead body," he replied.

Oberon stared at us. When we noticed, we stopped the banter and approached Grace on the bed. Dylan clamped down on her leg holding it still. Taking a deep breath, I wrapped my finger around the head of the nail. Her body bucked in pain. A maid appeared at my left, but kept her distance. She laid a small cotton bag on the bed.

"Pull it out quick. Don't hesitate," Dylan said. "Move to the second one immediately."

I nodded yanking the first nail out quickly. She screamed, and her body writhed in pain. Dylan ended up holding all of her down. I wrapped my finger around the second nail feeling resistance. "I think it's in her bone," I groaned.

"Yank it out! Now!" Dylan ordered.

Pulling with just a bit of power behind it, the nail released as I stumbled backwards away from the bed. Her scream filled the room once again. As soon as I put the nails in the bag, the maid rushed up to tend to the wounds. She cleaned the blood quickly. I gripped the nails in the bag as I tucked them in my jean pocket. Within moments, the wounds stopped bleeding. As if they'd never been there in the first place, the tiny holes disappeared without a scar.

Dylan spoke softly in her ear as her body relaxed once again. The pain didn't wake her up. She slept deeply. My arms shook as I realized I'd never released the spell tracking her. My jack-in-the-box exploded releasing the power I'd held in. I backed against the wall sinking to the floor. Dylan watched me, but kept speaking in her ear.

I shook my hands to release the spell like she'd taught me to do. Like I'd seen her do so many times.

Exhaustion took over, and I slumped to the floor falling asleep with my cheek against the stone. It reminded me of the night I moved to Shady Grove. We'd found the two missing children in the woods torn to bits by an aswang. Grace held so much power that when it released, she seemed like a drunken basket case. She fell asleep on the floor in the kitchen of the first trailer. I'd done almost the exact same thing as the power fizzled in my body.

"Who tells the story when we are both asleep?" she
    asked.

"No one," I said. "We leave that part out."

"This seems more and more like our story and not
    just my story," she said.

"It's your story. I was just along for the ride," I said.

"Hmm, well, do I get to take it from here?" she
    asked.

I sat back in the chair flexing my tired fingers. "Yes,
    but I need some rest. My hands hurt."

"Oh, poor baby," she smirked as she pulled a couple
    of orange sodas out of the fridge. Tossing me
    one, she lifted her eyebrows and the twinkle in
    her blue eyes glared at me. God, she was the most
    beautiful thing I'd ever seen.

I smiled at her teasing me. "If you don't mind, I'll
    pick it up in the morning," I said.

"As you wish, Dublin. But tomorrow, I expect less
    bellyaching," she grinned.

CHAPTER EIGHTEEN

THE SURREAL FEELING WASHED OVER ME AS I OPENED MY EYES TO MY room in the Otherworld. The tapestries hung on the walls just as I'd left them hundreds of years ago. In the next room, I could hear the running water of the Roman style bath. A new addition to the room was perched on the edge of my bed. Levi, my bard, staring at me. "Stop staring. You are making me uncomfortable," I said.

"Good to have you back, Grace," he grinned.

"I don't want to do that again, ever. It hurt like hell," I said.

"How are you feeling now?" he asked.

"Sore. Are you okay?" I asked. He looked like he'd aged. Perhaps he was just tired, but I knew all too well that my ordeal hurt him. Probably not as much as the poison that coursed through my veins, but his sensitive-self felt enough of it.

His hand found mine, and the connection between us tingled up my arm. "I'm fine now. Pulled power, crashed, slept and now I'm just happy to see you awake." I squeezed his hand.

"Pulled power?" I asked.

"To find you. I knew you were hurt, but finding you proved to be difficult. I held it all in until we got here. It wore me out," he said.

"I wore you out, huh?" I said, feeling much more like myself. "How long have we been here?"

He shook his head. "No way to tell really. I haven't been back to our realm."

"Crap. The election," I said.

"Do you care about the election now?" he asked.

Before I answered, I thought about everything that had happened since Stephanie Davis walked into the community center on that first night. I thought the Yule Lads were annoying, but we had lived through pure hell with her in town. Did I care?

"I made a promise to a lot of people. Seeing it through would be the right thing to do," I replied. My thoughts drifted to Dylan. Part of me didn't want to deal with it. The other part of me wanted to have a long fight and make-up sex. It sucked to be a fairy sometimes. Irrational bullshit. "Is he still here?"

Levi hung his head, and my heart dropped. If he was gone, I'd hurt forever. If he was here, then it upset Levi that he was here. Levi might be young, but I knew he would protect me fiercely. "He's sleeping in the next room. I finally convinced him to lie down. He sat in that hallway for hours just watching you through the healing," he said.

Taking a deep breath, I admitted to him, "The truth is, I don't even know what to say to him."

"Loss for words? That has to be a first," he grinned. "I'll go get him."

"No, let him sleep. I want to get a bath," I said.

"The bathtub is huge!" Levi smiled.

"I told you," I replied.

Slowly I sat up as Levi reached to brace me. "Do you need help?" he waggled his eyebrows. So damn cute.

"I think I'll manage," I replied.

The chemise the servants put me in did little to hide my body, but Levi had seen me naked enough by now. He didn't gawk or leer. Placing one bare foot on the floor, I winced at the pain. "Whoa, easy there." He steadied me. Healed or not, it still hurt like hell.

"Thanks," I muttered as I put a second foot down. I expected the pain this time. If I could just get to the bath, I knew the healing waters would soothe my pain. He blushed when I kissed him on the cheek. My hormones went wild at the sight. I suddenly remembered that I was full winter queen in my own realm. Cold tendrils of power surrounded my body starting at my legs and working their way up to my chest. I shuddered at the influx of raw energy.

"What's happening?" he asked.

"The realm is welcoming me home. Just being here strengthens me in ways that the trees in our world can't do. It's almost like a living creature in itself. The magic of the world knows me and feeds me power. It's like a drug," I sighed. "We don't need to stay here long."

"Well, then, go get your bath, and we will leave," he said. "If you need me, I'll be right here." He grinned like a schoolboy, but I knew in his heart he meant it.

The pain no longer stabbed me with each step because the magic dulled its intensity. As I dipped down into the warm, healing bath, my aches subsided. Leaning back on to the edge of the giant pool, I closed my eyes, letting the healing and power sink into my body.

The bathroom stretched long and wide to host the Olympic sized bath. Two currents of water fed the pool on each side. Everything was smooth stone with a mosaic above the bath on the ceiling. The mosaic depicted a snowy scene with a stone castle. My father's castle. It was breathtaking. I stared up at the beautiful sight, resting as much as I could before we left for home. I loved the bath, but because of the court, its politics and mostly my father I was happy to leave here.

"You are up," a voice came from behind me.

Turning around, I pressed my naked body up to the edge of the pool. It was only about four-foot-deep around the edges where a small ledge was built to sit on. I looked up into the piercing blue eyes of Dylan Riggs.

"Hey. Yeah, I needed to clean up before we go home," I said.

"How are you feeling?" he asked, keeping his distance.

"Better. Actually, the realm is feeding me power," I replied.

His brow furrowed as a strand of sandy hair fell down upon it. He wanted to say something, but he struggled to find the right words. He sat down on the stone floor several feet away from me, burying his face in his hands. "I'm sorry I wasn't there when you woke up."

"Levi said you'd kept a long vigil. You needed to rest," I said. Something about being home made me feel responsible and calm. No matter what happened back in Shady Grove, I didn't feel the need to jump down his throat. His pain-filled eyes met mine. Part of me knew that no matter what Stephanie said that Dylan hadn't done anything with her. He didn't know what to do to make everything right. Neither did I.

My body longed for his touch, but my heart ached over the trouble between us. I reminded myself that we both had flaws. By no means was I perfect. My hormones had just went wild looking at my blushing bard. I resisted that urge. Had he truly resisted Stephanie? Misaki? Even Kady?

"You should know that your mother came after me," he said. "I have got to learn to just tell you everything even if I think you are going to get mad. Your mother tried to seduce me with you dying on that bed in there. Right there in front of your father, Levi, everyone," he said.

"Tried?" I asked. If my mother came after him, there was no way anyone resisted that kind of seduction. No one.

"Grace, I cannot be seduced by magic. It's part of my heritage. I am the seducer. Over the years, I played that part. A womanizer for hundreds of years. At some point, after all of it, I looked back and asked myself what had I gained? I still didn't have an heir. My natural instincts to protect only served people on an individual basis when I found someone to help along the way. Overall, I had failed my father and mother. I met Jeremiah. He told me about Shady Grove, so I bought the house and land. I moved in without even a thought. The first week I met Stephanie at the bar. From that point, she lived with me for five years, but you know that. I'd made up my mind to fulfill the destiny that my parents wanted for me. I just picked the wrong girl," he said, pouring his heart out. He revealed more about his past in those few sentences than he'd ever said to me.

"Dylan, we can talk about this when we get home," I said.

"Actually, things happen at home. We have a daughter, the election, your new job, and a plethora of fairy problems that keep us from talking. We've spent our free time in bed," he said. "Not that I'm complaining, but it leaves little time to talk."

"So, while I'm standing naked in a bathtub while you sit on the floor is the best time?" I said.

"Now is the best time," he said.

I sighed. "What else?" I asked. Clearly, he had more to say.

"To answer you directly, no, I did not take your mother's overt offer. I was horrified that it even happened. Of course, Levi proceeded to tell me that you'd done the same thing to him when I died," he said looking away.

"Damn it, Dublin!" I yelled. I knew he was just outside in the room. I could feel his presence.

"No, leave him out of it. I'm not mad. I just wanted you to know that I knew. Heck, I wouldn't have blamed you had it gone further. I told him that I considered not coming back to Shady Grove after I died, but I couldn't let you go. Perhaps you and he would have been together," he said.

"It's not like that," I said looking around for a towel. Suddenly I felt completely vulnerable before him. "Will you get me a towel and a robe over there?" I said pointing to the supplies stacked neatly on a shelf behind him. Levi peeked around the door from the other room. "You! I'm going to bust your ass!" He grinned ear to ear. I flipped him off as he shut the door. Calm and collected Grace didn't apply to Levi. Making my way to the stairs, Dylan laid the towel and robe down for me to retrieve. He turned his back on me which seemed extremely strange after all the naked moments we'd had together. It was weird for him to turn his back on me, but perhaps he sensed my vulnerability. In fact, he made me angry observing such things about me. If it were true, that he watched me for so long, I needed to realize that there were very few things, if any, that I could hide from him.

As if he could read my mind, he explained, "If I look, I'll want it."

"No willpower?"

"Right now? None," he said.

"Okay," I said tying the belt on the robe. "I'm covered. What else?"

He told me about finding Stephanie at the house. The power was off, so she probably got back into the house easily after he left. She was a piece of work. I hated her. Not just for what she was doing to me, but what she'd done to Dylan all those years. What she was still doing to him. "I know my promises don't mean much right now, but I promise that I won't hide anything else from you. My fear of losing what we have made it so easy to just hope you never found out that I even saw her," he said.

"It's not like you did anything wrong," I said.

"No, not in the sexual sense, but if we are going to do this, then I've got to tell you everything. That is if you ever put that ring back on," he muttered.

"I have no desire to rehash every relationship that the two of us have had. A string of one-night stands for hundreds of years is not the kind of pillow talk I dream of," I said. He still kept his distance from me.

"Grace, there are some things I expect from you, too," he said.

"What?"

"This has to go both ways," he said.

"I tell you everything," I said. As the lie passed my lips, I dropped to one knee. Fucking fairy. I couldn't lie as Gloriana without paying for it. Alarm crossed his face.

"Grace, you should be sitting down. The poison almost killed you. You are right this can wait," he said not realizing what I had done. He approached me slowly to help me up.

I swatted him away. Hurt settled in his eyes as they turned a deep shade of cobalt. "If I lie in this state, I pay for it."

"You just lied?" he asked.

Instead of getting up, I sank down to the floor shaking my head. Disappointed in myself. I couldn't hold him to a standard that I didn't reciprocate. "You don't know everything about Levi and me," I said.

His jaw flexed. "What about Levi?"

"Ever since we shared power the first time, I can feel his presence. We are connected on a magical tether. I'm sure it's how he found the truck. When he pulls on that power, I can feel it. Even though I was mostly unconscious as someone dragged me through the woods, I knew Levi was looking for me. There is nothing I can do to break the bond. We aren't intimately involved in any way. He's like my best friend. If he hurts, I feel it. Every time Kady tortures him, I feel it. The only way to break it would be to forsake him as my bard. He's a servant to me as much as Kyffin is to Stephanie. I love him dearly. However, I have no intentions of ever being with him like that. I didn't tell you about the connection because I didn't want to upset you. I didn't want you to send him away or beat the shit out of him."

"That's why he hit me," he said.

"What?"

"When he told me about the truck, I flew back from Montgomery. My car is still there. As soon as I got to the truck, he laid the hardest punch I'd ever taken across my jaw. He looked like he was in pain. He feels it when you hurt, too. Right?"

I nodded. "Did he apologize?"

"Yes, we have reconciled. I didn't get why he was so angered. You being missing was enough to upset both of us, but this was pure rage," Dylan replied. "I know about fairy servants. I should have known it was like that for you. I'm not concerned about your relationship with Levi."

"I'm not concerned about your past with Stephanie," I said immediately. He looked surprised.

"Really?"

"She or any other woman you've seduced over the years," I admitted. I couldn't believe I was going to give into him this easily, but we had come to an understanding for the first time in our relationship. I knew there were things about him that I didn't know, but I did not intend to let those things keep us apart. I stood up to face him even though I was several inches shorter. "You said you needed things from me."

"Just that when things come up, you will tell me. I also need to know you aren't going to run when trouble arises. If we run, we run together. Promise me that we will face whatever it is together. I don't tell you things because I hate when you get mad. You are irrational and impulsive," he spouted without holding back.

"You are right. I am," I said. "I promise to discuss things with you instead of getting into a fit of rage. I was so angry when I left your house. It was dangerous to drive like that, and look what happened," I said.

"You were set up. I think she had something to do with all of this. She is trying to take you out completely. Not just the election, but you. She wants you dead. I don't know why. This is new to me. I knew she was a vindictive whore, but this need to destroy you is beyond what I know of her," he said.

The wreck was a blur to me, but he was right. There was someone there waiting on me. It wasn't a coincidence. "Maybe I should give up on the election," I said.

"No. You have to do this. You can't let her have Shady Grove, and if you don't stop her, I will," he said defiantly.

"Really? Because I've heard you more than once claim to want to bail on it," I shot back at him.

"Yes, because of you. But I can't let that cloud my judgment. I love you, Grace. I want to do this together, but if you don't want to go back, I'm going back without you," he said stepping toward me. I stepped back out of instinct because I felt the fire growing within him. However, there wasn't a step behind me, just the bath. My toes brushed the edge of the bath, slipping backwards I tried to steady myself.

His body burst into flame as large wings spread out behind him. He covered the distance between us in an instant. Warm fiery limbs wrapped around me, and we floated on the edge of the bath. I tensed at the sensation of fire lapping around my body, but realized that it didn't harm me. The icy cold protected me from the flames. His eyes burned into my soul. "Dylan," I whimpered.

He leaned forward as his white-hot lips brushed my neck. I moaned at the sensation. "This is who I am, my love. An eternal flame. I cannot stand by and watch as the evil inside of this woman takes over our town. She will enslave all of them to her will. What I need to know is if you are with me or not?" he spoke in a firm, steady voice. Its warmth and strength reverberated through me. His touch didn't force me back into my glamour. It seemed to bolster my natural gifts. Father said he was my foil, but not as my antithesis as I thought he had meant. Dylan was my perfect compliment.

"Perhaps what Shady Grove needs is a Queen and a King," I said. His body jolted in surprise at the statement. As he lost grip, we both tumbled into the tub. I surfaced in the water laughing as it boiled around me. I still wore my robe, but the phoenix had burned all his clothes off leaving only the superb body of my fiancé. At least, I hoped he still was my fiancé. He grabbed the belt of the robe jerking it loose. The robe sank to the bottom of the bath.

Pulling my naked body to his, he asked, "Is that a proposal?"

Distracted by our mutual state of undress, I stammered over my words, "Um, yes. Maybe."

"Why are you so flustered, Grace? You've seen me naked before," he laughed.

"I've just not seen you so hot and bothered like this," I joked.

"Do you mean it? We will do it together," he said.

"Yes, you fool. Of course," I replied. His hand pushed my lower back into his body while his other hand tangled in my hair. He pulled gently tilting my head back. His lips, mouth and tongue assaulted mine hard and strong. The force of it caught me off guard. It was more than the day before when I thought I'd seen his true force. I was wrong. There was more there that he hadn't shown me. The seducer could play a silly game of pool or he could smolder enough to melt my insides. My feet slipped out from under me, but it didn't matter. He had me wrapped up. Balance wasn't needed as the water sloshed around our movements.

Pausing for only a moment, he rested his forehead on mine. "Grace, I'm not a fool," he said. Before I could protest his lips were on mine again. He needed to be in control, so I didn't resist.

However, I knew my world. Someone was always watching. Using the power that naturally flowed into me, I traced runes with my fingers around us creating a barrier to outside influence. I rarely used runes, but I knew the powerful implements were a necessity here. A private bubble for us to make love in. He needed it. I wanted it.

Here in my world I saw myself clearer than ever before now. Independence had saved me over the years running from the Sanhedrin. Pure instinct to protect myself. However, if I truly wanted this partnership to work with Dylan, I needed to adapt. He needed me to depend upon him and share everything. With everyone else, I would be the same old brash, impulsive Grace. That part of me first attracted him to me, but for our relationship to work, I had to give a little. No, I had to give it all to him. It wasn't a surrender to his will or power, but a realization that it would become our will and our power.

CHAPTER NINETEEN

When he was finished with me, I was exhausted. After the week we'd had, I needed some downtime, but I knew we had to return. He lounged back on the edge of the bath. Seated on the ledge, he held my body close to him as I sat across his lap with my head resting on his shoulder.

"Look at me, baby," he said. I leaned back locking eyes with him.

"You plan on ordering me around all the time now?" I asked.

"Yes," he grinned. Damn it. He knew I'd let him too. "When we go back, you need to go back like this."

"Naked and straddling your lap?" I teased.

"No, like this," he said as he took a strand of platinum hair curling it around his finger. "The town needs a Queen."

"So, no more trailer trash Grace?" I asked.

"For now. I know who you are, but remember when you thought you were alone in the town with no other fairies? You were skeptical of everyone. They feel the same thing about you. I can see it in their eyes. People need to know you aren't going to hide your royalty. That you will be the Queen that they need. For now, you need to be Gloriana."

"You know my given name. What is yours, Dylan?" I dared to ask.

"My father was a Spanish explorer in the New World when he met my mother. They named me, Serafino Taranis."

"Taranis was a thunder god," I stated.

"Yes. Serafino was a form of Seraphim, the fiery angels of God. The name isn't catchy," he laughed. "My mother also gave me an Algonquin name that I used occasionally, Keme Rowtag which basically means thunder fire."

"Why Dylan?" I asked.

"I wanted to be as far from my real name as possible. Dylan Riggs is a name I made up after looking through the phone book one day. Jeremiah made me pick a name. It's what I picked. Sounds good right?" he smiled.

"You will always be Dylan to me," I said. His lips met mine gently.

"Time to go," he said. "I'm going to miss this bath."

"You! Now you know why I love the garden tub. It's a poor substitute, but at least it's something!" I laughed.

"We've got to try it out," he grinned.

"Yes, we do," I replied.

Father met us in the corridor of roots that would lead us home. We were all anxious to get back. "Gloriana, you should know that I slowed time here while you visited. You should return only a few hours after you left," Oberon said.

Something like love swept over me for my father. He noticed it in my eyes and smiled. Oberon, King of the Wild Fairies, smiled. "Thank you, Father."

"Take care of her, Phoenix," he ordered Dylan.

Dylan nodded.

Levi stood next to us with a lute strapped to his back.

"Where did you get that thing?" I asked him.

"I gave it to him," Father interrupted. My smiling father gave a gift to my bard. I stood astonished. "Goodbye, my child."

"Goodbye, Father," I said grasping the root closest to me. The tree spoke to me as I told it where we wanted to go. It seemed to be confused that we had two different destinations. The truck was destroyed. Dylan chided me for being difficult on objects with wheels. My truck, my trailer, and now his truck all demolished within a few weeks. He swore to buy me a tank when we got home. I sent Levi back to Shady Grove, and Dylan and I landed in a small park about a block from where his car was parked in Montgomery, AL. The rain still fell as we ran to his car. Slumping down in the passenger seat, I took a deep breath to prepare myself to go home.

"Try to rest. How much power do you retain from being there?" he asked.

"Some. Not all of it," I replied.

"Save it. We might need it," he said as he fired up the car. The ride home was quiet, so I dozed off.

I woke up as we pulled into the driveway at the trailer. Winnie ran out the door. "Daddy, Daddy! There is a funny man here."

Sucking in a deep breath, I worried about who we were going to find in the house. I knew Levi had to be here, so maybe it was just Winnie playing a game with him. But as we walked into the kitchen, I stared across the room at the fiftyish man who sat on the sofa grinning like a billy goat in a briar patch. Rufus ran around my feet, greeting me.

"Jeremiah Freyman! You picked a fine time to come home," I said to him, as he approached us.

"Grace, you are looking as lovely as ever. I'm happy to see that you weren't permanently damaged by your ordeal. Good evening, Dylan," he said reaching out to shake Dylan's hand. Levi stood at the kitchen counter sipping coffee. I eyed the cup, and he smiled at me.

"That remains to be seen," Dylan replied.

Jeremiah's face darkened with worry. "I'll be okay," I assured him. "I've missed you, Jeremiah. Why are you here now?"

"Caiaphas called me when the word spread about the video," he said.

"Video?" I asked. "Oh, shit. I remember the red blinking light now."

"Whoever it was tried to sell you on the black market," Dylan explained. "Remy called Levi to give him a heads up."

"Why would Remy know about it?" I asked.

"They knew he'd pay good money to get you back. I suppose," Dylan replied.

"Damn good money. He almost won the auction, but at the last minute, he didn't," Jeremiah explained. He always had a way of knowing everything even though he wasn't here much anymore.

"You bring any strays in with you," Dylan asked, because Jeremiah had a bad habit of picking up wayward fairies and dropping them off in Shady Grove. He'd done that with all three of us.

"Not this time, and if Stephanie wins this damned election, I'm going to have to stick around. She aims to misbehave," he said.

"Tell me about it," I said, as Levi slipped a warm cup of coffee into my hand. "Thank you, Dublin."

"Levi tells me that Oberon gave him a lute. A royal stag lute," he said.

I nodded as I sipped the coffee. Levi handed Dylan a cup too.

"It's a nice instrument," Levi said. "I had no idea how I knew how to play it. I just did."

Pausing for a moment, I turned to look at him. "You know how to play it?" I asked.

"Came natural to me," he said.

"Well, I'll be damned," I muttered.

"What?" Levi asked as he sat down on the couch. Winnie crawled up next to him. Jeremiah joined him with a knowing grin on his face. Dylan sat down in the side chair, pulling me down on his lap. I rolled my eyes at him.

"Levi, did you take a gift from a fairy?" I asked like I was his mother.

"Grace, I did, but he swore that I owed him nothing in return," he said.

I laughed. Father tricked him, but thankfully the damage wouldn't be too bad. "There hasn't been a royal bard since Taliesin."

"Royal bard?" Levi asked.

"Yes, dear. My father gave you the Lute of the Royal Bard. You are now the official bard for the Unseelie Court. Not only will you tell my stories, you will tell the stories of the entire court," I said.

"Oh, shit," Levi muttered. Jeremiah laughed. "Shut up, old man."

"Levi, I'm proud of you. You were a lost changeling running from a witch and a demon. Now you are a Royal Bard!" Jeremiah said.

"Is it a good thing?" he asked.

"Just means you have a lot of work to do. My story isn't done, so you can't start telling mine," I said.

"Ours," Dylan interjected.

"Ours," I conceded, as I sat my empty coffee cup on the side table. I leaned back into Dylan. His hand traced down my arm to my hand. I felt the cool metal of my engagement ring slip onto my finger. Jeremiah's keen eyes caught the movement. When he looked at me, he nodded in approval. We both had felt all along that Jeremiah matched us together. I sighed. "My father has thousands of years of stories to tell."

Winnie sat quietly listening to all of us talk. I watched her innocent eyes as each one of us talked, discussing Stephanie and the election. Finally, she became impatient. She threw her hands up, "Everybody be quiet. I have something to say."

Dylan chuckled behind me because it was adorable. "Go ahead, Winnie," I urged her.

"Aunt Grace, you are playing dress up again. Are you going to stay that way this time?" she asked.

"For now, I am. Is that okay with you?"

"Yes, ma'am. I like the costume," she smiled. "One more thing."

"What's that?"

"Are you going to marry Daddy?" she asked. Dylan flexed his hand. The one that held mine with his ring on my finger.

Levi mouthed the word, "Daddy?" I shook my head to let him know I'd explain it later.

"Yes, Winnie, I am," I replied.

"Can I be in the wedding and have a pretty dress? If you are going to be the Queen, does that make me a Princess?" she asked. The questions were coming freely now.

"Yes, you have to be in the wedding. I will buy you the prettiest dress in the state, and it doesn't matter if I'm the Queen or not, you are already a princess," I replied.

"One more thing," she said again.

Dylan continued to laugh behind me. "Yes?"

"When you marry Daddy, does that make you my Mommy?" she asked.

Jeremiah looked down to the ground. Levi's eyes widened as he stared at me waiting for my answer. I gripped Dylan's hand tightly. My voice came out shaky. "Winnie, your mommy is in heaven."

"I know, but I need a mommy in Shady Grove. If you aren't too busy, being Queen, you know," she said.

"If that is what you want, then yes, I will be your mommy," I choked out. A tear rolled down my cheek as Dylan rubbed his free hand up and down my back. His warmth spread over me. Levi smiled, and Jeremiah wiped a stray tear.

"Okay, I'm out of questions now," Winnie said without ceremony. We laughed at her. "What's so funny?"

I stood up, went over to the couch and wrapped my arms around her. "I love you, Winnie."

"I love you, Aunt Grace," she said.

"I almost died when she said it," I told Dylan as I sat on our bed later that night. He picked through the closet looking for something to wear tomorrow. He had a few sets of clothes here. We'd planned with Levi and Jeremiah to stroll into town tomorrow for a big campaign push. I would go into every business on Main Street, shaking hands with the owners and customers. Then we would visit some well-established neighborhoods in town, going door to door. We would encourage people to vote.

"You had to know it was coming," he replied.

"Actually, no, I didn't. She asked you before me," I said.

"That's because she's never had a father," he said.

He was right. She needed to have a father figure, and I was the added thought to that. "Do you want me to set a date?" I asked.

"Yes. Tonight, please," he said as he set out a white dress shirt and a red tie. "Is there a date that means anything to you?"

"October 21st," I said without hesitation.

"Good answer," he replied staring at me. That was the night I made love to him the first time after a flirty game of pool at Hot Tin Roof. "I will call Matthew in the morning and set up for him to perform the ceremony. You want to get married in the Grove?"

"Yes," I replied. "But I think I should avoid wearing white."

"It doesn't matter what color you wear," he said, taking his clothes off to join me in the bed. "I'm going to take off of you whatever it is."

He crawled into the bed, laying to face me.

"I'll get up in the morning and take Winnie to school. You rest," he said kissing me lightly on the lips.

"Sounds wonderful," I sighed. My body still ached, and I needed the rest. I snuggled up next to him quickly falling asleep.

CHAPTER TWENTY

"We need to buy a truck," Dylan said, as he drove us into town. We looked like a political power couple. I wore a red sheath dress with a strand of pearls and black pumps. He wore a black suit, white shirt and red tie that matched my dress. It was ridiculous. He'd taken Winnie to school allowing me to sleep a little longer. We were going to meet Jeremiah in town. If he followed me around as I spoke to people, it would be like the Sanhedrin were endorsing me without them actually making an official statement. Every fairy in Shady Grove knew Jeremiah.

"A red one," I said.

"A red one," he laughed. "You look nice."

"You said that already," I replied.

"Yes, but I know you are uncomfortable," he said. "I'm trying to ease your discomfort."

"I am. This doesn't feel like me," I replied. "But it can be."

"I've got to get used to the blonde hair," he laughed.

"Most men prefer blondes," I said.

"I'm not most men," he said. Sitting silent for several minutes as he pondered something, I relaxed back in the seat watching us pass blue sign after blue sign. "Look at it this way, I've seen you with people that you consider friends. When we talk to people today, pretend they are your best friend even if you hate them. We will start at the diner."

I groaned, because I hadn't reconciled with Betty. Running from the problem seemed to suit me more, but it needed to be done. Part of the reformation of Grace Ann Bryant. "Just slap me if I get out of hand," I said.

"I would never hit you, Grace," he mumbled.

"You know what I mean," I teased.

We pulled up in front of the diner. Walking in holding hands, he greeted Betty. Surprisingly, the diner was empty. "Howdy, Betty, how are ya?" he asked her.

"I'm finer than frog hair split three ways. How are you, Handsome?"

"About the same," he said.

"Hello Betty," I tried to say pleasantly.

"Surprised to see you here, Grace," she said. "Actually, I shouldn't be surprised you are running from your commitments."

"What?" I asked. "What do you mean?"

"Stephanie challenged you to a debate today over that community center. I thought you'd be over there instead of here with Dylan. We were about to lock up and head over there," she said.

I looked at Dylan. "She thought you'd be out of town or dead," he said. "Come on."

"I can't debate her. Dylan, I'll say something vulgar," I replied.

"Dead?" Luther asked as he appeared from the back of the diner.

"At least you know your limitations," Betty interjected.

"Dead?" Luther repeated.

"Look, Betty, I don't know who pissed in your cornflakes, but at one time, we were friends. I've done best I can for Shady Grove. I'm going to continue to do it for all fairies. You think that Stephanie, the Seelie princess, is going to protect you and Luther? Really? She despises all of us who come from the darker side. She always has. I don't know what kind of slick moves she put on you, but you should know that when I win, I will protect everyone."

Her jaw dropped open. I tried to keep it clean, but I did mention urination. Sigh.

"Grace, we know you will," Luther said from the back. "Now get down there and tell everyone else what you just told Betty. And what's this dead thing?"

"Thank you, Luther. I'll explain later," I said. "One day, Betty, we will be friends again, but only after you apologize." I said it teasingly. Luther laughed, as she smacked him on the arm.

"You shut-up," Betty hissed at him.

Looking at Dylan, he grinned as he pulled me back toward the door. We hopped in the Camaro, driving like bats out of hell to get there. "Grace, just be yourself. Don't worry about the vulgar. That back there came off as endearing. You will be fine. Speak your heart."

"I don't have a heart, Dylan Riggs," I smiled. He didn't respond, but I knew the memories flashed in his mind as well as mine.

"You ready?" he asked as we pulled into a full parking lot. I could hear her voice speaking through a microphone.

"Yes, I think," I said, walking to the door.

"No, wait. You can't think. You have to know," he said. "She thinks you were sold on the black market. Or that the poison killed you. She does not expect you to walk through those doors. Secondly, those are your people in there. Go in there and be their Queen."

Jeremiah pulled up in his Buick land yacht. He jumped out of the car, but realized Dylan and I were having a serious conversation. He stood back waiting for us to finish.

I swallowed, but feared to speak. Dylan kissed me quickly, then slung the door open in a flourish. I stepped through waiting for him. Stepping up beside me, he took my hand, and we waltzed down the aisle like we owned the place. Stephanie glared at us. Each step I took, her face wrenched in anger. She tore her eyes away from me. They landed on Kyffin Merrick and her fiancé, Sergio Krykos. Both of them bowed their heads.

Then it hit me. Sergio was the man who dragged me through the forest. I should have known it was him, but the deep olive tone of his skin. I heard his voice in my head taunting me.

The crowd watched silently as I joined her on the stage. I knew I didn't need a microphone. Dylan stood at the edge of the platform. She looked at me like I was as welcome as an outhouse breeze.

"Good afternoon, everyone. Please forgive me for being a tiny bit late. I suppose my invitation got lost in the mail," I smiled. Her upper lip twitched causing her nose to crinkle. I suppressed a laugh, looking back to the crowd. I saw that Jeremiah had positioned himself near the back door. Betty and Luther slipped in quietly followed by Levi. Deacon Giles stood at the microphone at the center of the room. "Deacon, did you have a question for us?"

"Yes, my Queen," he replied with a slight bow. His blue jean overalls were dusty, but his flannel shirt looked new. It was a bold red and black block plaid. "Before you arrived, I asked Stephanie if she planned to restrict the movements of fairies in and out of town."

"Do you?" I asked her.

"Before I was rudely interrupted, I said there will be limitations on movement. A simple form can be filled out stating your business out of town. My office will approve the leave. If someone comes into town, then they will meet with myself or another council member to determine if they will be allowed to stay. We will have limits on groups based on the current population of the city. If there are too many of a certain group, new residents will not be allowed in. We will establish safe quotas." I knew she was talking about Unseelie fairies like myself. We were banished from the realm more often than the Seelie. Most of us were badasses.

"How do you plan on determining the current population of the city?" I asked her.

"Census, of course. You aren't dense, Grace," she said.

"You are right. I'm not. Nice hole you dug there. I appreciate it," I smirked, then turned to speak to the crowd. "Deacon, fairies are free to come and go as they please. The burden of aiding or policing will fall upon the council and their leader. Who am I to tell you that you can't go to town to buy new clothes or supplies for your child's school? Who is the council to tell you that you can't go visit a relative or friend? That's utter nonsense. I won't allow such a terrible policy to be put in place. Also, there will be no census. It isn't necessary because everyone will be treated the same. Well, that is, if you vote for me." Deacon smiled, clapping along with many people in the crowd.

A man I didn't know approached the microphone. He wore a dark blue shirt with jeans. His shoes were worn, but the laces were bright white. His dark hair covered part of his face as he spoke. "How do you plan on policing when things get out of hand? The days leading up to Christmas were chaotic," he said.

Waiting for Stephanie to respond, she said, "Go ahead, Grace. I'm interested in your answer."

I thought for a moment about why she would let me answer first. It makes it easier to formulate her answer, so I had to make mine good enough to last through whatever she had in rebuttal. "Thank you, Miss Davis. First, what is your name, sir? I'm trying to learn everyone's name. It will take some time, so I apologize for not knowing."

"I am Sylvester Handley. I own a small fabrication shop just outside of town," he said.

"Ah yes! You were the one that made the frame for Hot Tin Roof's new sign when it was rebuilt recently," I recognized him by the business he owned.

"Yes, ma'am," he replied politely.

"Fine work that was. Thank you. As for policing, I know that during the holidays, Sheriff Troy Maynard and his small crew were overwhelmed with the fairy problem that presented itself, but also with the normal uptick in police matters surrounding a holiday. I propose that the council outsource policing. My fiancé, most of you know Dylan Riggs, recently completed his paperwork to become a private investigator licensed by the state. Add to that his experience with the Sheriff's department, I think he would be the right man for the job. Also, I don't intend to do any of this without him. We are partners. I think there are other individuals here that we could rely on when the police are strapped with human issues. People that we all trust to be fair and unbiased. We need to handle our own problems. Thankfully, Sheriff Maynard is one of us. If the need arises, he is more than willing to help. The council should decide issues on a case-by-case basis and act accordingly, but perhaps once we are convened we might discuss hiring our own law enforcement that way we would control fairy issues, keeping them separate from the state courts," I replied.

"Really?" Stephanie scoffed. "How do you intend on paying such a force?"

"It would be voluntary at first, but hopefully we could think of ways to generate revenue much like the volunteer fire department that adequately serves the city. They have wonderful fundraisers that generate cash for equipment and other needs. We can do the same thing," I replied.

"When I am Queen, I will see to it that each council member will be paid, as well as any outsourced contractor. You cannot expect people to work for free or to generate enough revenue doing car washes and bake sales. For example, while I am tending to business here in Shady Grove, my law practice will suffer. I need compensation for that as well as any other council member who will have to take time away from their jobs," she said.

"It's called a public servant for a reason," I interjected. There were snickers through the crowd. I already knew that the mayors in small towns like Shady Grove didn't receive a salary. Walter Jenkins, the mayor of Shady Grove, who stood along the right wall of the building next to his daughter Ella, didn't receive a salary. His accounting firm encompassed the money that he made to live on while supporting a child in college.

"I know that it will take time to establish these things, but soon, we will all get used to a new sense of order within the town. We need rules because as you all know some of us can be extremely deadly. Everyone needs to feel safe and secure. The events at Christmas were astonishing. Those things will not happen as long as we keep tight control of who comes and goes from Shady Grove," she said.

"How much do you think is a fair salary for council lead?" I asked her.

"We are running some analytics on the pay for local mayors and council members. I think we can come up with some fair numbers very soon," she replied.

"I will work for free," I quickly followed her statement.

"Miss Bryant, we all know you have no money other than your father's. Well, plus the money you syphon off of Dylan Riggs. You have never worked a day in your life, nor have you had to worry about money. Not everyone here can say that. I think you forget that you have been very fortunate to be the daughter of a King," she said.

"Will you work for free?" I asked, ignoring her comments. I'd spent my life listening to people whisper about me behind their backs. To have her say things to my face was refreshing in a way. The digs stung, but she kept digging the hole. At some point, I planned to push her in it.

"As I said, we are running analytics."

"The answer is no," I said.

"There should be compensation," she replied.

"I will work for free," I repeated. "Will you?"

She leered at me, "We should take questions from the audience. You aren't allowed to question me directly."

I turned to look at the microphone. My bard, Levi Rearden stood there grinning like a possum eating green persimmons. "Miss Davis, would you work for free?"

I bit my top lip to keep from laughing. Damn, I loved that boy. Man. Whatever.

"Mr. Rearden, as a servant of the winter queen, I should suspect you to do her bidding and ask questions for her, but this is a fair debate. You cannot ask that question just because she compelled you to do so," Stephanie said.

"Grace doesn't compel me to do anything," he said.

"He's right. He's as stubborn as a mule. I'd be wasting my

breath if I tried," I said. The crowd laughed.

"Who else here wants to know if Miss Davis will work for free?" Levi said to the fairies around him. Hands shot up all over the room. He turned back to her, lifting his eyebrows. We waited for her answer.

She sucked in a breath with a lip twitch and a nose wrinkle. "I suppose I can work for free," she conceded.

"Thank you, Miss Davis. That is very kind of you," Levi said. I shook my head because he was just rubbing salt in the wound. I remembered a few days ago when the thought crossed my mind about being paid to be Queen. I was glad it was a fleeting thought. I didn't voice it to anyone, but it was arrogant for me to even consider it. These people didn't owe me anything. I made a promise with no conditions. I couldn't expect to change the rules on them.

As Levi sat down, a young woman approached the microphone. Slender and lithe, I knew immediately that she was a Seelie fairy. Her green shirt flowed down in bell sleeves with bits of lace at the ends. A golden belt sat low on her hips, but was aesthetic only as her tight jeans hugged every part of her lower body like a glove, then tucked neatly into brown cowgirl boots.

"Hello, I am Riley MacKenzie of the summer realm. When one of you is elected, there will be four council members working with you or against you. Not everyone will be on the same page. How do you plan to unite the council over long standing arguments and issues?" she asked with a hundred years of wisdom behind her voice. She wasn't as young as she looked.

Stephanie began speaking immediately, "This is why there are four seats, plus the Queen. The Queen will decide disputes. We won't have any split votes. There will always be a majority." Even I know condescension is a tactic only used when you want to piss someone off enough to slap you silly.

Taking a deep breath, I hoped this one went my way. "Nice to meet you, Riley. I love your boots."

"Thank you. I got them down at the tractor supply," she said turning them sideways to see. Stephanie cleared her throat loudly.

"Sorry, Miss Davis. It seems to me that you missed the point of

Miss MacKenzie's question. Yes, there will be times when the council lead will have to decide, but I'd like to see us agree on things before that ever happens. Trust me when I say that I know I cannot please everyone. There are people in this room that I love dearly, but we do not see eye to eye on the issues. For example, Betty Stallworth and I have been friends since the moment I first stepped into the Diner. She feels differently about how the factions of fairies are divided. I'm stubborn when it comes to getting my way." I stopped to look at Dylan who shook his head in agreement. The crowd laughed. "Thank you, Darlin'. I knew I could count on you," I smirked.

"Anytime, my Queen," he grinned. They laughed more.

"Betty, would you mind coming to the microphone?"

"What is this?" Stephanie started to lose her cool.

"You had your chance. Now it's my turn," I said dismissing her, as Betty cautiously approached the microphone. If anything, I knew how to control a room full of people. I'd done it for years from one pub to the next bar. It's easier to pick the mark, if you control the whole room. Of course, I wasn't aiming to sleep with anyone in the crowd, but the tactic was the same. I had to control them. "Thank you. I know you feel very strongly that lumping all Unseelie fairies together in one group is the wrong thing to do, correct?"

"That's right. I've never killed anyone unlike *some* in this room. I was banished from the realm for something my spouse did at the time. I know I'm different. Luther and I are not violent," she stood her ground.

"In your mind, what is the separation point? If we split Unseelie into two categories, what defines the two categories? Murder? Maiming? Torture? Assault? Where would you draw the line?" I rattled off offenses as I stared into the dark brown eyes of Sergio Krykos. His gaze was fixed with mine. He knew that I knew. He didn't shy away from my stare, but I saw his hand twitch. My eyes rolled back to Betty when she spoke.

"Murder," she replied.

"So, intent to kill? Or accidental deaths as well?" I asked.

"Intent," she replied.

"Based on actions here or in the Otherworld? The basis of their exile?" I asked.

"Yes, not what happens here, because I know we have to do things to survive sometimes," she explained.

"This is true. I know all too well," I sighed. This would be tough, and if I didn't play my cards right, I might as well get that new triple wide cruising to the next town. "Alright. If you were banished from the realm because you committed murder with intent, please stand and walk to the right side of the room. If you are anything other than an Unseelie fairy, please stand and go to the left of the room." This would leave Betty and her group seated in the middle. A murmur crossed the room, and no one moved immediately. "I suppose I could call my father here and ask him about each one of you individually."

"I ain't movin'," said a man in the back.

"Neither am I!" another voice added.

Before they became unruly, I put my hands in the air with no power behind it. Just a gesture to indicate that I had more to say. "I don't want any of you to move. Betty, look around you. You know these people better than I do. Please point out the ones that need to move to the right side of the room," I replied. She winced, but didn't speak.

I didn't want her to seem like a fool. Walking to the front of the stage, I gingerly sat down on the edge trying not to flash everyone in the process. I dangled my legs seeming informal as I could. I wanted to project that I was still Grace. Seated in front of her, it put me within distance to speak to her so that the whole room couldn't hear us.

"I can't do that, Grace," she said quietly. I was sure only a few people closest to us heard her.

"I can't either, Betty. I won't. We've all been exiled. We are all the same," I said quietly back to her. The murmur in the room increased in volume. Speaking in a louder voice, I said, "It's not simple to separate any of us. Look at me. Before I moved to Shady Grove, I moved from place to place. I broke up marriages, using men as toys. I lived my life the way I saw fit and didn't give a rat's

186

ass about anyone, but myself. I've changed. This town and the people in it changed me." I looked over, smiling at Dylan. The light of approval in his eyes encouraged me to continue. "Now, I'm a one-man woman, a mother, a best friend, and a Queen. We aren't the people we used to be. However, I agree with you, Betty, about separating the groups."

"Agree with me?" she asked.

"Yes, the way I did it was wrong. I would like to redefine the four groups I mentioned on the first day of the election. There are no groups. No Seelie or Unseelie, no lycans, no miscellaneous. We are fairies. When we go to the polls in a couple of days, no one will ask you your faction. No one will group you. The lines between the candidates are erased." I started to get up from my position as I saw a tear roll down Betty's face. Dylan walked over, offering his hand to help me stand. "When you vote, vote for the best person for the job. The top four people will win. We are all Grovians."

As I rose to my full height, holding Dylan's hand tightly, I waited for their response. The hall was quiet. Then, one by one each one stood up and clapped. The whole hall erupted in applause. I breathed a sigh of relief as Dylan leaned into my ear.

"You are magnificent," he said. "My one-man woman." I blushed. Damn it. I elbowed him slightly.

"You can't change the rules now," Stephanie growled. The roar in the room ceased.

Spinning around on her, I suppressed the desire to yank the hair out of her head like we were on Jerry Springer. However, I smiled, because I had her right where I wanted her. She knew it too. She looked at me from the bottom of the hole she dug for herself. I didn't have to push her in. She jumped. "Riley MacKenzie," I called the name of the girl who asked in the first place. She stood not far from where she'd vacated the microphone for Betty. Stephanie's nose crinkled up as she breathed through it hard. She looked like a bull that was about to charge.

"Right here," Riley said waving her hand. I turned toward her.

"Riley, the answer to your question is what I've just done here," I said waving around to the crowd. "We will negotiate, because I know that we can find common ground." I felt Dylan's hand squeeze mine in approval. Luther made his way to Betty, hugging her from behind. She swatted at him playfully. He smiled and winked at me. I winked back.

Riley's eyes lit up, as she leaned into the microphone, "Thank you, *my* Queen." A Seelie fairy subjected herself to me. I never thought I'd see the day.

"You are very welcome," I said. "I'm past my comfort level with this debate business. You all can stay here and ask Miss Davis questions if you would like. I'm going to head over to Hot Tin Roof. If you have any other questions for me, please come and see me. Dylan will buy the first round." The room cheered. Nestor planted his palm on his forehead, then sprinted for the door. Mable followed him closely. I nodded to Levi who took his eyes off the slender Riley MacKenzie for a moment, then took off behind Nestor to help.

"I'm buying drinks?" Dylan asked as I looked at him. We ignored the scowling Stephanie Davis behind us. I wanted to strut my legs behind me like a dog covering poop. Everyone started exiting the room. It seemed no one else had questions for her.

"I'll pay you back," I said.

He dipped his head close to me. I sucked in a breath, because even now, he made me tremble. "In kisses?" he asked.

"If that's what you want," I said.

"I need a down payment," he said as his lips met mine. I heard a whoop from the back of the room which caused both of us to blush. I giggled like a schoolgirl. "We should get to the bar."

"Nestor is going to kill me," I said.

"Not before you pay me for all these drinks," he said.

"We can just use the campaign budget," I replied.

"What campaign budget?" he asked.

"How big is your bank account?" I asked. His mouth dropped open.

"Big enough," he retorted.

"That's what she said," I replied.

"Come on, you," he said flustered.

"Oh, Darlin', I love it when you get discombobulated," I teased.

He pulled me behind him toward the door as people stopped to shake my hand promising their support. I knew that they all meant well for the moment, and if we all went to the voting booth now, I'd win. There were several days left until the election. I knew anything could happen. This was Shady Grove after all.

CHAPTER TWENTY-ONE

DYLAN AND I STOOD BEHIND THE BAR TOGETHER SERVING DRINKS. Nestor took a break sitting at a corner table talking to Mable, Levi and Miss Riley MacKenzie. The bard was making his next move. I smiled as I watched him.

"Think he will get her?" Dylan asked in my ear.

"He already has her. Watch," I said. Dylan tried to look without staring. Levi said something to Nestor who died laughing. He turned to look at Riley. As she tucked a strand of hair behind her ear, she blushed under his gaze.

"Well, I'll be damned," Dylan said.

"That's my boy," I said proudly.

"You didn't teach him to seduce anyone," Dylan said.

"How do you know?" I asked.

"He comes by it naturally," he said.

"Yeah, he does," I admitted.

"You've set a date?" Betty asked from the stool across from us. Luther was up playing pool with some guys from the church.

I smiled as Dylan pulled me close to him. "Yes, October 21st."

"Wedding dress shopping?" Tabitha asked. She'd come in a little late after her shift at the med center, but she'd already heard about the meeting.

"I guess," I said.

She laughed at me. "Every woman gets excited about a wedding dress," she said. "But not you?"

I bit my bottom lip, rolled my eyes for emphasis, and said, "Maybe a little."

Dylan chuckled beside me. "I'm looking forward to it." I remembered what he said about taking it off of me, and I blushed. Tabitha and Betty both giggled as if they knew what he meant.

"So, what's it going to be like Dylan while Grace is the Queen of Shady Grove? Are you the official concubine?" Tabitha asked.

"Actually, there won't be a decision that I make as Queen without his advice and approval. I'll have to negotiate with him before ever taking on the council," I said.

"Thank you," he muttered in my ear. Chills rose up on my arms as his breath brushed my ear.

"He will be King," Betty said realizing the implication of my words.

"Yes," I said.

"Girl, you gotta use that," Betty said.

"I agree," Tabitha said.

"What?" Dylan asked.

"Run as a couple. We need to change all the signs!" Tabitha said.

"But we aren't married yet," I said.

"Doesn't matter. You are engaged. Every one knows you are a couple. Granted we've all seen you argue too, but running together will put any doubts out of people's minds about your brash ways. We all know Dylan tempers you," Tabitha said.

My lips twisted into a scowl. Dylan started laughing, but tried to hold back. Calming myself I said, "Yes, Tab, you are right. Dylan really keeps me in check."

"Oh, you are in so much trouble," Tabitha said.

"I didn't say it! You did!" he protested.

"You laughed," she supplied.

"Yes, you laughed," I agreed.

"This isn't fair," he pouted.

"Life's a bitch, but sometimes it has puppies," I said as I high fived Tabitha and Betty.

"What's all this?" Luther said, as he joined us.

I poked my lip out at Dylan, and his face turned from defeat to I'm going to bite your lip if you don't quit in two seconds flat. I winked at him as he shook his head at me. "Luther, save me. They are ganging up on me."

"Come play a round of pool with me," Luther said.

"Sure thing," Dylan responded. He kissed me on the cheek. The warm sensation of his lips on my skin surged deep into me, and suddenly I wanted to skip this little after debate party.

"Watch out, Luther! He cheats!" I teased.

"You are next," Dylan said, walking away and pointing at me.

"No, sir, I've played my rounds with you!" I called back.

"Want me to go get Winnie after school?" Tabitha asked while grinning at Dylan teasing me.

"Yeah, if you don't mind. Take her for ice cream or something," I said, pulling some cash out of my pocket to give to her. She smiled, accepting the money.

Tabitha liked spending time with her, and Winnie said she was her new BFF. "We always have fun," Tabitha said.

"I hate to leave when there are so many supporters here. We need to make a big push over the next couple of days. I'll talk to Dylan about changing the signs, but I'm serious about us being a team. I don't want to do it without him," I said.

Betty smiled. It seemed to calm her last fears about me taking over. Not in that Dylan would have control over me, but that I valued his input so much. "You have changed, Grace. Even in the last few months, you are so much different from when you didn't know what any of us were."

"I hope so. A lot has happened," I replied.

"What was the dead thing back at the diner?" she asked. I grimaced, because I'd hoped she and Luther had forgotten about it.

Remington spoke to me briefly after the debate. He was relieved to see me alive. I thanked him for his efforts to buy me. He was researching who actually won the auction, and if Stephanie had anything to do with it. I told him my suspicions that it was Krykos who dragged me through the woods. He said he would look into it. Dylan agreed to let him handle it until he received his official private investigator license in the mail soon. Remington told Dylan that he could throw a lot of business his way from his law firm. It was good to see them getting along.

I looked up to Levi who briefly met my gaze. By this point, I expected to see him completely enamored with Riley, but instead I saw confidence that he had her instead. Nodding my head slightly to him, I felt the connection between us move. It was his way of nodding back. Ah, yes, my bard was finally becoming a real fairy. I was so proud.

"I wrecked Dylan's truck," I said.

"And…" She knew there had to be more to the story.

"And, I think it's best we don't talk about it here. Except to say, I had to visit my father and his healers or I would not be here right now," I replied as Betty's face turned grave.

"Who?" she asked.

"Not sure, but we believe she was involved somehow," I replied.

Betty hung her head, shifting her white curls forward. "I'm ashamed of the way I acted to you, and to think I'd considered voting for her.

"You weren't voting *for* her. Just voting against me," I smiled.

"Yes, mostly," she smiled back. "You really aren't mad?"

"No, I told you that you would apologize," I teased.

We laughed together. I'd missed my friend.

Levi walked up to lean on the bar. "Well, hello Handsome," I said to him.

"I'm going to drive Riley home," he said.

"In what?" I asked, because he drove a Harley, the truck was wrecked, and no one drove Dylan's car.

"In her car," he grinned. "See you in the morning."

"Don't do anything I wouldn't do?" I said.

"So swapping gravy is fine," he grinned. The devil. She stood to meet him, as they walked out the door, she flashed her eyes back to me. I narrowed mine at her. That's right, Sweetheart, you may take him to your bed, but he's mine. I smiled and waved.

"Laid that on pretty thick," Betty said.

"Don't hurt my bard," I replied. Dylan and Luther ended their game. It looked like Dylan won. Didn't surprise me. I was sure he cheated.

"A kiss for the winner?" he asked.

"Luther, come here," I said.

"Hey! Not him! Me!" Dylan exclaimed. I gave him a little peck. He groaned at the weak prize.

"More later," I promised. His face lit up.

"You gotta pay for all this alcohol," he said.

As the crowd dispersed, we helped Nestor clean up. "Are you sure you are okay?" he kept asking me.

"I'm fine. Better than fine. Dylan and I are on the same page which means more to me than a couple of nails in my leg," I said as he grimaced.

"Are you okay?" I asked remembering his glass dropping incidents.

He shook his head. "No, I'm not, but there isn't anything you can do about it."

"Are you sick? Cursed?" I asked.

"No, Grace. I'm old. I've been on this earth since the ancient days. The longer a fairy spends in the real world the more it wears on them. My power is waning."

"So, I'll take you back home so you can recharge. I'm pretty sure father will let you come back if I asked," I said.

"It's not that simple," he replied. "Leave it for now. Please." I conceded to his wishes, but I would ask my father soon if I could bring Nestor to the Otherworld. I knew it would help him.

"Where is Levi?" Dylan asked realizing he was gone.

"He took Riley home," I said.

"Atta boy!" he whooped. "Are you ready to go, my dear?"

"Yep," I replied. "But can we go to the trailer? I don't think I'm up for cleaning up the house yet." I left it in the mess that Stephanie had made. She knew how to put on one hell of a show.

"Yes, of course, I'll go take care of the house tomorrow," he said.

When we arrived at the trailer, Tabitha pulled up behind us. Winnie bolted out of the door of the car running to Dylan, "Daddy, Daddy! Look at my new wolf," she said letting out the cutest howl I'd ever heard.

"I see that. Cute gift, Tabitha," Dylan said to her.

"They were fresh out of firebirds," she replied. "I'll see y'all tomorrow."

"Later! I'll call you. Thanks again, Tab!" I shouted to her. She waved as she pulled back out of the drive.

Winnie told us about her "super fun" time with Dr. Tabitha, as she called her. She practically yawned through her story. I got her dressed for bed, and Dylan read her a story.

"Goodnight, Daddy," she said to him.

"Goodnight, Sweetheart," he said, kissing her on the forehead.

His face glowed in the praise of the little girl. "You are a wonderful Daddy," I said.

"Please remember that the next time you get mad at me," he smiled.

"No more, Dylan. Looking at her in there, I realize what we might have lost. No more," I said. His arms wrapped me up spreading warmth all over my body.

"I know what I almost lost," he said. "It scared the crap out of me. This was worse than the curse at Christmas. I still feel like I caused all of this."

"Time to stop that. We have an election to win. Do you want to change the signs?" I asked.

"I think it's too late for that. You acknowledged me on the stage, and at the bar. People know we are together. That will make the difference," he said.

We settled down in the bedroom, exhausted after the long day. I curled up next to him as he stroked my platinum blonde hair. I had scared myself in the mirror earlier because I just wasn't used to seeing myself this way. I started to drift off to sleep when he spoke.

"Levi took Riley home?" he asked.

"Yes," I mumbled. I didn't reach out for Levi's presence. I was afraid of what I might get in return.

"His first fairy, right?" he asked.

Raising up in the bed to look at him, I gasped. "It is."

"He won't be able to walk tomorrow," Dylan laughed.

"Oh, shit! No, he won't." I said. "He will be addicted to it." I started giggling. I could just see him walking in tomorrow, dragging his ass. I hope she worked him over good.

"He needs it," Dylan replied.

"Yes, he does," I giggled, then yawned.

"Goodnight, Beautiful Grace," he said.

I sighed. Only Dylan called me that. "Goodnight, Darlin'."

CHAPTER TWENTY-TWO

Levi strolled into the trailer around noon. Actually, he limped into the trailer, groaning like he'd been through three wars and a goat roping. "Well, hello, Dublin," I said to him from the kitchen counter. Dylan sat in the recliner smirking behind a newspaper.

"You! You could have told me!" he barked at me.

"Told you what?" I feigned surprise. "Levi, what on earth happened to you?"

"I barely survived! That's what happened," he groaned, as he leaned on the wall outside his bedroom.

"Fairy looks good on ya!" I laughed, as Dylan tried to remain neutral. The knuckles on his hands gripping the newspaper turned white as he fought laughter.

"It was so good," he moaned. I thought he was going to orgasm right there in the hallway. "I'll never sleep with a regular girl ever again. I had no idea what she was doing when she…" he stopped mid-sentence looking at me. "Nevermind." He skirted into his room, slamming the door.

"My bard's all grown up, Dylan," I said. "I'm prouder than a bitch whose pup got his first flea."

Dylan kept laughing, but ignored the whole situation. "Are we going campaigning today?" he asked. "The vote is tomorrow."

I'd been thinking about the best thing to do all day. Shady Grove wasn't a big city. I couldn't do an interview with a television reporter or a radio spot. We just didn't have those things. The closest thing we had to social networking was Hot Tin Roof and The Grove Diner. Everyone that frequented those places, I already knew.

"Got any ideas?" I asked, because I was plum out.

"I do, but the question is, do you trust me?" he waggled his eyebrows at me. Trust wasn't optional anymore, if I was in for a penny, I was in for a pound. I just wished it was the kind of pounding that comes in the bed, not at the ballot box.

"Absolutely," I said.

He laughed as he pulled out his cell phone. "I almost believed that! Go put on something pretty and red," he demanded. He started making calls while I picked through the clothes that I bought with Tabitha. I wasn't sure when we would go back to Dylan's house. After the last two days, I don't think either of us was eager to be there. Rufus was here. I hated that Winnie's favorite room was there, but we wouldn't stay away forever. I picked out an apple red dress with a v-neck and long sleeves. The bottom flared out which looked cute and fun. It looked like me. If anything, today I would be me.

As I got dressed, Dylan continued to talk in the other room. I heard him say, "Great. I'll meet you there." I slipped on some cute heels, then strutted into the living room. His eyes locked on me. Twisting his hips sideways, as if he could coax that bad boy down, he stalked to me. "Grace Ann Bryant, you look damn good."

"Good enough to eat?" I asked.

"What kind of question is that?" he said nibbling my ear.

"The kind that will get us out of campaigning today," I admitted, as his hands found their way up my thighs. Instead of kissing me, he bit down on my bottom lip, pulling it away from my teeth. He growled like a tiger on the prowl. My lady bits shivered with delight. "Damn, you, Dylan Riggs. How the hell am I supposed to think about anything, except making love to you now?"

"You can do it. I know you can," he whispered in my ear. "Are you ready to go?"

"Um, no," I replied with flushed cheeks. "I think I need fresh panties!"

With his hands still under my dress, he hooked the side of the sensible cotton panties I put on and slid them down my legs with a simple tug. "Go ahead. I helped," he grinned.

Oh.

My.

God.

This was the seducer. I hadn't tingled this much since we played pool the first time. He fully intended on leaving me wanting. Bastard!

Slowly I stepped away from him, locked in his gaze. Azure flames seared into me. Quickly I turned away, his hand grazed the edge of my skirt flipping it up at the last second. I grabbed my bare ass as I turned to face him again. "Dylan!"

"What? My hand got caught in a loose string," he smiled, not so innocently.

Utterly confused whether I need to jump him or run away because we needed to get to town. I realized that Levi was standing at the end of the hall, flushed and staring. "Levi!"

"Shit," Dylan muttered, turning to look at him. "Shouldn't you be sleeping that off?"

"Um, yeah. Nice ass, Grace," he said, slipping back down the hallway.

"Rearden, I'm going to kick yours, if you don't get moving," Dylan threatened. There was no intent behind it. I thought. Maybe. "Sorry."

"Levi has seen my butt before, but I'll let you come in here and apologize properly if you want to," I offered. Stepping toward me quickly, I stumbled back from him. He caught me and slammed the door at the same time.

"We don't have time for this," he grumbled, as his hands found their way back under the dress.

"I know, and you will wrinkle my dress," I said, as I unbuttoned his shirt.

"They will be waiting on us," he mentioned.

I didn't care who he meant as I pulled the dress off over my head. I laid it carefully over a chair. Holding back no longer, he pressed me against the wall. Campaigning could wait for a few minutes.

❧

Seventeen minutes to be exact. We were both so wound up that it didn't take long. He helped me back in the dress, but picked out a less than sensible pair of panties to wear underneath. They were red and lacy. I indulged him, because as far as quickies go, that was fucking hot. He put on black slacks with a white button up shirt. Helping him with the buttons, he brushed my hair back behind my ear.

"Sex hair?" I asked, because I hadn't brushed it yet.

"You are beautiful," he said. "Strong, sexy and beautiful."

I blushed, because of the intensity of his stare. The hardness of his voice revealed the deepest feelings. "Thank you. I needed that," I said.

"Why?"

"Because this election just doesn't feel like me. It feels like a game I've been dragged into," I said.

"You were great yesterday," he said.

"Can I do that all the time? Do I want to?" I asked him.

"You can't do it all the time, because I want many repeat performances of mind-blowing sex. You have a daughter that you want to spend time with every day. It will not consume your life, but we both know that you are the one for this job. Even if Stephanie wasn't here, it's yours. It's always been yours, Grace," he said with a confidence that I couldn't seem to muster.

"Who is waiting on us?" I asked.

"Your supporters," he replied. "Brush your hair. We need to go."

As I stared at myself in the mirror, the brush flowed through my platinum locks smoothing out all the tangled bunches made by Dylan's hands. His confident gaze stared at me in the mirror. He believed in me. My heart was finally back to the place it needed to be. The place where I knew without a doubt that Dylan was the best man on this earth, and that if he believed in me, then I must have done something to deserve such praise. "Good?" I asked.

"Perfect," he said offering his hand. Grabbing it, I laced my fingers with his hoping his support would boost my tenacity. When we walked into the living room, Levi sat on the couch in dress pants and a red polo.

"What are you doing?" I asked.

"Going with you guys," he said.

"Don't you need to rest?" I asked, knowing he was tired despite the bravado. Fairies have very little need to stop, slow down or rest between sex. Levi was a changeling, so while I imagined his libido was stronger than a normal male, a fairy would wear him out.

"I'll be okay. This is important," he said, as he grabbed his helmet and jacket.

We climbed in Dylan's car, and Levi followed on the Harley. Finally, when I couldn't stand it any longer, I asked, "Dylan, where are we going?"

"One final rally before the vote," he smiled.

"How did you organize a rally in such a short amount of time?" I asked.

"I didn't. I started arranging it last night," he admitted. My jaw dropped. The light in his eyes flickered, "In fact, had we left the first time you came out of the bedroom in that dress, we would have been about seventeen minutes early."

"Liar!" I accused him.

"Complete truth for you, my Queen," he said.

"Seventeen minutes to be exact," I scoffed.

"You remember when you used to torture me with an allotted time for making out and fondling?" I gulped. "Well, I became really good at counting and doing *other* things at the same time. I'd say I've mastered it now. What do you think?"

"Yes, I'd say so. I'm a great motivator," I laughed.

"You would turn this around on me!" he laughed too.

"Of course, I have to win, Dylan. One day you will learn. I guess I'll have to continue your education," I replied.

"I look forward to it," he said as we pulled up to a massive gathering at the gazebo in the town square. It was adorned with red, white and blue bunting. People walked around the square talking and laughing. There were balloons tied to light posts. "Wait right there." He exited the car, circling around to help me out. As he lowered his hand for me to grasp it, I took a deep breath. My hand shook as I reached out for his steady one.

"Dylan," I hesitated.

"You've got this. Come on," he said confidently. Laying my cool hand into his warm one, I rose out of the car with, well, all the grace I could muster. As we approached the crowd, I was more nervous than a cat in a room full of rocking chairs.

The people cheered and clapped as we approached the main gazebo. Shaking hands as I went, I looked into the faces of the people of Shady Grove that I loved. Jeremiah was first, waiting on the edge in his full Sanhedrin robe. He bowed slightly, kissing my hand instead of shaking it.

"My Queen," he said.

"You, old coot," I laughed. A smile twinkled in his eye as we continued to walk.

Next in line, Remington Blake stood by Niles Babineau. The both bowed slightly.

"Grace, you look lovely. Good afternoon, Dylan," he greeted us both.

"Thank you for coming," I said.

"Wouldn't miss it for the world, honey," he said.

Lamar and his Yule Lad brothers waited to speak to me. I talked to all of them. Phillip didn't speak as he and Brad, the BBQ King, were chowing down on sausages. Lamar proudly showed me the crown he'd added to his peg leg in support of my campaign. I kissed him on the forehead. He cheeks turned twenty different shades of pink.

Cletus and Tater stood among the fairy folk which threw me off guard. "We wouldn't miss a party for nothing!" Tater exclaimed.

"Grace, whatever this queen business is, we want everyone to know that we support you," Cletus added.

"You are too kind," I smiled at their crazy, oblivious gesture.

Matthew Rayburn stood alone. Kadence was missing. I didn't expect her to support me, but I winced at Matthew's expression knowing that I noted her absence. "I couldn't convince her," he said.

"Matthew, it's nothing. Kady has always been headstrong. She has to figure things out on her own. You have done such a good job raising a beautiful daughter. She actually reminds me a little of myself," I said. "And it doesn't matter what happens to me, there is a part inside of me that will always love my Daddy." I might have laid it on a little thick because I wasn't sure I actually loved my father. However, since the true world of Shady Grove had opened up to me, he had been supportive and caring.

"Thank you, Grace," he smiled.

Dylan and I exchanged pleasantries with the Mayor and his daughter Ella. We also spoke to Troy and Amanda who showed up in their police uniforms just to prove a point. The others who showed up to support me were Deacon Giles, Caleb Joiner and even Malcolm Taggart.

"Mal, good to see you," I said.

"I should apologize for my bad behavior," he said.

"Oh, honey, if I had to apologize for every time I acted out, we'd be here all day," I joked.

"That's very nice of you, Grace. I promise it won't happen again," he said.

"Damn straight it won't," Dylan interjected. Malcolm shifted his weight as if he were prepared to run from Dylan who reached out and patted him on the shoulder.

Behind Malcolm there were many citizens of Shady Grove that I knew in passing like Sylvester Handley and the Santiagos'. There were other cops, firemen, business men and women. I even saw Mrs. Frist standing in the back with her arm around a gorgeous, young fireman. She waggled her fingers at me, and I just laughed. At least she wasn't still after Levi.

Dr. Tabitha stood in her lab coat smiling at me. "That was my favorite of the dresses!" she squealed as I got close.

"It's my favorite, too," Dylan said. Tabitha's eyes widened when she saw the blush rush over my cheeks that matched the redness of the dress.

"Oh, I see," she said. "Good luck."

"Thanks," I said gathering myself.

Betty and Luther stood with Mable and Nestor. We all shared hugs. Nestor hugged me last, whispering in my ear. "I know he isn't here, but your father is proud of you. I am so proud of you." I felt the tears building up in the edges of my eyes. "Don't cry. You've got a speech to make."

"Speech?" I said.

"Yep, you can do it," Dylan said.

Finally, Levi left the side of Riley Mac Kenzie long enough to wrap me up in one of his bone crushing hugs. "Grace, I don't know where I'd be in this world without you," he said.

"Oh, don't go all mushy on me," I teased him.

"I know you never want to say it out loud, but I'm going to," he said.

"Say what?" I asked.

"I know the connection between us is because I'm your servant," he said.

"Levi, you are not my servant," I interjected.

"Yes, I am, and I want to be," he looked back at Riley who nodded. "I understand this world better now, because of what you taught me. No matter what happens in the future. I will always stand by you."

Damn allergies struck me in the eyes as tears rolled down my cheeks. I felt the grip of Dylan's hand flex, releasing mine. Slinging my arms around Levi's neck, I felt the tingle from the top of my head to the tips of toes, and everywhere in between. "I don't know what I'd do without you," I said.

"You were fine without me for hundreds of years," he laughed at my assertion.

"I couldn't do it now," I said.

"Quit crying," Levi said suddenly becoming uncomfortable. I brushed away my tears as I reached for Dylan's hand again. I dared to look in his eyes to see if there was jealousy there. I saw none. Levi retreated to Riley's side. She laced her arm through his. The power of her touch on him rippled through our bond, and my eyes widened at the raw intensity of it. I had no idea how he survived her, but he had. Not only that, she was back for more. Well done, Bard.

Dylan saddled up next to me as all the eyes in the square turned to me. "Grace, you are the strongest woman I've ever known. Step up there and knock 'em dead. Not for real, but you know what I mean."

I heaved a laugh out at his assertion. It wasn't entirely inaccurate. Thinking back to the days of my Father's court, I realized for every exile standing before me, there were a dozen that didn't get the reprieve to live. Father told me once that killing those who disobeyed him was part of his job as King. He had to keep the peace between the courts, sacrificing his own miscreants when necessary. He assured me that the Seelie did the same to their wayward lot. Clearly the Queen of the Seelie fairies missed an opportunity to put Stephanie down.

"Good Afternoon. I'm so overwhelmed that all of you are here to support my run for Queen. I stepped into the role thinking that I wouldn't be challenged, but over the last week, I've realized that my challenge hasn't been Stephanie Davis. It's been myself. Remembering all the days I sat in my trailer, I minded my own business, friendly enough to all of you. But I never put myself out there for anyone, except maybe Winnie. The world suddenly altered my reality. A changeling was dumped at my door for which I am eternally grateful," I said, nodding to Jeremiah. "Things happened that forced me to open my eyes and see what was really here in this town. Even before accepting my role here, I began to see that Shady Grove was all about friends, family, good food, and a place to relax. A place to call home."

I locked eyes with Betty, Luther, Nestor and Mable as I spoke. Their smiles knew my indications were about them. "Whether I'd admit it in public or not, I had an unhealthy infatuation with the sheriff in this town." The crowd laughed when I paused. Dylan stepped up beside me. "Who showed me after all these years of roaming the world, that love is real. It's tough and glorious all at the same time." He squeezed my hand.

"This job is harder than I expected. My father used to tell me that being in charge wasn't all it was cracked up to be. Not in those words of course. I assure you it was much more formal, but still he was right. To be honest, I don't know how good I'll be at it. I may fall flat on my face, but if I do, I'll do it while giving you, the people of Shady Grove, everything I have to give."

The crowd cheered and clapped. I waited for it to die down. "I am humbled and honored that you would choose me as your Queen," I managed to choke out, as Dylan kissed me on the temple.

They clapped and cheered again. Dylan put his hand up to draw attention. Much like my gesture on the first day of this debacle, they silenced, waiting for him to speak. "All of you are invited to my home tomorrow evening for a victory party. There will be food, beverages and fireworks!"

"What?" I mouthed. He winked at me. I loved that man.

My supporters ecstatically patted each other on the backs. The roar grew as we stepped off the gazebo to join their excitement. Betty started introducing me to people that I'd never met before who were supporting me. Each name I tucked in the back of my head. I would remember them all. Father said he knew the names of each of his servants and peers. It seemed as though all I needed was a name with the face, then they were engrained in my mind as the people I'd sworn to protect.

We circled the crowd greeting everyone. Dylan ate sausages with Brad and Phillip while I talked about potential council members with Tabitha and Mrs. Frist.

"Grace, I must say, I never expected you to turn out so well. Oberon must be very proud," she said.

"You know my father?" I asked.

"Know is a relative term, child. Yes, I knew him once or twice," she smiled.

"Information I didn't need to know," I smirked. Tabitha and Mrs. Frist laughed. "Wait, is that why you got kicked out?"

A smile crossed her lips. "Maybe," she laughed. "Doesn't matter now, does it? You said we are all the same."

"I did say that, but I say a lot of things I end up regretting," I laughed.

"We all do, honey," she said. "Let me go find someone to entertain me. I see the lovely Miss Riley has latched herself on to your bard. Pity. I would have loved to educate that one."

"Me too," said Tabitha.

"What?" I said, surprised at her admission.

"Awe, come on, Grace. I may be a respectable doctor, but I'm not blind. Levi is hot."

I shook my head. She was right. He was damn good looking. I hadn't realized the fairy women of the town were all gunning for him. His education might just be starting. I laughed at the possibilities. Poor Levi had no idea.

"What's so funny?" Dylan asked, returning to me.

Ducking away, Tabitha said, "I'll catch you later."

"She and Mrs. Frist just were lamenting the loss of being able to educate Levi," I said.

Dylan laughed. "You didn't know that half the women in this town wanted him?" I shook my head in denial. "So oblivious, Grace. It's almost endearing if it didn't scare the crap out of me."

"Scare you? Why?" I asked.

"Because, you need to be more aware of what's going on around you. As much as I'd like to stick to you like glue, you've got to be able to recognize danger. There are some very dangerous people in this town."

"Am I one of those *dangerous* people, Dylan Riggs?"

The crowd silenced as we all turned to face Stephanie Davis standing on the gazebo flanked by Kyffin Merrick and Sergio Krykos.

CHAPTER TWENTY-THREE

"You know, I'm pretty sure you weren't invited to this party," I smirked at her. Today, she would get the full Grace. No holding back. I would be me even if it killed me. I should have said, "Here Dylan, hold my beer."

"It is the town square. Soon to be my town," she grinned, waving her arm about like she was Vanna White. The men stood behind her in the shadows. Kyffin's stout frame jiggled with laughter at her snide remarks. Krykos' eyes bore holes in me, but he did not react to Stephanie as she spoke. In fact, he never once glanced at her. Something in his ardent gaze felt off.

"What is he?" I asked Dylan quietly.

"Sergio? A dick?" he shrugged.

"No, what kind of fairy," I pressed, looking back at Krykos, his eyes brightened. He watched me intently.

"Why is he looking at you like that?" Dylan asked. I could see a hint of jealousy at the way Krykos leered at me.

I grabbed the front of his shirt with my fist. "Look at me! Dylan, what is he?"

"I'm not sure," he said, shaking off the anger. "I've never asked."

A cold darkness settled inside of me. Gloriana's power flared as a portal from the Otherworld flashed open in my head. Someone was feeding me power from the other side. It had to be my father, of course, but why did I need it?

I snapped back to Stephanie who stood before my supporters. "I've come to talk to you all about Grace and the things she's been hiding from all of you."

"We know her. You have nothing to tell us that we don't know about her," Betty said.

"Oh, Betty, she has you so fooled," she purred. "Have none of you wondered what happened in the woods that night to Demetrius Lysander?"

Lysander was my lawyer, and a servant to my father Oberon. He brutally killed two children. I hunted him down, turning his life over to my father at the end. My father obliterated him.

"Lysander killed two human children," Dylan snarled.

"Oh, my sweet Dylan. So, enamored with her that you can't even see the truth," she said. "Lysander did kill two children, but instead of taking care of the murderer, she turned him over to her father. Oberon thanked her for turning Lysander over to him. Then he squashed him like a bug. His own servant." She emphasized the word while locking her gaze on Levi. He'd stepped between Stephanie and Riley, watching the Seelie elf closely.

She wore a blue lace overlay dress and tall black heels. She swirled around to the crowd watching them. They all watched her. "How many of us here have unsettled grievances with the almighty Oberon?"

"I am not my father," I spouted at her.

"No, dear, you just have to be your father's daughter," she sneered. "Who is to say that one by one you won't turn us over to him for our due retribution? I know if he could get his hands on me, he'd kill me."

Behind her Sergio shifted his weight, it was subtle, but I saw it. Stephanie did not concern me. He did.

"I think you forgot I'm an exile too," I replied.

"Are you? Because I heard of a wild tale of fairy trafficking and how your bard whisked you off to the Otherworld where your father's healers nursed you back to health. He also made your Bard, your Levi, the Royal Bard of the Unseelie. Are these rumors true? Can you pass into the Otherworld without consequence? Are you really an exile, Grace? In that form, you have to be honest," she said.

Clearly, she knew more than I thought she would. I knew that things that happened in fairy, never stayed in fairy. Very much the opposite of Vegas. However, she had spies in my father's house. "I was kidnapped and poisoned. My father's healers did heal me. And yes, my exile was lifted many years ago, but I chose to stay in this realm," I replied. "I have nothing to hide." As I looked around me, I started to see doubts in the faces of my supporters.

"Isn't it also true that Amanda Capps was working with Demetrius Lysander, but instead of punishing her as you did your own lawyer, you let her go without a reprimand? And now she is fucking the sheriff who staunchly supports your candidacy? Seems awfully convenient," she said.

"I do not have to explain myself to you, but I will to anyone else here that wants to know the reasons I made the choices that I did that night," I replied. "Dylan was there. He can vouch for me."

"No, he can't," Stephanie said. "You've enthralled him."

"I have not. He can't be enthralled," I replied.

She crossed her arms over her chest. "Is that completely true, Dylan?"

He tensed next to me. "I am not enthralled, Stephanie. I love Grace."

"Are you sure you aren't enthralled?" she pressed.

"I am sure," he said.

"Prove it," she smirked. "Because you once told me that the only being on this earth that could enthrall you would be a fairy queen. Were you lying? Your powers can be negated by royal fairy blood."

I didn't look at him because she was twisting my words. I knew she had to be twisting his as well. He chuckled. "Actually Stephanie, I said that to you, because I already knew what I felt for Grace. It was irony, but I'm sure it escaped your self-centered vision. The joke was on you."

"Then prove it. Walk away and leave her here. If she is truly capable of being Queen, then she can do it without you," Stephanie said.

Before he spoke, I turned to him. He looked down at me questioning. "You stay and shut-up. I've got this. Keep an eye on the Greek with the staring problem," He nodded to me. Maybe I did have him enthralled. I was sure he had me.

"See! Look! He obeys," she called to the crowd who looked on the situation.

"Shut the fuck up," I said. Dylan suppressed a laugh.

She shot daggers at me. "Who do you think you are?"

"I am the current Queen of the Exiles, and you will cease!" I said releasing power.

She blinked as the wave rolled over her. I watched the magic in with my sight, but it rolled past her. An evil grin crossed her face. "Tisk, tisk. I think maybe you aren't the queen after all," she smiled.

"You will listen. I can't do this without Dylan, and I won't. I can't do this without the people standing behind me, and I won't. This isn't about me, Stephanie. It's certainly not about you. Who am I without them? There is no Queen without her people," I replied.

"There is if you are married to a King," she smirked, flashing her hand at me. I'd seen her diamond engagement ring, but this time, tucked under it a solid row of diamonds. It flashed brilliantly. I turned my attention back to Krykos who moved slowly toward her. With each of his steps, the cold darkness I sensed moved closer to me. He was Unseelie, but there was only one King. My father. When he touched her outstretched hand, she sank to her knees in supplication. Kyffin Merrick hit his knees as well.

"Gloriana, you were always such a waste of beauty. You could have been Queen of the Otherworld, but your basic desires for human flesh outweighed your sense of family, and you were ousted from the realm. Your father's heart grows weak to even allow you to re-enter that realm. Of all of us, you are the least worthy," his voice shook inside of me.

Levi made a move toward us, but I threw up my hand. I felt this man's power. He would squash Levi. My bard stopped, but snarled at the power I'd used to still him. Dylan's warm hand rested on my back, as Krykos continued to speak.

"You would think after hundreds of years of fucking humans, you would crave something worthy of your love, instead of this wretched excuse for a man. He's not even human. He's a fucking animal," he prodded Dylan, who did not flinch or move.

"Not only that, but you are the *mother*, and I used the term loosely, of a human child. Where is the cold, heartless daughter of Oberon worthy of his crown?" he asked.

"You can make remarks against my bard, my fiancé and my father, but when you brought my child into this, you crossed a line. Buckle up, Buttercup, you just flipped my bitch switch," I said pulling the power that had been fed to me from the Otherworld. The square froze over causing my supporters to scurry away from what was to be a massive fight. Pushing the power out of me and forward to Krykos, a flash of arctic wind blew the kneeling Stephanie and Merrick over on their sides. However, my opponent was unmoved.

"No, dear, like this," he said making the same motion I had, but instead of wind. He pressed a full wall of ice toward Dylan and me. Dylan's hand flashed before me in a burst of flames that melted through the block before it reached us. While we held our defense, Krykos pushed another block of ice to us. This one moved faster knocking us both off our feet. Dylan jumped to his feet engulfed in flame. Krykos snapped his finger turning him to a block of ice. "You know how to do that one, right?"

"He is mine, and I am his," I claimed Dylan formally on the spot. If Krykos harmed him, as a fairy, he would have to face the punishment of my father and the council. I wasn't sure of his ties to the Unseelie Court, but it was glaringly apparent that he was extremely powerful.

"I should destroy him anyway. I do miss Oberon. If I blast

Serafino into a billion pieces of ice, do you think your father would care? Trust me, he wouldn't," he laughed.

"No, I will give you anything. Don't harm Dylan," I said as I faced the reality that I might have to choose between my own freedom and Dylan's life.

"Oh, but he will return. He is a phoenix after all. Right?" he smiled. I remembered what Dylan told me. Only the power of a royal fairy could destroy him. I knew he was talking about me, but for some reason it never occurred to me that another royal fairy would do it. Krykos was a relative. I could feel his darkness coursing through my veins. "Ah, you know I can kill him. Permanently."

My heart dropped. "Grace," Levi said behind Krykos. "Don't."

Levi knew me. He knew that I would give anything, including my life, to save Dylan. Krykos snapped again freezing Levi. "See. Two for one," the bastard laughed. Kyffin and Stephanie laughed too.

"What do you want?" I stammered, as I shook my hands, releasing the power. Nothing I held could go against him.

He circled around me. My skin erupted in disdain and hatred for him. His power pulsed around me. "You feel the call home. You feel what you truly are inside. Oh, Gloriana, you've forgotten the hateful, snide, sexy little wench you used to be. You've replaced it with a simpering, weak woman. It's very sad to see one of my own blood so lost. Let me remind you of what you are."

"What. Do. You. Want?"

"All in good time, my dear," he said, tracing his cold fingers up my arm.

"If you are going to fucking touch me, then I'll say just get on with it. Kill them both," I said, knowing he still had a game to play, and he wasn't ready to kill Levi and Dylan, yet.

"So impulsive. You do remember, don't you? The nights in the realm. Masked parties. I should say masked orgies. Oh, how I miss it so? Your young tight ass wearing next to nothing. Such beauty as the realm had ever seen. The only daughter of the King. Dragging fairy men into the hallways, closets and side rooms to fuck their brains out. You turned more than one fairy man into mush. I'm surprised you haven't done it to poor Levi over there. But that wasn't enough for you, human men were putty in your capable hands. Giving them the ecstasy that they could never get from another human, leaving them wanting for the entirety of their pathetic lives. You were a bad little fairy. I loved it. You were perfect in every way, but now, you've forgotten that wonderful time in your life."

"I was wrong. I deserved to be banished. If you are looking for that fairy, she is gone," I said defiantly.

"Actually, if you want me to let Dylan Riggs and Levi Rearden live, you will bow before me. Declare that I am the rightful King of the Otherworld, and become the vixen I know you to truly be," his tall form leaned over me, leering down my shirt. As he reached out to grab one of my breasts, I ducked to the side and raised my leg to knee his nuts, because even as a last resort, it is a sure thing. However, he was faster than me, dodging my leg by swatting it to the side. I spun away from him. He pressed up behind me grabbing my throat. Squeezing slightly, he twirled me around to look at the fairies hiding behind bushes and cars. The people of Shady Grove. My people. I couldn't protect them from this. He spoke in my ear. A chill raced down my spine. "Look at them. If you do as I say, you will have the power to protect them as you promised. I swear it. You will own them all." The ground shook with the oath.

"No, my Father's throne is not mine to give. Who the hell do you think you are?" I asked.

He spun me around to face him, pulling my body to his very aroused self. "Oh, Gloriana, how could you forget me? Well, I was wearing a mask the night that I tried to take you for myself. You pushed me away, but I got a glimpse of that glorious body. It's a shame you've marked it as you have," he said as he clamped down on my wrist over my tattoo. The power I had stored in it straight from the Otherworld, flowed into him freely. I could not stop it. He tilted his head back, moaning in pleasure. As he pressed his hips into me, my body responded, but my will was strong. I tried pulling away as far as I could with his hand around my neck.

"Stop," I said through gritted teeth.

"No, you will be my servant, just as the Bard is yours. I will feel you whenever I want!" he growled.

"Who the fuck do you think you are?" I growled back with all the effort that I had left.

A silent whoosh swept over the square. Snowflakes dangled in the air. The surrounding fairies did not move. I saw Riley MacKenzie blink, so the people surrounding us were completely aware of what was going on. I only knew of one person who could stop time in this realm. Oberon, King of the Unseelie Court.

He stood to the side of us. His silver tunic stretched to his knees covering charcoal pants. Black boots covered his calves to his knees. An antlered crown crusted with diamonds sat on his head, flashing brilliantly in the winter light. His cold blue eyes stared at the man who had me.

"He's my brother, Brockon," my father's steady voice said. "Release her, little badger." It wasn't a request, because Krykos flinched at the order, but he did not let me go.

"Hello, brother. I hoped you would visit us," Krykos said. I'd remembered tales of my Uncle Brock who was the biggest debaucher in the entire kingdom which wouldn't be so horrible if he didn't put his hands all over my father's concubines. Father didn't take kindly to it. "You must see that now I have pieces of your power, that you foolishly fed to her. You cannot make me do as you wish." He squeezed harder on my neck. I coughed, straining at the pressure.

"Release her, now. Do not make me destroy you," Oberon said.

"No. You will give me your crown for her life. My Queen and I will waltz into the Otherworld and return it to its glory," he sneered at my father.

"Daddy, don't," I choked out.

"What Queen do you speak of?" Oberon asked his brother.

"I'm sure you know the lovely Raine, daughter of Rhiannon, Queen of the Seelie Fairies," he said as Stephanie stood obediently behind him. The bravado she wore on her sleeves I now knew to be a construct of Brock's vanity. A reflection of himself that he cast on her. Raine bowed deeply to my father. I knew now that the Queen of the Seelie didn't dispose of Stephanie, because like me, she was family. Her child. My father couldn't do to it to me. Neither could Rhiannon.

Oberon looked at her through the eyes of a lustful man. I saw my father admire her curves. "She is lovely, and I remember her naked body quite well. I found her in my bed once. She tried to seduce me to prove to her mother how worthy she was as an heir. Raine, you were banished for those actions, correct?" Father asked her. Two royal daughters banished for basically the same thing. Fairy daughters were worse than a preacher's daughters.

Could this get any more fucked up? Yep. "You had her banished! You demanded it like she was an intruder in a foreign land. A spy sent by the Seelie Court to ensnare you. She wasn't. She was a woman trying to prove her worth to her mother. She is just like Grace!" Brock screamed at Oberon, tightening his grip on my neck.

"Those things were true. She was a spy, an intruder, and mostly a whore. Things didn't change when she came to this realm. She's fucked everything with a dick," Oberon laughed, as he walked through the stilled square. When his body touched the fallen snow, it attached to him, then fell to the ground leaving a void wherever he walked. His eyes intently watched Brock, waiting for his moment to strike.

"So, has Gloriana," Brock spat back at him. He was right. I couldn't deny what I used to be. Things were different now, but that didn't matter to Brock. He just wanted my father to relinquish his crown.

"In that, you are wrong, little brother. Gloriana is a Queen in her own right. You stand in her land. You may have taken my power from her, but you can never take the power that these people have given to her. I am proud to call her my daughter," Oberon said.

I knew it to be true. The power I felt at the meetings wasn't so much Gloriana, but the power of the people who trusted me to act on their behalf. Taking the hint, I reached for power, but not from the Otherworld. I found it in Shady Grove, and its people. The Diner, Hot Tin Roof, the Druid's grove, Dylan's home and my trailer. The people swirled through my mind. Well, butter my biscuit, the power I found under my command was stronger than anything my father had funneled to me. It was time for some gravy.

"Put me down," I ordered. His grip released me against his will. I stared into his eyes as I snapped both fingers. Dylan and Levi gasped for air as the ice around them melted into puddles. Brock reached for me again, but shrank back when my glamour popped into place. Gloriana wasn't Queen of Shady Grove. Grace was. I narrowed my gaze at him. "Leave this place and take your whore with you. Never step foot in this town again. How dare you threaten my people!" My voice was steady, but forceful.

"Gloriana, we should talk about this. We could be a team. We could rule here and in the Otherworld. Return it all to the glory of the Unseelie. Don't you remember what the Sanhedrin have done to you? You ran from them. Now you keep one as a friend? You are flirting with danger, and it will ruin you. Please, Gloriana, come with me," he said reaching out to me.

Flashing my hands out before me, a cold force pressed toward him much like his ice wall on us, but unseen. He stumbled and fell to the ground, surprised at the power. It flowed over him like a crushing wave.

"My name is not Gloriana. It's Grace. Get the fuck out of my town before I squash you into little fairy bits," I growled.

Gathering himself off the ground, he straightened his coat and his shoulders. Stephanie stood to take his arm, but he pulled it from her. She bowed her head to him as a servant. He spun on his heel. Stephanie and Kyffin skulked away, but he stood immobile with his back to me. He was only a pace away. I saw the flash of fear on Dylan's face, but before I could react, he spun lunging toward me with a gleaming gray knife. It plunged into my stomach as I tried to dart away from him. Immediately, I felt the effects of the cold iron coursing through my veins.

Dylan rose up, as ball of flames barreling at Krykos who laughed. Touching the tree beside him, he slipped into Otherworld as I sank to my knees. I looked to where Stephanie and Kyffin once stood, but they were both gone too. I stared at the knife in my gut. Dylan's arms engulfed me in warmth before I hit the ground.

"Fuck. Grace, how bad is it?" he asked.

I coughed up blood which trickled down the edge of my mouth. Levi knelt next to me clutching his stomach. He felt the pain of the knife through our shared power.

"Move," my father ordered. Levi moved away, but Dylan didn't. I focused on his eyes. "You take care of her. You tell Winnie I love her," I choked out to him.

"You will tell her. Oberon's healers can fix this," Dylan assured me. I knew he was wrong. The nails in my leg turned my blood to ichor, but this blade turned my entire body into the black inky substance.

"Not this time. I love you," I said.

"She is right. It is a Thokcha blade. Thunderbolt iron. She will not recover," Oberon explained.

Dylan's eyes filled with tears. He knew the cold iron wrought by lightning would pierce not only my body, but my soul with its supernatural elements. The world swirled around me as I tried to focus on Dylan. I felt Levi's hand brush mine. The tingle lingered for a moment and passed.

"Give her to me," my father demanded. I didn't want my father. I wanted Dylan. My last moments on this earth, I wanted to be in his arms. Knowing I couldn't protest, my father leaned over me, stroking my face. My attention was drawn to him for a moment. "She is mine. I am hers." He claimed me as I had Dylan. The bond between us surged open filling me with his magical power.

The pulsing cold cut through my lungs, making me gasp. It wasn't like swapping power with Levi. This power consumed my mind, pushing the limits of what I knew. It opened doors to knowledge that I never knew I had. I saw the fairies around me for what they truly were. The power went beyond anything I'd developed over the years. The power of a King. My Father's inner strength. The passion of his love. The resolve of his mission. The fire in his cold, dark soul. He opened himself up, pouring all of this into me.

As the light left him, he drew runes with his hands around us.

Each one an icy snowflake hovering around our bodies. When he finished, they circled our bodies in a winter dance. He closed Dylan and Levi off to us. Dylan lurched at the barrier, causing icy dust to explode around us. Even in full fire form, he couldn't penetrate my father's wall. The orb glistened around us as the snow inside swirled. I kept my eyes on Dylan who desperately tried to reach me. The barrier did not give into his flame.

"He loves you, Grace," Father said, using the name I preferred.

"I love him, Daddy. Please don't separate me from him," I said.

A sad smile crossed his face. "In my many years, I've found that love is fleeting. It is found, but rarely, then moves on. But once in a while, you find forever. I cannot stand in the way of forever. Not even the immortal that I am."

"What do you mean?" I asked, looking at Dylan's kneeling form outside the snowy globe. His fire burned out, leaving him in tears at the edges of the barrier.

"I cannot stand by and watch my child die. The one I loved the most," he said.

"You let them banish me," I choked out as the darkness closed in on me.

"I did, because I knew, if you stayed in fairy any longer, you would become as cold and vindictive as those who are still there. Standing before the council, a fire ignited in you that I'd never seen. One that shouldn't be possible for the darkness of our people. It was hope which I knew would be quashed the moment I let you stay. I let you go, and now you will become the greatest of us," he explained. "I love you, Grace."

"No!" I protested. Slowly, he withdrew the knife. A magical tether coursed between us. The black darkness latched to the blade as he pulled it from me. Ebony tendrils slithered out of my body locking to the knife. It wobbled in his strong hand, seeking its victim. He didn't feed me power for me to use. He fed me power to bind himself to me like Levi was bound to me. "Daddy, no." Tears ran freely down my face. In that moment, Oberon, King of the Unseelie Fairies, chose to be my servant, thus giving him the power to take my place.

Holding the knife above him, he looked to Dylan. "You take care of my girl," he said. His eyes turned to Levi flashing to a brilliant silver, then back to icy blue. Levi shook his head slightly, but never diverted his gaze from us. The blackness cascaded down from the knife, like obsidian vipers snapping for their prey. They writhed and twirled around each other in a sensual death dance.

Horror filled Dylan's eyes as he watched the slithering arms latch on my father's chest. They spread across him devouring him as they went.

"This implement of death meant for my daughter, I take on her behalf. All that is mine belongs to her. All that I was, she now is."

Plunging the knife into his own stomach, he slumped over. I grasped for him as if I could hold his life in this realm with me. "Daddy, please don't go. I'm so sorry," I whimpered. The connection between us ceased. His icy blue eyes turned white to match his flowing locks. His body was rigid, and the surrounding globe exploded sending shards of ice around the square.

Hunched over his body, I felt the earth shift as time started moving at a normal pace once again. The fairies around us came out from their hiding places to stare at the dead King. A warm arm wrapped around my waist. Dylan's warm body leaned into me. Levi moved across from me. His eyes widened when I looked at him. I didn't ask because suddenly I felt tired.

Hearing voices around me, I leaned back into Dylan.

"It's okay. I've got you," he said.

Oberon, King of the Unseelie Fairies, died in the square in Shady Grove, Alabama. His power rose up from his body in tinkling ice crystals. Floating over me, as I rested in Dylan's arms staring at the lifeless body of the one man in the entire universe that I thought would never die, the crystals slammed down into me with force settling my father's power and realm on my shoulders. A responsibility that I never wanted. More than Shady Grove was now at stake. The entire Unseelie realm laid open before me.

CHAPTER TWENTY-FOUR

THE PEOPLE OF SHADY GROVE APPROACHED THE DEAD BODY OF MY
Father. I expected to see a few smiling faces since he sent most of
them here in the first place. However, I didn't. I saw tears and
sadness. Mable's face glistened with tears as Nestor held her close to
him. Trying to stand, Dylan held me in place.

"No, don't move." He reached through the hole in my dress.

"What are you doing?" I heaved through sobs.

"Making sure the wound is closed," he said.

"There is no wound, Dylan! He took it all," I gasped. My anger
toward him was only the frustration of watching my Father give up
his life for me. Not just his life, but his power, his kingdom. Everything. The deep realization of what happened hit me.

"What is it, Grace?" Levi asked.

"There is no King in fairy," I said, shoving out of Dylan's arms.
I rushed to the oak that Brock used. The tree spoke to me in kind
terms, but denied my request. "Why!"

Dylan stood next to me. "What the hell are you doing?"

"It's too late," I said.

"Brock," Levi growled, realizing my frustration.

"He's taken the Unseelie," I said. My vision blurred, and I heard Dylan's frantic voice before blacking out.

"Can I tell this part?" I asked, as she sat down on the sofa. She leaned back in it exhausted with telling the tragic end to her father's long life. "You know what, let's just take a break instead."

I got up from the laptop. As I sank down in cushion next to her, I wiped the tears off her cheeks. She clasped my hand in hers and kissed it, sending waves of fairy tingles through my body. "Levi, I'm still not sure that we did the right thing," she said.

"That is neither here nor there. It is done," I said. "And now we tell the story so everyone will know."

"It will just be another fairy tale. They will make a cartoon of it, perverting its truth," she scowled. Grace always had a way of finding hope in things. The bright spot in the darkness, but sometimes I had to remind her of those things. I considered it my Bard duty to not only tell her story, but to remind her of the finer points.

"Grace, I doubt they will make any cartoons about a fairy queen in a trailer park," I said when she elbowed me in the ribs.

"Levi, I swear," she said.

"You swear what?" I teased.

The devil flashed through her eyes, "I'll curse you again."

I remembered the last time she cursed me, but we hadn't gotten to that part of the story yet. It was awful. I hated her because of it. Thankfully, I got over myself and realized she was right. "I beg of you, my Queen. Please don't."

"Hush your mouth," she said, leaning over on my shoulder. "I don't know if I can do this. Tell it all. Relive it all again."

"Okay, we will stop writing it completely, depriving me of my one true mission," I conceded, knowing she didn't mean it.

"Or you could just finish it for me," she offered.

"You are going to let me tell it my way. With no interruptions? No interference?" I asked.

"You are right. There is no way I'm letting you tell it all," she said. "Are you even writing down everything I tell you?"

"Well, I might be embellishing some of it and leaving out other parts," I admitted.

"I figured as much. What are you embellishing? Your sexual conquests?" she laughed.

"Actually, I'm leaving yours out of it. Nobody needs to know the details of what you and Dylan did in bed," I said. "Gag." I shoved my finger down my throat for good measure.

"Levi, seriously? You should have told me, so I could skip those parts. Unless you are getting off on it. You know that kiss still haunts you," she teased.

"Grace, that was a long time ago," I said, shaking my head about the kiss with Dylan, the one she never forgot. I would never hear the end of it. For eons! Joy.

"Sigh. Yes, it was," she said. "Go ahead. Tell your part, then we can get to a good stopping place before I decide to lose myself in my garden tub."

Returning to the laptop, I began again.

Dylan always impressed me with how fast he was. Something of the bird in him knew exactly the right moment to swoop in to catch her or arrive in a conversation just as he was mentioned. I suppose it could be creepy. Grace always said he had an uncanny sense of the future, almost like he lived a few seconds ahead of us.

"We are doomed," Mable exclaimed.

"No, we aren't. Calm down," Nestor assured her. "However, this is very bad. We need to get them both out of the square."

"Levi, run to my car and get my extra set of clothes," Dylan said. The hazard of igniting into flames was that he ended up being naked afterwards. I didn't care what Grace said about Dylan and I kissing, seeing him naked was more than enough to never question which side of the fence I was on. Naked man was gross. Not that it was a question in the first place. Damn that woman knew how to get in my head.

Naked Dylan sat on the ground holding Grace's limp body. I ran off to the car as fast as I could. I didn't want to miss any of the conversation. If Brock already took over the Unseelie part of fairy, it meant one thing. With Stephanie as his servant, he was only one royal from owning all the Otherworld.

"Um, guys?" I said, as I threw Dylan's clothes at him.

"What?" Dylan growled, trying to catch them. He shifted Grace toward me, and I bent down to steady her while he dressed. We'd all see him naked now. It's not like it mattered.

"If Brock has Unseelie and Stephanie is Rhiannon's daughter..." I started.

"He plans to take it all," Nestor finished.

"Shit," Dylan mumbled. "I'm taking her home. Get him out of the street. Take his body to my house. We will do a pyre out there. Levi, go get Winnie."

I nodded. "Are you going to your house or the trailer?"

He looked down at Grace in his arms. "The trailer. It's closer." It wasn't his first choice, but I knew Grace was still wary of his house since Stephanie had been there.

"We will get Winnie," Nestor said. "You forget that you are down a vehicle."

SNAKE IN THE GRASS

"Right. My head is scrambled. I guess the damn election doesn't matter anymore," Dylan said.

"It still matters. We will need a council. If Brock makes waves in fairy, there will be more exiles here. Not less," he explained.

"Holy crap," I muttered, knowing he was right.

"Fine. Go get her. Just tell her Grace is sick. I don't want her upset," Dylan instructed, as he hoisted Grace up into his arms. He paced toward his car, and I walked along with him. I grabbed the passenger door, swinging it open so he could put her inside.

"Meet you there," I said.

"What about Riley?" Dylan asked.

"You know that no one is as important to me as Grace is, right?" I responded.

He nodded with approval. I hopped on my bike to follow them home. As I rode, I could feel Grace inside the car. Her mind racing with knowledge. She was beginning to see the whole picture. She had shut herself off from all that was fairy for good reason. Now it was all thrust upon her without permission. Oberon spoke to me in those last moments. A strong, steady voice in my head. Resolved to save her. He loved her.

When we arrived, we got the torn dress off of her, putting her in something comfortable. He stood over her, stroking her forehead. "Can you feel her, Levi?" he asked.

I knew that she had told him about us in her Father's home, but I never expected Dylan to accept it, much less ask me to use it. "She's overwhelmed," I said, describing it the best way that I could. I felt the rush of power into her as her father poured all of his knowledge and will into her. Some of it bubbled over to me. Not in a form that I could use, just the force of it through her. Her mind zipped in a million directions trying to make sense of the information that it now held. It was too much at once. Dylan stared at me, hoping I could give him more. "Did he say anything to you? At the end?"

"Just to take care of her," he said. "Why? What did he say to you?"

"In my mind, he said that one day I'd tell this story, and when I did, he wanted everyone to know that he never intended to lay it all on her at once. He believed in her more than she ever realized," I said sadly.

"This is bad, Levi. She will be torn between here and there now. She's the rightful heir to his throne," he said, watching her rest.

"Grace never wanted that, and he knew it. Perhaps he never meant for her to take over the Otherworld, perhaps he meant for her to just be here," I suggested.

"Did he tell you that?" his voice laced with disdain.

"No, but you know as well as I do, Grace doesn't do what everyone expects her to do," I said with a smile. I tried to disarm him. The last thing I wanted was him to be upset when she woke up.

He released his frustration with a snicker. "No, she doesn't. I think most of the time, she tries to do everything the opposite on purpose."

"It's Grace," I said.

"Beautiful Grace," he responded.

He watched her sleep. When Winnie arrived, she came in and hugged us both. She looked at Grace with sad eyes. "Is Mommy okay?" she asked. Grace would have melted to hear those words come out of that little mouth.

"She's just resting," Dylan told her.

"Okay. I got a happy meal," she explained. "Uncle Levi, you want some French fries? I'll share." I couldn't refuse her. Dylan nodded for me to go with her. I felt Grace, so I didn't have to be in the room with her. Although her body rested, I felt her mind sorting out the knowledge. She would get a handle on all of it, but I didn't know how long that would take.

After putting Winnie to bed, I gave Dylan a break. While he was up, Troy arrived at our door. I heard them talking in low voices in the living room. When Dylan walked back into the room, he looked awful.

"What's happened?" I asked.

"My house is gone," he said.

"What?"

"Troy said it looked like someone just plucked it off the foundation, stuck it in their pocket and walked off," he said astounded.

"Stephanie," I replied.

"Yes, the fucking snake. She probably was in the house for more than just to taunt Grace. She wanted to rip everything from us. One day I'll kill her," he growled. His anger was exposed through his flaming eyes.

"Welcome to the trailer park," I smirked.

He turned those burning eyes to me, and I flinched. Shaking his head, he released the anger. "She will love it," he said, looking back at Grace.

"That's all that matters, right?" I said.

"Absolutely," he replied. "Oh crap! Where is Rufus?"

"He's in the bed with Winnie," I said.

"Geez, I almost had a heart attack," he said.

"Your house is gone, and you are worried about the dog?" I asked.

"Levi, I don't worry about anything, except Grace," he said turning his attention back to her. I knew the feeling.

"You are so sweet, Dublin," she purred.

"Shut it," I said. "Finish the story."

"It's a long way from done," she replied.

"I mean this part. The election," I said.

"Yes, Bard," she smirked.

When I woke up alone in my room in the trailer, I admit that I was perturbed. After finally getting a grip on everything my father passed on to me, I expected to find Dylan by my side. Even more disappointing was the absent Levi, who I knew wouldn't abandon me. Perhaps Riley MacKenzie was better than I thought. A shadow crossed the door, and brooding blue eyes met mine.

He tilted his head at me, "You know. Sometimes I hear your thoughts quite clearly, and while Riley is good, you are my Queen."

"Oh, hush your mouth. Where's Dylan?" I asked, as Levi crossed the room to the chair opposite of the bed. He nodded toward the door.

"Well, she's awake," Dylan said from the doorway.

I sighed. They were both there and fine. Everything was not fine though. When my father opened himself up to me, I saw him for who he truly was. So many years I spent in anger, but my father was probably the best fairy in the world. His decisions were made with the utmost care and wisdom. I'd been so wrong about him. Although I knew it hurt him deeply, he still loved me. Just like a father should.

"Is Winnie okay?" I asked. "What day is it?

"Grace, she is fine. Congratulations are due," Dylan said.

"For what?"

"You won the election," he said. "You are the official queen."

"I'm not sure that matters now," I said.

"It matters now more than ever," Dylan replied. "Nestor and Mable made some inquiries. Brock has taken over Unseelie. Those loyal to your father, the die hards, are being hunted down. We expect that Shady Grove will become fairy central. It's a good thing you have a council now, too."

I raised up in the bed. Dylan shifted the pillows behind me to prop me up. He kissed me lightly on the cheek. Worry filled his eyes, all of it directed toward me.

"Who?" I cringed to know.

"Nestor, Tabitha, Diego Santiago and Betty Stallworth," Dylan said.

"No Seelie," I reflected.

"Grace, Tabitha is Seelie," Dylan prompted.

I slapped myself in the forehead. "Ouch! Of course, she is. Damn, I'm an idiot. I know the differences now. I can see it. Looking at the both of you, it's very clear to me now what you are. My father could see like this all along."

"How do you tell?" Levi asked.

"I don't look, search through the knowledge, and come to the conclusion. It's just there. I look at you and see bard changeling. Dylan is Phoenix. There is no guessing. It's like he downloaded the book into my head. Along with a crap ton of shit I didn't need in my head," I huffed.

"Like?"

"Fairy history. The great fairy war that split the races. Rulers. Servants. Exiles. The dead. The extinct. The missing. You get the idea. The names of all his servants. It goes on and on," I said, as a tear rolled down my cheek. "Are both of you okay? There is something you aren't telling me."

"Oh, hell," Dylan cursed.

"What?"

"You all of a sudden super intuitive?" Dylan asked.

"No, I can look at your face and see something is wrong. What is it?" I demanded.

"It's not important right now," Dylan replied. He looked at Levi who shrugged.

"Don't you piss on my leg and tell me it's raining," I exclaimed, shaking my finger at him.

"The house is gone," Dylan blurted out.

"Gone? What did it grow legs and walk away?" I asked.

"Maybe. Troy went out there to take your father's body. I thought we'd set up a pyre, but the house was gone. The foundation is there, but it's like a tornado came through and kicked it to Oz," he said.

"Oz. No, it's in the Otherworld," I said. "Isn't it?"

"It had to be her," he said. "However, I have no idea what she did with it. Just another way to meddle with us."

"What did you lose? Other than the building? Important things?" I asked.

He sat on the side of the bed. I watched Levi slip out quietly, but at the last moment his eyes met mine. Suddenly, I was lost in the mind of my servant. I realized things that I didn't want to know. He turned his back to me to walk out the door. A shiver ran through him because he knew that I knew everything. His fears of the future.

His admiration of me. His love. This was how my father knew all of his servants. He saw their souls. Levi's soul was filled with uncertainty, except for one thing. Us. He knew we were solid. I understood then how important I was to him. How important he was to me.

Withdrawing from Levi's consciousness, I realized Dylan was talking, "I have you and Winnie. That's all I want. I haven't had the heart to tell her that her room is gone." He hung his head in defeat.

"She is a good girl. She will be fine. Where's Rufus?" I asked.

He smiled. "In the bed with Winnie," he said. "The pistols you gave me were in the trunk of the Camaro. Other than that, my clothes and things that can be replaced. I told you that I gutted it. I took everything out of it before remaking it for you."

"That's why she did it," I said. "Petty bullshit."

"Maybe. Probably," he said. "I'm homeless."

I raised up, forcing him to look at me. "Guess you get to stay in the trailer park now," I said.

"Thrills you to death, doesn't it?"

"Sends all kinds of chills up and down my body. Utter pleasure," I grinned.

Finally, he returned the smile. "As long as I have you. I'll live in a shack."

"If I keep up with my track record on houses and cars, we might just be living in the shed behind Nestor's bar," I said.

"Levi would have to move out," he laughed.

"Agreed," I said.

"I heard that," Levi said from the living room. We laughed.

"He's been around you for too long," Dylan said. "He could tell what was going on while you were sleeping. I was thankful to know that although overwhelmed, that you were okay in there."

"We have work to do," I said. "Are they already arriving? More exiles?"

"Yes. Remy called and said Niles would have the apartments done by next week. He will start on a second set right after that if you approve," he said. "I suppose the trailer park will expand. You can do this, Grace."

"We can do this," I replied. "I will make them pay for this bull-shit. I'm not done with Brock and Raine."

"Good, but right now, I just want to be with you," he said, laying down next to me. He wrapped his warm arms around me, and I felt safe. However, he shifted his legs away from me. I tried moving back to him. I wanted to cuddle. I needed it. "Grace, don't."

"I'm just tying to spoon. Don't go buy any ladles," I smirked.

He cleared his throat. "I can't lay next to you like this and not have a reaction."

"Oh really," I said, sliding myself back to him. He'd reached the edge of the bed, so he had no choice but to allow me to touch him.

"I wasn't trying to do this," he protested.

"Why the hell not?" I asked.

"Because, your father just died. The world has gone to hell in a handbasket," he said.

I rolled around to face him. "I will mourn my father, and the world hasn't gotten that bad yet. Neither of those things have anything to do with loving you."

He kissed me on the lips. "I love you," he whispered in my ear. Goosebumps ran down my arms.

"I love you, too," I said, reaching to unbutton his jeans. "Now, show me that snake in the grass."

A Message From the Author

I'm always thrilled to hear from a reader. The feedback for Grace's story has been so positive. I'm glad you all love her and her merry band of exiles. As an independent author, I'm in charge of everything from writing the story to registering copyrights to marketing the book. One of the biggest marketing tools for an author is an honest review. If you truly enjoyed my stories, would you mind taking a few moments to review the books on Amazon or Goodreads? I would greatly appreciate it. Visibility increases with more reviews. As that happens, I'm able to produce more books.

Thank you so much for loving these stories. I'd love to hear from you anytime. Please message me on my Facebook page or through my email.

Facebook: www.facebook.com/kimbraswainofficial
Email: kimbraswain@gmail.com

Reviews on Amazon:

Bless Your Heart
Tinsel in a Tangle
Snake in the Grass

OTHER BOOKS IN THE SERIES

GOODREADS:

Bless Your Heart: https://www.goodreads.com/book/show/
36730556-bless-your-heart

Tinsel in a Tangle: https://www.goodreads.com/book/show/
37457023-tinsel-in-a-tangle

ACKNOWLEDGMENTS

First and always, Thanks to my loving husband, Jeff, and my beautiful daughter, Maleia. You are my dreams come true.

Thanks to my Canvas Crew who look over the books and badger me to death when I don't have a new one to read. I love you guys so much! Larry, Tabitha, Mike, Kristie, Chris, Sandi, Moragan, Allana, and Carol.

Thanks to Hampton, my wonderful cover artist, who has embraced the idea to be different. I get giddy every time I get a message from him with an update on a cover.

Thanks to the wonderful indie authors who have encouraged me along the way. You guys really set the bar, and I plan on catching you all eventually. Your support has been phenomenal.

ABOUT THE AUTHOR

From early in life Kimbra Swain was indoctrinated in the ways of geekdom. Raised on Star Wars, Tolkien, Superheroes and Voltron, she found herself immersed in a world of imagination. She started writing in high school, and completed her English degree from the University of Alabama in 2003.

Her writing is influenced by a gamut of favorite authors including Jane Austen, J.R.R. Tolkien, L.M. Montgomery, Timothy Zahn, Kathy Reichs, Kevin Hearne and Jim Butcher.

Born and raised in Alabama, Kimbra still lives there with her husband and 5-year-old daughter. When she isn't reading or writing, she plays PC games, makes jewelry and builds cars.

Follow Kimbra on Facebook, Twitter, Instagram and Pinterest.

www.kimbraswain.com
www.facebook.com/kimbraswainofficial
www.twitter.com/kswainauthor
www.instagram.com/kswainauthor
www.pinterest.com/kimbraswain